Sons and Brothers
(Legends of the Family Dyer)

David W. Thompson

ALL RIGHTS RESERVED

Publisher's Note:

This is a work of fiction. All names, characters, places, and
events are the work of the author's imagination.

Any resemblance to real persons, places, or events is
coincidental.

Solstice Publishing - www.solsticepublishing.com

For my friend, mentor and personal hero.
Fellow author "Boogie Woogie"
The instigator of my lifelong love affair with the written
word.

J. Leonard Thompson, Sr.   06/07/1921- 1/17/2019

Miss you, Dad

Part I

Chapter One

Night descended on the mountains, thick as molasses and corrupting all it touched. The full moon floated above the tree-line, bloated as roadkill left in the sun. If he stretched, he might snatch it from its perch. It emitted little light, a scarred pumpkin with its jack o' lantern face mocking his torment. Barren branches were fleshless fingers grasping to ensnare the jeep, and rip out his soul...

St. Mary's County, Maryland. September, 1990
Brodie Caine

The trotline cord glided through the johnboat's roller system. The stains of dredged mud and deep-water slime gave testament to many trips here. The trolling motor was locked at an angle to maintain the boat's course, compensating for the incoming tide's pull.

He felt the jerk on the line, gentle at first as the creature took hold, then a stout pull as it latched on to his offering. He peered through the murky depths and saw the creature's mouth open and close, savoring its victim's flesh.

As if sensing danger, the sea dweller flailed one claw from side to side in warning, prepared to defend its right to the captured prey. Its smaller claw and saber-tipped legs skewered the exposed meat and fat, unwilling to share.

As it was pulled toward the surface, greed trumped caution, and the predator became the prey. He readied his net as the ghostly crab floated closer to the surface until...

With a flip of his wrist, he moved his net under and up. The large blue crab broke the surface in a clacking frenzy of legs and claws. He noticed the long thin apron and smiled, then reached out to squeeze its carapace.

"Good, no more sooks or paper shells." He hoisted the crab over a bushel basket and flipped the net over, dumping his latest catch in with two dozen other large bodied 'jimmies'—adult #1 male crabs. He pulled the chicken neck off the trotline's slip knot and rolled the line into a bucket for storage. It would be his last run this year. The nip in the air signaled the changing season and the crab run was slowing anyway—even if they were fatter. Maybe his mother would make them some crab cakes for dinner...

He stowed the rolled trotline behind his seat, pulled the trolling motor prop out of the water and reached down for his paddle. There was time to explore before his mother came home. He dipped the paddle, breaking the water's surface with a moist whisper, no more than a wet kiss. It reminded him of Uncle Jim's visits. His tobacco juice spit made the same sound hitting the porch floor in front of their house trailer.

Just south of where he ran his trotline, a small creek dumped its waters into the bay. It was a famous creek—at least by local standards. His best buddy, Mike Cusic, claimed it was a haunted stretch of water, cursed by a vengeful witch because of some atrocity committed by colonial settlers. Mike said it happened like a thousand years ago, yet strange things still happened there and on the surrounding property. Ghostly wisps of fog that followed unnerved hikers, boats flipped upside down by unseen obstacles, and even a few dozen car wrecks on the nearby state road over the years.

He turned the bow of the johnboat into the creek and wondered what it must've been like then—years ago when the country was still new and raw. This stretch of the creek looked just as it must have then. Invasive phragmites reeds covered banks once populated by wild rice and cattails, but otherwise…giant maples and sycamores, hundreds of years old, stretched their branches toward him in a welcoming embrace. And the people then? Were they so different? Perhaps they caught crabs from this same stretch of water and feasted that night on food earned by the sweat of their brow. Sustenance drawn fresh from the sea and land. Independent—leaning on no one, a man's value based on the strength of his back and his husbandry of the land—not an unearned birthright.

He sucked in a great draught of salty air, stretched and slid down to the floor of the johnboat, resting his head on the abandoned seat. The push of the tide reversed the water's flow and pulled his small craft deeper into the creek and its surrounding woods. His mind drifted to that other time and the mist of a dream shrouded his eyes.

The marshy banks gave way to more open woods, and beyond he saw a small field or large garden. A 30-ish man and a woman his age worked the ground between the rows of what looked to be very anemic tobacco plants. Their hoes moved up and down tending the scrawny thin leaved plants—thwack, thwack, thwack. They worked with the tenacity and rhythm of machines, only stopping to wipe the sweat from their eyes. On this warm late summer day, the man was dressed in long sleeves, pants with suspenders, and heavy work boots. The woman wore a bonnet and a dress that bunched up at her ankles—although she worked in her bare feet.

Did he drift up to a Mennonite farm or was it a historical reenactment the county sponsored for tourists? He grabbed a branch to pull his johnboat to the bank while he observed.

Although in clear view, the workers (or performers) feigned ignorance of his presence. Bent at the waist, the cadence of their hoes increased, creating a beat not unlike tribal drums. The man stood to full height and twisted back and forth to work a kink from his back. He shielded his eyes and stared in Brodie's direction.

"Zachary? Are you being careful down there?"

A splash to his right and he turned to see a dark-haired boy, no more than five years old, sitting at the creek's edge. He would've sworn the lad wasn't there moments before. The child was dressed like the adults in the field and slapped at the water beetles scurrying over the water's surface.

"I'm careful, Uncle." The boy raised his eyes and his mouth flapped open.

"Sorry," Brodie said, "I didn't see you either. Did I scare you?"

"No, but you're bigger than I thought you'd be, Mister."

"Huh? What do you mean...?" but the boy's attention was already back to the water. He slid his hand in the creek and pulled it out with a splash. He ran toward him, his right hand cupped in front of him.

"Look what I caught, Brodie." He opened his fist to display a tadpole. The immature frog's vestigial legs dragged it across the boy's palm. "This is gonna be a baby frog. You ever seen one before?"

He nodded and leaned over the johnboat, holding the boy's wrist steady to admire the prize. "What's your name, buddy? Do we know each other from somewhere?"

The boy shook his head and jerked his hand away.

"What's wrong, little man? You look like you've seen a ghost or..."

The woman from the field was suddenly there and snatched the boy from the water, stood him on the bank and pointed to the field. "Go home, now."

"It's okay, ma'am. He was just showing me…"

The woman grabbed the bow of the johnboat and swung it around against the current as if it was weightless. "You don't belong here, Brodie. This isn't your time."

"Huh? What's that supposed to mean?"

"These new lands and waters are bountiful, but blood is thicker. Do you not find it so?"

"What in the hell are you talking about, lady?"

Her eyes bored into his. "Stay out of the mountains, Brodie. Only evil waits for you there." With that, she gave the boat a herculean shove that propelled the vessel sideways downstream. It slammed into a submerged widow-maker log and flipped.

He woke coughing up water from his lungs. Standing in the waist-deep creek, he wiped his eyes. The johnboat was floating away, already at the first bend, and he raced to catch up with it. Trotline cord drifted behind the boat and he gathered it up as he reached the boat. He wasn't as lucky retrieving the crabs. The hard-won dinner was gone, but his paddle and crab net floated just ahead. The expensive trolling motor battery was also gone.

God, what a crazy dream. It had to be a dream, yet he couldn't help looking back for reassurance. Upstream no opening in the woods indicated a field, no one stood on the banks—and he looked…*really* looked. He heard a distant thwack, thwack, thwack…hoes slapping the dirt? He tuned his ears towards the sound. The awkward flight of a pileated woodpecker provided a triumph of sanity.

"Sweet Jesus, I sure need this trip to the mountains."

Chapter Two

Hampshire County, West Virginia
Anna Hirsch

She never imagined a single knock at the door could upend her life. The knocking indicated some urgency, and she rushed from the shower, donning her robe as she descended the stairs.

Flashing red and blue lights filtered through the cigarette stained curtains over the foyer windows. *Oh no, Mom…?* But no, her mother was sprawled out on the couch. Her snores echoed through the small house like pigs rooting in a garden, sleeping off whatever she'd put in her system this time.

"Hampshire County sheriff. Open up or we're coming in."

"I'm coming." She turned the corner towards the door and loose threads from the well-worn carpet snagged her toe.

"Ouch, ouch, ouch."

Another rap at the door. "Ma'am, is everything all right in there?"

"Yes, I'm coming." She limped to the door and threw it open.

"Miss Hirsch, is it?"

"I'm Anna Hirsch."

"Ma'am, is your mother at home?"

"No…I mean yes, but she's sleeping." She nodded toward the living room. "What's this about, Officer?"

"I'm Deputy Stiles, Miss. I have a warrant for the arrest of Madeline Hirsch. Please step aside." The deputy didn't wait for her to comply, but pushed past her to the living room. Clumps of red clay mud fell from his boots marking every step. A second deputy moved past her, nodded an apology and joined his companion. They bound her mother's wrists together with tie wraps.

"Madeline Hirsch, you are under arrest for the murder of John Clarke." The second deputy pulled a card from his shirt pocket and read her Miranda rights. "Do you understand your rights as they've been read to you?"

"What? No...no I don't understand. Oh, I get it. Did my friends send you here for my birthday next week? You are lookers, I'll give you that." Her mother smiled and winked at the deputies. She offered them no resistance... until they led her from the room.

"Wait, no wait...what's going on? Where are you taking me?"

"Ma'am, I repeat, you are under arrest and charged with murder."

"Anna, call your grandfather. Tell Mika we need his help."

"I will. Stop, you're hurting her. Mom, stand up and walk. We'll get this straightened out."

Phone calls to the sheriff's office provided little information. The following morning, Mika's lawyer called to fill her in.

"The sheriff's office claims your mother drove into Martinsburg last evening. That she was trying to get money for drugs and...this isn't very pleasant, Miss Hirsch, but your grandfather said to tell you the truth..."

"Please do..."

"Well, apparently, she'd tried to turn a trick. The potential john ended up concussed in an alley behind the liquor store. There was a bourbon bottle covered with his blood beside him and your mother's fingerprints were all over it. His wallet was taken and it was found in your mother's vehicle last night."

A cornucopia of emotions consumed her: concern, betrayal, the pain of desertion, and yes—guilt. Could she have helped her somehow? Was she too wrapped up in her own drama to see her mother's need?

The next phone call she received was from Social Services. They deposited her at her grandfather's cabin that night. Lovestown, West Virginia, was her new home.

***

She closed her eyes and let the spray from the shower soak her hair and wash away the remnants of tears from her face. The water pressure was stronger than at her mother's house. She felt her eyes well up and she allowed herself a moment of self-pity. It was too much to deal with, even for someone accustomed to the pains of betrayal: her mother, Mr. Simmons, and Garren. Dear God, even Garren.

She shook her head to clear her mind and bit her upper lip to brace herself against the world. The hot water quit before she finished, but she didn't have the luxury of time today anyway. She rushed, not in anticipation of the new day, but in a hurry to put it behind her. Stepping from the shower, she felt for the towel rod.

"Damn, forgot the towel." Water dripped from her raven's hair (Garren's description) and formed a small puddle on the tiled floor. Shivering, she hugged her arms around her chest and dashed to the closet, snatched a towel, and vigorously patted dry. She tossed the towel to the floor and pushed it about with her foot to mop up the puddles. Her grandfather needed bathroom rugs.

The morning marked a new beginning in a short life full of new beginnings, none pleasant. Her existence remained in constant flux since her father walked out of their lives two years before. It seemed to her that the dust from the moving vans had barely settled in Martinsville, and now her mother's adventures left her homeless—a virtual orphan. Her grandfather welcomed her into his home with the full sanction of the state, and of his heart. The one constant in her life, he had the stubbornness common to a man of his years, and the wisdom that old age is often given credit for, even if undeserved.

The thought brought a smile to her lips that transformed her eyes. She wiped the fog from the bathroom mirror, and flipped back her hair. Heavy and wet, it swished and slapped the small of her back. Feeling as shallow as the girls she silently mocked at her former school, she stared at her blurred reflection.

Although less than a quarter Native American, her skin was nearly the same tone as her grandfather's. It was a source of great pride to her, a tie to her past and to ancestors she held in high regard—an admitted albeit clandestine vanity. Her skin reflected who she was but was also a banner celebrating non-conformance. A flag setting her apart in a world that paid token homage to what it secretly abhorred—diversity. She blushed, stuck out her tongue at her reflection, and smiled. At the knock on the door, she pulled the towel tightly around herself.

"Anna, are you nearly done?"

"Almost. Washing the sleep from my eyes."

"Don't want to be late on your first day. Hustle up."

Great, another new day in another new school, but maybe it would turn out better this time. As she dressed, she allowed her mind to wander to kayaking the South Branch River with Garren—experiencing it in a way most people missed. The gentle pull of their paddles drawing them around each bend to absorb every new vista. Dragonflies used their hands and feet for landing pads as they performed their mating dance. Majestic raptors soared toward the mountain peaks, and in the span of a single breath were gone. Blue herons clumsily walked the banks on stilt-like legs, but when alarmed, displayed their grace in flight. The memories were so intense; she could smell the sweetness of the water, and even stare into the depths of

Garren's blue eyes. She knew she'd miss those times together…that she'd committed the ultimate blunder from the look in his eyes, and the stiffness of his body. She'd forfeited a friendship she treasured more than any other.

She released the memory before a half-formed tear could fall, and finished brushing her hair. As she pulled on her bra, she felt the pinch of her birthmarks, the three raised parallel lines imprinted under her left breast. Probably need a larger cup size, she thought, but not something she'd talk to her grandfather about. She finished dressing in black jeans and a matching blouse. An antler amulet completed her trademark uniform.

Her mind drifted off to Garren again. He said she shouldn't let the xenophobic fools get under her skin, and that her differences were what made her special. He said people might see her for who she was then, and not the caricature of her they'd created in their minds. It would be nice to fit in somewhere, with someone. But she knew people would see what they wanted to—no matter what she did.

Before her faux pas, he'd told her to put Mr. Simmons in his place, knee him where his momma never kissed him, or even punch him in the jaw! It was all easy for him to say. He'd never known prejudice…never seen the smirks on faces of a majority unlike himself…never been the focus of a dozen sets of eyes from a hostile clique. Still he was her Garren…or had been.

But she was no hero. No warrior against injustice. No, she'd stalked from the room wet eyed, and timid as a rabbit.

"Anna!"

Chapter Three

Hampshire County, WV
Garren Doyle

The crosshairs moved over his intended prey, then steadied as he squeezed the hair trigger. The sharp crack of the .243 caliber rifle shattered the stillness of the morning.

"Ha, clean kill!" He smiled. The rifle's echo bounced from valley to hilltop and back again, heard mostly by the animals living in those hills. The blast from a firearm was not an unusual sound here. In fact, it was a sound common on any given weekend in the rural Appalachians. The immediate fear it might cause among closeted city dwellers was not felt here. It was certainly of no import to any of his neighbors, furred or otherwise. He felt the weight of the rifle in his hands, admired the artistry of wood mated to metal, and knew the significance.

His whoop of joy created an acoustical double exposure as it merged with the last weak echoes of the rifle's shot. It felt childish getting so excited over a target, but when your talents are few, you celebrate what you do have. Shooting was the one thing he excelled at.

He drew in the smell of burnt gunpowder, savoring its acrid flavor. Autumn in the mountains...how could anyone live anywhere else? The trees displayed vibrant oranges, reds, and yellows in tones never created on any artist's palette. The colors danced and came alive in the breeze.

"Garren? You doing okay?" his mother yelled from the back porch of their cabin.

"Great, Mom. Three targets, three bullseyes, can't beat that."

He ran to the house, targets in hand. As he approached the back porch, his mother placed a half-peeled apple and her paring knife on the table. She pulled her blonde hair out of her eyes and looked at, or rather through him. He knew where her mind went when that faraway look entered her eyes. How had he grown up so fast? Just yesterday, Adam was killed in the car wreck. Just yesterday, she'd endured birth pains. Just yesterday, he was potty trained, started school, had his first crush…now her only son would join the men in deer camp for a week.

"Earth to Mom…?" He waved his hand in front of her indigo blue eyes. Eyes matching his own.

"Your father would be proud." Diana took the targets from his outstretched hand. "It looks like you're a pretty fair shot."

"Don't forget your promise."

"I keep my promises, young man. Assuming your Uncle Jim promises to keep you safe, that is. Sixteen does seem young to be up there with a barely civilized pack of men though. Are you sure you don't want to wait until next year?"

He felt his jaw drop, then saw she was biting back a grin.

"Do you think he would?"

"He who? Uncle Jim?"

"Dad. Would he be proud of me, you think?"

"Of course he would. I wish he could see you now…but then, I guess he does…"

He wondered what his father would think. In fact, he wondered about the man period. Was he glad when his mother got pregnant with him? Did he want a child? He'd heard the gossip—whispers from people not quite in earshot. Snippets of conversation suggesting his father's accident maybe wasn't an accident at all. Maybe Adam Doyle couldn't handle the pressures of fatherhood. Sometimes he questioned the story himself, and then he'd feel like a traitor to his father's memory for allowing the thought to come to fruition.

For a change, his mention of his father brought a smile to his mother's lips. Often he came home to find her crying for no reason, usually with a framed picture of his father in her lap, repeating over and over, "Why Adam, why?"

He was worthless to help when melancholy overtook her. Sometimes she'd remain in the dumps for several days after her tears dried. She weathered a lot by herself, and when she needed him most, he couldn't help. He felt useless, ineffectual, and immature. There was nothing worse than being unable to help someone you love, to have to stand by while they suffered. He grabbed the crucifix hanging at his chest. Holding it brought him comfort, a tie to a father he never knew. His mother said Adam was never without it and she passed it to him after one of her crying marathons.

The worst part about his mother's pain was that it was entirely his fault. He was like a deer tick: sucking the life from her, and leaving nothing of value in return. He was the reason she worked so hard, and why she never had any boyfriends. After all, everyone talked about Diana's beauty. He admitted it was true, even if she was his mother.

"Earth to Garren, now who's spacing out?"

"Sorry, just daydreaming about the hunt. Will you be all right while I'm gone?"

"You had to grow up too fast, didn't you, Garren? I think this poor decrepit old woman can look after herself for one week. I'll be fine. I'll never forget the first week your father and I hunted that mountain together. I never felt more alive."

"Come with us then. Show us a thing or two," he suggested.

"Not this year. You check it out, and do your male bonding thing. If you see a lot of deer and bring home some venison, maybe I'll go next year and show you how it's really done."

He smiled and hugged her. This hunt would be the best week in the history of man. He turned, and headed inside to clean his rifle.

"Oh, hey Garren? Your Uncle Jim said he worked out a way for your cousin Brodie to go to camp. Aunt Lily couldn't afford the money the men put up for the cook, so Jim set Brodie up as cook's helper so he can get in some hunting too. I'm sure Mika could use the help too."

His mother's eyes darkened as they always did when she spoke of her sister Lily, or Lily's son Brodie for that matter. He knew there was bad blood between them, but it wasn't something his mother cared to share.

His Aunt Lily called last May to see if Brodie could stay with them during the last month of school. Lily said her job required her to go on 30 days of travel. He'd heard their phone conversation, or at least his mother's end of it.

"Since when are grocery store clerks required to go on travel? Um hmm…um hmm.

"You can be straight with me, Lily. Did you get another DWI? Um hmmm…sure, right—whatever you say. But yeah, Brodie can stay with us. None of it's his fault after all."

He wondered if that side of the family were always the black sheep. He had little in common with his cousin. They didn't like the same video games or TV shows, and where Brodie was, trouble was sure to follow.

Brodie said his mother trusted him for the length of his leash, so maybe he was proving her right. Or maybe some people were just born bad…all he knew was if Brodie was around, he was at the heart of any mischief…or was blamed for the same.

They did find one interest in common: the outdoors. Still, he wasn't very close with his cousin and he wasn't sad when Brodie went home after school ended for the summer. But by mid-summer, they were forced to be bunkmates again.

Again he heard his mother and aunt arguing on the phone, his mother's phone left on speaker as she bounced around the kitchen fixing dinner.

"Diana, the two boys hardly know each other."

"They just spent the last month of the school year together."

"Yes but they were in different schools. How much time together did they have with homework and all? And Brodie was in Hampshire High and Garren was in that fancy hoity-toity private school…"

"Don't you dare, Lily…"

"Sorry. That was uncalled for. But hey, just for the week? I know Brodie would love to show Garren off to his friends and take him crabbing. And I'd love to see my nephew. What do you say?"

Finally, Diana agreed that a week in the trailer park wouldn't scar her child for life.

***

St. Mary's County, Md.

Their week together started out rough. The first morning, Brodie told him to hang around the trailer and play video games as he had yard work to do in the neighborhood. He played a few games and ran through the TV channels but the rabbit ears didn't pull in many channels. He wandered outside and found Brodie two trailers down—pulling weeds from a tiny patch of flowers.

"Busy?"

"Yeah."

"Doesn't look like fun."

"It's not but it's something I do to help Mom pay the bills. What do you do to earn your keep?"

"I help some around the house…"

"Hmmm, must be nice. Guess you had a dad that took good care of you. Sure wish I'd had a dad like that."

"That the way you see it? There was insurance when he died, so yeah, I guess he took good care of us that way. I'm sorry you and Aunt Lily have it so bad, Brodie."

"Don't worry about us, cousin, we'll make out just fine even without the silver spoon."

He felt the blood rush to his face, and involuntarily felt his hands draw into fists.

He saw Brodie's eyes move past him as another boy approached.

"Hey guys. What's going on?"

"Not much, Mike, just catching up on some side hustles. Figured I'd get it done today so my buddy, Garren, and I can enjoy the rest of the week."

"New around here, Garren?"

"No, I'm from…"

"Garren's my blood, Mike—my favorite cousin, but he thinks I'm the black sheep of the family."

The cousins glared at each other, fists clenched and nostrils flared.

"All righty then. Let's get to it." Mike grabbed a handful of Johnson grass and pulled. They spent the rest of the day yanking weeds together and making plans for the rest of the week. When Mike ran home to get them some cold Cokes, Brodie slapped him on the back. "No hard feelings Garren. I was just joking around."

The next day, they trekked through the woods to a small swamp behind the trailer park. Small pools of murky water dotted the area. Poison green moss and cattails covered the surface wherever islands of soggy earth emerged from the muck. As they walked, the clinging mud sucked at their boots making a slurping sound when they pulled them free. Bubbles popped to the surface as water filled their tracks.

A sticky sweet smell permeated the entire area, made stronger by their disturbance. He thought of rotten potatoes covered with strawberry syrup. But everywhere they looked the water teemed with life. Raccoon tracks at the edge of the pools showed they weren't the first to enjoy what the water offered. Frogs leapt to safety as they approached. Water striders skimmed the surface as minnows, tadpoles, and crayfish flitted about under water. Brodie had brought along two aquarium fish nets, and they whiled away the afternoon catching and examining the small creatures.

The second day, Brodie borrowed a neighbor's rust bucket truck and they went crabbing. He'd never run a trotline before and the excitement of the catch almost matched the salty sweet taste of the crabs that evening. The boys were left to their own devices for the most part. Aunt Lily made rare daytime appearances.

Their fourth night together was on a Saturday and Brodie had a plan.

"I think we should try something a little different tonight…unless you're scared, cousin?"

"Scared of what? A 'coon hunt, maybe? I noticed your neighbor has a pair of black and tans."

"No, a different kind of hunt."

***

Brodie's friend Mike Cusic showed up as they were locking the trailer door behind them.

"You sure you know how to get to Nickel's through the woods?" Brodie asked.

"Sure do. I went last week, didn't I?"

"What's Nickel's?"

"It's like a country style nightclub. Bar, game room, dance floor, and best of all—lots of ladies."

"Won't they card us?"

"Don't worry, Cuz. Mike knows the bouncer."

After a mile walk through dark woods, he saw the lights of the night spot ahead. The bouncer stood as a lone sentinel silhouetted at the door. The man reminded him of the actor in an old porn film he and Chris Gale watched in his father's barn. He waited for an ID request but it never came. The huge mustached man poked Mike in the ribs and waved them in. "But you get in trouble and I *will* hurt you."

Mike led the way and bellied up to the bar. He bought three Bud Lights and held his up in a toast. "To good times…" They clicked their cans together.

"Hey, let's go check out the ladies, men," Brodie suggested.

They skirted the foosball table and negotiated the waving sticks surrounding the pool tables.

"Let's hit the bowling machine," Mike said. "It's just outside the ladies' room and they all have to pass by there, sooner or later."

Walking in the back of the trio, he was the last to pass the tables. A bearded 30-ish man, built like a pro-football linebacker, moved towards him with two fists full of beer mugs. Brodie stopped to stare towards the ladies' room and he couldn't move forward or around him.

"Gangway, coming through." The man didn't wait for an opening, but barreled through, and knocked him into a pool player's cue. The pool player gripped his stick in a white knuckled grip, sat it on the table and jerked the bill of his orange Baltimore Orioles ball cap to the rear. The man turned his scarlet red face to him, so close he could feel the heat of his breath.

"What…the hell…is wrong…with you? Boy!"

"I'm sorry."

The man grabbed him by the throat and squeezed. "Can you see there's men playing here, punk?"

"Let him go," Brodie said.

"Just who the hell do you think you…"

Brodie grabbed the '8' ball from the table and smashed it into the man's wrist. The man's ball cap sailed across the room as he dropped to one knee, holding his wrist. But Brodie's victory was short-lived. He turned his head towards the ladies' room and his cousin's eyes opened wide. The man stood and slammed his fist into Brodie's face, and a head butt followed. Before Brodie hit the floor, he saw the bouncer grab Brodie from behind.

"You okay, Garren?" Brodie asked. The bouncer dragged him toward the door.

His throat was constricted and he took great gasps of air, trying to catch his breath but gave Brodie the thumbs-up sign.

"You two, with me." The bouncer's calloused finger pointed at him, then Mike, leaving no doubt who he was addressing. He dared a quick glance to see what had drawn Brodie's attention. Aunt Lily stood outside the bathroom door. Some greaser had his tongue in her mouth as he worked a handful of her skimpy blouse.

At the door, Porno-man gave Brodie a shove, then each of them in turn as they exited.

"Don't come back."

"As if…" Brodie yelled.

***

He thought about that night often and wished he could go back in time to make it right. He often consoled himself with the knowledge that he was out of his element and that Brodie took him there—into harm's way. Maybe Brodie had earned his bad boy reputation honestly, but regardless, Brodie defended him. He wondered—would he have done the same for Brodie?

Chapter Four

St. Mary's County, Md.
Brodie

Brodie stomped the mud from his boots on the trailer steps, flung open the paint chipped door, and stalked into the living room. The odor of stale cigarette smoke and alcohol filled the air. His mother was stretched out on the sofa, still dressed in her robe. He reached down and pulled the front of it closed, then tightened its belt.

"Mom, it's eleven in the morning; are you drunk?"

Lily stretched, and absent-mindedly tugged at her robe.

"Not yet, baby, just took the edge off a little bit." She gave him a dazzling smile.

"Whatever…did you remember I'm going to hunting camp with Jim Doyle and the men next week?"

"How can we afford it, baby? The men all put up fifty dollars apiece for the cook up there. Then there's a non-resident hunting license to buy, tags and gas money too. Did you rob a bank or do you want me to skip the lot payment this month?"

"Jim and I have it all worked out. I'll be helping the cook with his chores and whenever he doesn't need me, I'll be hunting. I saved my money from mowing lawns and selling crabs. All the expenses are covered."

"Jim's been known to make promises he can't deliver. Guess it is an occupational hazard for a used car salesman. When did you stop calling him Uncle Jim anyway? And more importantly, can you afford a week away from school?"

He realized the trip would take a little more selling than anticipated, but he knew which buttons to push. He wouldn't let her take this away from him.

"Look Mom, I know you want me to be able to do this but you're worried. It will be great for me, and Garren will be there too. You know I have no problem playing catch up at school, and it won't cost you a thing." Under his breath he added, "Or any of your boyfriends."

"I don't know, Brodie. What if I need you?"

He wasn't ready for that question, and for a moment felt sorry for her. She totally lacked confidence, self-reliance, or commitment; she was a child at heart.

"I know you work hard," he said, "and I know the grocery store isn't an easy place to work. You're on your feet all day, so I've got this. If I can help with the bills like I did this summer, then I can handle paying for things I want too, right?"

Lily's face fell, deflated, conveying the memory of lost paychecks and her shame. She'd said her supervisor gave her time off for showing up late, but he knew it was because of a long series of days late. New boyfriends always disturbed her mental equilibrium. It didn't help her attendance when her nights ended at sunrise. It was amazing she'd sobered up enough to get there at all.

"It's okay, Mom. Don't even worry about it. It's just between us, a family secret." Her eyes watered and he sat on the couch beside her, placing an arm over her shoulders.

"I just don't know, Brodie…"

"Mom, there is something else I wanted to talk to you about too."

"What, Brodie?" she asked, looking for any reprieve from the memory he'd summoned.

"We're learning about genealogy in school. I just thought this might be a good time for you to tell me about my father? I think Aunt Diana and maybe even Uncle Jim knew him… just from things they've said. Will you please tell me about him? All I really know is that I inherited his hair and eyes, and that's not much to go on for this class."

He bit his lip, and felt some shame at causing his mother to squirm.

Lily jumped from the sofa, tears cutting furrows down her cheeks, her face blooming like a crimson rose. She took a deep drag of her cigarette and ashes fell to the floor.

"Oh God, Brodie, not now, I just don't want to talk about that now. Just when you finally stopped having those awful dreams, you want to start in on me about that again?"

His brows drew together as his eyes tried to capture hers, but she stared at the couch pillow instead.

"Maybe we can talk about it when you get back from hunting camp, son. And Garren will be there so you'll have someone your own age to talk to."

"Yeah, Garren," he said. "Thank God my 'never does wrong' cousin is going to be there. It should make it interesting anyway."

He didn't really have anything against Garren. Actually, he imagined him to be an all right guy. He just needed a little real life maturing and some education of the kind not found in any book. He'd spent too much time with those fancy kids in that private school of his. Acting a little high and mighty was the norm for folks born with a silver spoon. Most of them did nothing, and earned nothing on their own. They were just well financed leeches.

He admitted, though only to himself, that a good part of his resentment was jealousy. The one thing he envied about his cousin. Garren never knew his father either, but Brodie's father left…deserted his mother and his unborn son. He'd made a conscious decision to desert them. Garren's father had an excuse—death forgives all. But Brodie's father? Would he have loved his son…*if* he'd stayed? Would he be proud of him today? Or shamed at the mention of his name? Would he be pleased to see his flesh and blood renewed in his progeny? Or would he deny the kinship…perhaps hiding his existence from some other legitimate family? One he'd deigned to love and care for? Had he been too young to assume responsibility for a new life? His mother did so, albeit poorly, but it was nonetheless the most she was capable of.

Thinking of Garren reminded him of the month he'd spent at their cabin at the end of the school year. He made friends easily, or acquaintances…always had. After the first week in the new school in the mountains, he and George Ferris were best of friends. George had an established reputation as a bad boy. He and George gravitated to each other like iron to magnets.

He learned what his other classmates didn't know—that George's father was an abuser. Not that George came out and said so…but he'd seen the signs. George's explanations about his old man showing him how to box didn't hold up.

The week before school let out, he was suspended for an incident in the girls' locker room. Diana and Garren never found out and he was home in Maryland before his mother was released from her stint in county lock-up. It was a simple matter to clear the answering machine and filter their mail.

He wasn't the main perpetrator. Hell, he didn't even know what George was planning until he snatched the snake from the burlap bag. Still, he was the beneficiary of the prank, and George's old man would've beat him senseless if he'd been the one suspended. The whole thing wasn't a big deal, the girls had towels and everything…

But when he saw Lenore Bauer…God what a hottie she was! Long auburn hair, green eyes, and a body that could fuel a young man's dreams by its very existence. He'd been attracted to her since he'd first laid eyes on her, but with what she did next, he fell in love—an incurable abiding addiction. That at least, he got from the school suspension. Knowledge never comes without a price, and Lenore was worth it!

George tossing the black snake in the showers was a stroke of genius. The girls ran out screaming with towels barely covering anything. They hadn't even noticed the two boys standing there—well, except for Lenore. She made a fast exit, but spied them gawking at the wet parade. She paused, calmly walked over and punched him in the jaw…hard, as hard as any guy ever had. His molars still ached at the thought of it.

He thought he could find his way into her good graces though. He'd tied some of the flowers he'd picked from Diana's flower bed with a note of apology reading: 'Dearest Lenore, I know we've never officially met and I wish the circumstances of our recent "exposure" to one another were different. Please accept my humblest apology. Do you believe in fate? I feel inexorably drawn to you. Take a chance? With Deep Affection, Brodie Caine.'

He attached the note to her locker in the morning, but he wasn't around long enough to see her reaction or hear her response.

The acting principal Percival Simmons called him and George into his office the next morning. He knew the man from seeing him in the halls and somewhat by his reputation. Simmons was a tall thin man with stringy black hair and a hawk's bill nose. Some students said his dark eyes absorbed all the light from a room. George said the man had a very negative charge in his fuse box, but then, George's dad was an electrician. Perhaps he wasn't as peculiar as the school painted him, not as strange as he appeared, but they weren't the ones to start it—who'd name their child Percival?

Simmons pointed at the two scarred wooden chairs in front of his desk. He and George sat down and prepared themselves for a tongue lashing. Simmons giggled, shook his head and stood up to pace back and forth in front of his office window.

"I don't know what to do with you two. This is not acceptable behavior, you know that, correct?"

They nodded but Percival didn't wait for an answer. "Still, this reminds me of a younger me. I know you aren't bad young men and I know boys will be boys, but this can't stand. I need a scapegoat, boys. Who's gonna be the man and 'fess up?"

He held up his hand.

"You, Brodie?"

"Yes, sir, Mr. Simmons. I instigated it, George was just along for the ride."

He was suspended, and Percival let George off with a warning. As they were led from the office, he saw Mrs. Burch, the English teacher, and Simmons' voice became very stern.

"…and if I *ever* hear even a hint of disrespect to women from the two of you again, expect the full force of…"

The man's voice trailed off as he continued down the hall to empty his locker. George nodded his thanks, but wouldn't look him in the eye. George didn't meet him at the pool hall to play video games after school either—even though they'd done so every day since they'd met. He knew how to adapt to being unappreciated though. His cousin taught him that.

Garren told him he was having a great time during their week together, but after that evening at Nickel's, Garren hardly spoke to him. Hell, he tried to help him that night. Did Garren blame him for what happened? Did he think he'd set him up? He acted embarrassed and wouldn't look him in the eye. But what could he be embarrassed about? So what if they snuck into a bar?

Maybe Garren was afraid of him, and maybe that was a good thing. He knew Garren always followed his lead, but hell, he could talk anybody into just about anything if he set his mind to it.

Chapter Five

Hampshire County, WV
Lenore Bauer

She smiled as Bridget Braden approached their shared locker. Bridget flashed her well known smile as the last bell of the school day rang. The two of them had been inseparable for as far back as her memory stretched, but their bond was tested over the summer. When her mother remarried, they moved from the old neighborhood. The new house was a modest, comfortable home but luxurious by their past standards. The Cape Cod had two acres of land with it and one other bonus—it was still less than two miles away from her friend. They couldn't meet every day anymore, but the summer saw many miles logged on their bikes visiting each other.

Classmates at Potomac High School referred to them as the 'Dynamic Duo' which was a big improvement over 'The Double B's,' a nickname only partially derived from the initials of their last names. Thankfully, it fell out of favor a few years earlier when Lenore 'blossomed,' as her mother described her embarrassing development at the time.

"So, what do you think of the new girl?" Bridget closed their locker door.

"Oh, I don't know, two words I guess—dark and unapproachable, but to be fair, it's her first day of school."

"Coppery skin, chocolate eyes, and dressed in black…that wouldn't have anything to do with your first impressions, would it?" Bridget continued. "I think we should get to know her, maybe take her under our wings…"

"Okay, I get it now. I was going to tell you the gossip on her, but my guess is you've already heard it, huh?"

She saw her innocent smile, the one she knew Bridget had been practicing on the boys.

"Well not really, what did you hear?" Bridget asked.

She rolled her green eyes in the manner usually reserved for her mother.

"Yeah, right…so, the story is they 'asked' her to leave her private school because of being disruptive in class. She's Native American or something, and into tribal religions, mysticism, and stuff. Whenever they tried to indoctrinate her—it was a Christian school—she argued with them. I guess they couldn't handle all that, so here she is."

"And you've been hooked on that paranormal stuff since we did the Ouija board years ago."

Bridget laughed. "Guilty as charged. Still, she seems really poised and sure of herself. Don't you think?"

"Guess you paid a lot more attention to her than I did, but one thing I do know is that you moved that Ouija board pointer!" She laughed. "But you could use a shot of that assurance yourself, Miss No Self-Confidence…"

"Ha, ha, so funny I forgot to laugh. Easy to say for a girl with knockers like yours. Nobody calls you BB anymore."

"They're your initials, Bridget…"

Bridget pursed her lips. "Hush, she's coming."

She looked over her shoulder and saw that Anna wasn't coming; she'd arrived. She stood staring at them, and likely heard some of their conversation.

"Hi. Anna, isn't it? We were just talking about you," she said.

"So I noticed. Comparing the fresh gossip about the new girl?" Anna's eyes clouded over. Her lips contracted into a tight line.

"Not exactly," she responded. "Being new and all, we wondered if you'd like to hang out with us sometimes."

"Why, are you lacking a token Injun? Trying to do your good deed for the day so you can tell your social club? Thanks a bunch, but no thanks."

"No, we just…oh hell, forget it. We don't need the grief or the drama," she snapped.

"Wait. No, it's not like that, Anna…" Bridget started.

"No, let's go." She grabbed her friend's elbow and pulled her away.

***

Anna

She glared at the two girls as they stalked away. They were pretty, she thought, perhaps the prettiest girls in school, but neither one of them seemed particularly aware of that fact. That was rare enough and normally would assure their popularity, and yet…

They had three classes together—that she knew of. Maybe there were more, but she hadn't noticed them until she became aware of them noticing her. Her impression of them, and of this school, was all more of the same. True, it was her first day, but this school seemed no different than the others. The boys leered at her, assuming an undeserved and uninvited intimacy. Their disrespectful stares reminded her of wolves drooling over a bitch in heat. But unlike a she wolf, she'd sent no signal to them, no invitation expressed or implied. No, she was just different, and therefore 'exotic.' That elicited their prurient desires even as it marked her as a pariah. Did they suppose their indecent remarks might win them her favors?

The female students were no better with condescending smirks and whispered secrets. But maybe these two girls were different, or maybe it was that they were poor? In this community there was poor, and then there was 'Poor' with a capital P. The hateful girls behind her in history class opened her eyes to that fact.

"God, she's so full of herself, isn't she?" one asked.

"Into some creepy stuff too…"

"Yeah, and pretty loose I heard, but that kind usually is you know. Certainly not like us, I guess evolution hasn't caught up."

Her hackles went up. Her face flushed and she wanted nothing more than to bruise her knuckles on their fat gloating faces. But she knew she wouldn't…best to keep her head down.

"Yeah, poor white trash, both of them."

"At least you can tell Lenore's a girl. Double B might be a twelve-year-old boy for all we know."

Her mouth dropped realizing it wasn't her they were mocking for a change. *Lenore? And Double B? Not Anna…not the new girl…or the Indian Goth chick…?*

She knew what it was like. She felt for the two girls disparaged by the snobbish clique, but admitted to herself that it was a nice reprieve. Were they as much of an outsider as she was?

God she missed Garren, her only friend, but his friendship was also in doubt now. Was she throwing away an opportunity with the two girls? A chance for new friends? If so, didn't that make her a reverse snob? No better than the bitchy gossip girls?

They might be more like her than she thought. She'd noticed that the red-haired girl had what her grandmother called 'the seeing eyes.' Was she also a Spiritualist? Or something else? What would her spiritual guide advise? Moll would say something like "*Someone finally takes an interest in you and you insult them? Take the chance, Anna, just be careful...*"

"Hey ladies, wait up." She trotted toward them. "Look, I'm new here, and I'm coming from a place that if it wasn't hell, was at least hell-adjacent. I'm sorry I was a bitch..." She extended her hand. "Does the offer still stand?"

The perky strawberry blonde girl was quick to grab it. "Sure, good to meet you, Anna. Doubt you remember all the names from class. I'm Bridget, and this is the White Witch Lenore."

Lenore stuck her tongue out at Bridget, paused and took her hand.

"White witch? What's that about? No disrespect, but you are about the whitest person I've ever met," Anna quipped, "but what's with the witch part?"

Lenore smiled, but her eyes did not. "Don't go there, Anna. It's the name this guy Brodie Caine tagged me with. You'd probably think he was gorgeous and sexy like the rest of the girls did, but he was a creep. I'm glad he got expelled. Anyway, Bridget and I are getting together at my place tonight. Want to join us?"

"What's the plan?" she asked.

"It may sound lame, but my new dad built a fire pit in our back yard. We sit around and talk. Sometimes about boys, sometimes about the meaning of life and man's inhumanity to man." Lenore grinned.

"Wow, very deep. Count me in."

Lenore wrote down the directions to her place, and handed them to Anna. "Seven-ish?"

She smiled. "Wow, the first day of school and I have an invitation to the lair of the White Witch!"

"Ha-ha. We do need our token you know." Lenore grinned.

Chapter Six

What a foul and fateful night! His life defined by one weak moment, one screwed up, selfish instant of time. All good will negated. Their love tainted...now only an empty rotted husk would remain. Help me, Lord—if you can hear me now through the blight on my soul. Death would be a kindness, Father.

St. Mary's County, MD to
Nathaniel Mountain Hunting Camp, WV
Brodie

"It sure is beautiful this time of year, ain't it, Uncle Jim?" He wound down his window to breath in the crisp autumn air.

"My favorite time of year, Brodie, that's for sure."

Jim pulled his old International pickup truck out of the trailer park entrance and squealed tires where the loose gravel met the asphalt—all the while grinning like a schoolboy. He glanced behind him and thought most of the vehicles parked there were in better shape than Jim's old primer gray war wagon. Anybody would think Uncle Jim down on his luck, and they certainly wouldn't suspect he owned the local car lot.

He pointed at the cross hanging from Jim's rear view mirror. It appeared handmade using two case-hard nails welded together. "Does that help keep this old truck from falling to pieces?"

"Don't mock the Big Guy, Brodie. The Good Lord can do wondrous things, but this old truck? They don't make 'em like 'The Tank' anymore, young'un."

"Yes, sir and it still gets the job done."

"It'll get us there and back, don't you worry."

They stopped once to stretch on their three-hour drive, then filled up with gas and snacks. Jim dumped a quart of oil in the Tank's engine and they hit the road again. Before Jim swallowed the last bite of his Twinkies, he flipped on his turn signal and followed the exit off Interstate 81.

He recognized the exit as the last leg of the trip to Garren's house and slapped the pickup's dash. "Woo-hoo, Jim. We're nearly there." He didn't much look forward to spending so much time with his cousin, but he wasn't about to let it ruin his hunt either.

The last section of Route 50 was a lazy stretch of road that, along with Jim's driving, rocked him to sleep. The sudden braking shook him awake, and he looked up as Garren yelled from the front step, "Ready for the deer?"

"Question is, are the deer ready for us, right Brodie?" Uncle Jim jabbed him with his elbow. He shook his head as Garren dragged his bags toward the truck. "Jesus, Garren. You reckon you've got enough gear for one week?"

"I packed Dad's old Army duffel bag with everything I thought I could possibly use, but then Mom got carried away."

Jim pointed at the gun case he toted. "Is that the .243 your father bought for you before you were born?"

"Yes sir, shined up, oiled down, and ready to go. It won't let me down." Garren grabbed his bags and threw them in back of the truck as Diana walked out of the house.

"Look at the three strong men heading out after poor little Bambi," she teased.

"Don't tell me you've been watching that Disney foolishness? You know better, Diana," Jim said. "Last chance to stretch before we hit the road again, Brodie."

He jumped out of the truck and waved Garren over. "C'mon Cuz, I want to show you the gun Uncle Jim's letting me use." He hustled to the back of the truck and lifted out a worn leather gun case. He slid back the paper clip that served as a zipper pull and removed an old lever action 30/30. The front barrel band was missing from the front of the stock, and a sloppy duct tape repair job held it all together. He tossed the weapon to Garren.

"What do you think, Cuz? Think this thing will shoot anywhere close to where I point it?"

Garren looked down the sights and worked the lever. "It has a smooth action anyway."

"Yeah, I'll give it that. Some might even say sloppy. I wonder who's likely to be hurt when I pull the trigger—the deer or me?" He laughed.

"Uncle Jim wouldn't let you use it if it wasn't safe."

"Maybe, but hey, help me out. I know Uncle Jim's going to get breakfast at the Springfield Diner on the way up. He always does. I've heard the other men say he doesn't get to camp until late because he flirts with the waitresses and drinks a couple pots of coffee. I need to shoot this thing to make sure I can hit what I'm aiming at."

"What do you want me to do?"

"Maybe prod him along some? He's your real uncle and all."

Garren nodded and they walked toward the cab of the truck. Diana hugged the two boys goodbye, then turned to Jim. Brodie heard her whisper, "Thank you so much Jim. I appreciate you doing this for the boys. It all started out so wrong for both of them, and Lily hasn't been..." When Diana's eyes met his, her thought froze on her lips.

"Everything's fine, Diana. I'll take good care of them. No need to worry," Jim said. "You fellows about ready? Everybody's got their hunting licenses, right? Tags?"

"We're ready to roll, Uncle Jim," Garren said.

The old truck bounced down the road, spewing blue smoke while running the Interstate for a few miles, then they were back to county roads, and a teeth jarring ride. He didn't speak a word, absorbed in his own thoughts. Jim rattled on about camp life and Garren asked if the other hunt club members were seeing any deer.

"Quite a few I'm hearing, and it's still early. The harvest was way down last year, not many hunters came up. Hope it's different this year."

"Better for us if they don't, isn't it?"

"Maybe, but not for the deer. There was a lot of snow up this way a few years back. The deer yarded up and stripped all the browse from the trees—all they could reach anyway. We found quite a few skeletons in the woods that year."

"Starved? Has the herd recovered?"

"Hoping so. We set restrictions the past three seasons to keep the kill down, only taking barren does and old bucks. The numbers are up now—maybe too many, so we've lifted the restrictions this year."

He pictured the deer bones scattered by the carrion eaters and rodents after the calcium in the bones... "That sucks, Jim. I sure do hate having an empty belly. Can't imagine starving to death."

"Yeah, starving's the last way I'd want to go. I'd take the bullet any day. And speaking of *not* starving..." Jim pointed at the curve in the road. The Springfield Diner loomed dead ahead.

Jim and Garren ordered breakfast, but he settled for just coffee and a muffin. He didn't want to take the time to eat.

After the food arrived, Jim motioned to the blonde twenty-something waitress.

"Helen, for some reason that coffee just ain't flowing as quick as usual, can you help remedy this situation?"

"No problem, Mr. Doyle. I look out for my favorite customers. Want some more eggs too?"

Jim placed a hand at Helen's waist and allowed it to slip down to her backside.

"Well, eggs are one thing I could go for," he said.

The waitress smiled, but looked like his buddy Mike's beagle when he was given a bath. He didn't like it, but knew he had to get past it. The waitress walked behind the food counter.

"What do you think about that gal, boys? She sure is something, isn't she?" Jim winked.

"Yes, she's pretty...somebody's daughter I bet. Isn't she about the same age as your daughter?" Garren asked.

He spit out coffee at Garren's remark. He felt embarrassed for the girl too, and for some strange reason, he was embarrassed for Jim as well. He winked at Garren.

"You think we should leave soon, Uncle Jim?" Garren asked. "We don't want to get to camp too late."

"What's your hurry there, young fellow? This is part of the pre-hunt ritual. Hell, if I didn't stop and have breakfast in Springfield, it might offend the gods of the hunt. We wouldn't want that now, would we? Are you afraid the deer won't wait on you?"

***

For the remainder of the drive to camp, he and Garren listened as Uncle Jim related the history of the camp.

"Your father and three of his closest friends established the camp twenty years ago, Garren. One of his wealthy clients originally owned the place. A newlywed, the poor feller bought 375 acres on the mountain while still in the throes of marital bliss. He hoped—with Adam's help—to turn the dilapidated old cabin there into a weekend retreat for himself and his new bride. The plans were barely set in motion before her moral code revealed itself—in the form of an affair—and their domestic tranquility ended. The divorce promised to be a long and nasty affair.

"The client said if Adam absorbed what he owed him, he'd sell him the land for a tenth of its value. He said he was selling it—whether to him or a stranger—but he intended to keep the money away from that 'whoring bitch' no matter what the cost. The deal proved so sweet that after three phone calls and two lawyer's appointments, the land belonged to them.

"The men spent a summer's worth of weekends fixing the place up. Well, the three men *and* your mother. Diana worked at their sides, hammering nails, pulling old planks, and scouring the inside walls and floors with bleach water. They added on the downstairs bunkroom and, as the final touch, a TV and outside antenna were installed. Diana teased them saying she was putting in a small flowerbed with garden gnomes out front...maybe a few pink flamingoes too.

"All that sound like your mom, Garren? And what you've heard of your dad?"

"Mom, yes...but Dad? I wish I knew, Uncle Jim. Mom tells me some, but I can tell how much it hurts her. Do you think any of the original guys will be coming this week?"

"It being opening week, I suspect Henry Gale will be there. I believe you know his son, Garren—I think his name's Chris? Then there's Bertram Campbell, he's a city feller, and not one of the originals, but he's an owner now and he's been coming up here for a few years. More money than he knows what to do with. Played the stock market I think. Now he's started some kind of airplane business in Martinsville, and something with computers too. He has a finger in so many pies, you'd think he was running a bakery. Bertram bought out Jack Farrell's share from the family when Jack passed. Jack didn't have any kids. But I bet the family got a pretty penny for it. I doubt we'll see Turnip Price. He had a by-pass operation this year. He's about 75 years old and ain't getting up to camp much nowadays anyway."

"The man's name is Turnip?"

"I don't know, Brodie. Price said they tagged him with that as a kid. They said his head looked like a turnip. I never had the heart to tell him it still does. Anyway, that leaves Mika. Don't know his last name; don't know if he knows it any more. He's the cook, not an actual member but might just as well be. He's been coming up as long as any of us. Brodie, you'll get to know him right well. Mika's part Indian, helluva nice fellow, and he's a pretty fair wood carver too. World class I've heard, whatever that means when it comes to whittling.

"Mika's a private sort, and you'll never hear him complain. He and your daddy were as tight as two ticks on a hound dog's ear, Garren. He lost his wife a while back. I hear he took up with some young gal, and that he really robbed the cradle. Doubt that place has plumbing or anything else, so I don't know how he enticed her up there, but Jimmy Coombs saw her in his yard the other day. Said she was a real looker too. It don't sound like Mika, but Jimmy swore it was the truth. Maybe Mika's just old and lonely. It happens. Don't let that happen to you boys, but don't be in no hurry to settle down either."

Jim's old truck ricocheted from one pothole to the next on the last leg of the drive. Jim pointed out areas of interest. To the right stood the fifty acres that some religious cult purchased the year before. Jim said when he came up this past summer, a half dozen naked folks were parading around the field. The boys craned their necks in hopes of a repeat view, but there was only an old sow guarding her piglets that stared at them as they passed. The next farm belonged to some folks only interested in turkey hunting. Jim said he'd never seen them there at any other time of year. They had a gentlemen's agreement with one another: if one group wasn't in camp, they could hunt off each other's property. An older man owned the final farm, still trying to eke out a living from the rocky, depleted soil. Deer ate a good part of what he managed to grow, and he hoped the hunters would 'kill every damn one of 'em they see.'

"I think my butt's growing roots into your seats, Uncle Jim," Garren said.

"Don't be ruining my fancy seats now, here? 'Sides, there's the camp drive dead ahead." Jim pointed to the dirt furrow.

"You might want to think on adding some new shocks on this old clunker, Uncle Jim." Garren rubbed his backside.

Jim maneuvered the old truck around a bright yellow pickup parked at the edge of the road, and partially blocking the cabin's access lane.

"That's Bertram's truck, nothing but the biggest and best for him. He can't park at the cabin like the rest of us; somebody might ding his paint job you know.

"There's sure a bumper crop of dogwood berries up here this year," Brodie said.

"They say that means a hard winter is coming, boys." Jim wrenched the gearshift into reverse and slammed home the parking brake.

The number of vehicles parked out front indicated a full house, and Jim hustled the boys in to introduce them to everyone. A heavy-set and partially bald man in his mid-fifties was introduced as Bertram. He nodded from his chair by the wood stove, busily engaged in cutting store tags from his new camouflage clothes. He didn't get up to shake hands.

"That's my guest Frank Harvey," Bertram said, pointing a thumb at the man warming his hands by the wood stove.

"We just got in ourselves," he said, "pleased to meet you boys." Frank held out his hand. "Brodie?"

"Yes, sir." He shook the offered hand. He noted Frank's greased down hair, and his genuine smile.

The back door of the cabin creaked opened and a teenage boy walked in.

"Chris? Son of a gun, what are you doing here?" Garren asked. "I thought your dad wanted you to wait until next year?"

Chris Gale grabbed Garren's outstretched hand and pumped it heartily.

"I did too, guess he wanted to surprise me, and it worked."

He felt Chris' eyes giving him the once over. He stared back, noticing he kept his dirty-blonde hair cut short, and his baby-face was topped with nerdy 'birth-control' glasses. Chris worked around the room shaking hands as he went. Garren introduced Chris to him and Jim.

"So are you related to Lenore?" he asked.

"My new sister," Chris said. "Brodie Caine, is that right? I think I've heard Lenore speak of you."

"New sister?"

"We don't like step-sister. My dad and her mom married and made us a family."

"What Lenore said...it was all good I hope?" he asked. Chris glared at him, and everyone knew whatever stories Lenore shared, they didn't cast him in a favorable light.

Chris's father Henry soon followed his son in, firewood cradled in his arms, and the introductions and handshakes began again.

A thin sinewy man entered from the kitchen. His skin was the color of an old penny, and flecks of gray streaked his short black hair.

"I'm hearing all this commotion out here, and I'm thinking there's hunters wanting to eat." The man walked over to him, and shook his hand.

"Don't believe we've met, but I reckon you're my help this week? I'm called Mika by my friends, and all kinds of stuff by everybody else.

"I figured you fellows might want a quick bite before you check out your stands, so I've got some sandwiches made up. I promise you'll be eating better the rest of the week."

"I've no doubt," Uncle Jim responded.

"Brodie, if you'll take a look at our two stands up the hill there, and make sure they haven't fallen apart, I won't need any help until tonight."

"Thanks, Mr...." he started.

"It's just Mika, that'll do fine."

Mika looked at him and then at Garren. "I knew your father, Garren. If you have any of him in you, you'll be a fine man."

"Thank you, Mika, and I'm pleased to finally meet you. My mother speaks very highly of you."

The men all pulled on their boots and headed for the stands. Uncle Jim pulled Garren aside, pointing out the two mounted deer heads on the wall.

"That's the two deer your mom and dad took the very first year they bought in to this place. I've tried to get your mom to take them to your cabin, but she says there are too many memories. Diana is the Greek goddess of hunting you know. I don't think she ever looked as happy as she did when she was hunting."

He saw Garren's smile and shared some measure of pride in his aunt and uncle.

"I don't think Diana's been to camp since your father died. Whenever she says, your daddy's share of the camp will pass to you, so we need to break you in right! I'm hoping you can get her back up here soon though."

The stands were laid out four to either side of the cabin, following the farm road in opposite directions, and all perched overlooking deer trails. Garren was on one side with Jim, Bertram, and Frank while Henry, Chris, and the two cooks hunted the other side. Still, they went as a group to check out all of the stands. Some of the hunters put out shelled corn to lure the deer to ambush. The two stands closest to the cabin were designated for the cook and his guest, or his helper, because the deer frequently moved through in the evenings when the cook had the most time to hunt. They were close enough to camp the cook could slip in quickly after breakfast in the mornings.

Evidence of deer activity was everywhere. The area around the last two stands past the cook's looked like they'd held a deer convention. Bucks anxious to get on with breeding season had shredded trees of their bark. Large areas of ground were pawed up leaving sexual signposts for the does. These were the stands hunted by Henry Gale, and this year his son Chris. The younger Gale made little attempt to hide his excitement.

"This is my year, guys! I can't wait until tomorrow. I'll be back in camp with my deer and sipping coffee by eight o'clock!"

"Is that a.m. or p.m.?" he teased.

"Well, there's a two deer limit this year, so I reckon I'll have both of my tags filled by 8 p.m."

"I hope that's true, Chris." Garren laughed.

The light left quickly in the mountains, and the men hurried back to the cabin looking forward to Mika's dinner, each convinced they'd be the first one back to camp in the morning, venison in tow. Some toasted in advance the next day's successes. Cards were dealt and they gathered around the table, joking, telling lies, bonding.

Jim Doyle sat his drink down, looked at his cards and made his bid.

Mika raised the bid and tossed in his markers. He took a long pull on his ice water. He glanced at him, then at Garren.

"I swear, boys, I've never seen two cousins look as much alike as you two. There must be some strong family genes in there."

Jim Doyle cleared his throat, coughed and took a long pull on his beer.

"What happened with those genes in you, Jim? You just look like plain old Jim."

"I suppose I'm a throwback, Mika. I know what you mean though. If you add a few pounds on Garren, and dye Brodie's hair blonde, maybe take an iron to that curly hair of his, then, yup, they could be brothers, huh?" He winked at Mika.

He noticed the wink, and also saw the questioning look on Garren's face. They both feigned ignorance, hoping Jim's alcohol-loosened tongue continued to wag.

The subject changed back to the morning's hunt, though, and the air became electric with anticipated excitement. All else was forgotten.

Henry and Frank soon followed Bertram to the bunkhouse.

"Okay, fellows," Mika said standing, "I'm going to call it a night. Brodie and I will be up at zero dark thirty, and we'll be stirring you bunch up shortly after for grub and opening day."

The hunters agreed, shutting down the lights and setting their alarms, impatient for the new day to dawn.

He tossed and turned in his bunk. It was comfortable enough, considering the circumstances, but his thoughts were at home. Was he too quick to accept Jim's offer to come? Too selfish? His mother had few friends and she didn't make the best decisions when left to her own devices.

He thought of her as she was in her younger days. A Southern Maryland girl through and through. He bet she was born with Old Bay under her fingernails and seeping from every pore. Fearless and independent she'd been, a lioness when defending her cub, and a comforting angel when nurturing his hurts. What happened? Was he the cause of her collapse?

He remembered her chilling out with fellow players after a victory in the women's softball game behind Nickel's. Toasting one another with a ten ounce can of Budweiser in hand, often making plans for a rousing game of cards…invariably that meant a game of pitch.

He wondered about Jim's comments. The circumstances of his birth were shadowy enough…was it his accidental birth that began his mother's spiraling descent?

Chapter Seven

Hampshire County, WV
Lenore

Peering through the picture window facing the road, she saw Bridget turn her bike into the drive. "If you need me, I'll be out back, Mom," she yelled. The screech and slap of the screen door drowned out the last of her words.

The girls greeted one another and hurried to the back yard to start the fire. She knew the fire pit was Bridget's favorite part of her new home.

"So tell me, what do you really think of Anna?" Bridget asked.

"She's cool. I'd say she's our kind of girl. And of course, there's the other thing." She grinned.

"What might that other thing be?" Anna approached from the trees behind them.

"Huh, how did you get there? Were you spying on us?" Bridget asked.

"We're friends, remember? Friends don't spy on one another. They might gossip about each other behind their backs, but spy? Never."

"But how…?" Bridget began.

"I walked through the woods. It's not far as the crow flies, or as the Indian walks…and what's the other thing, Lenore?"

"Look Anna, first off, I'm sorry. Seems whenever we see you, we're talking about you, but we were having a private conversation."

"Excuse the heck out of me, but I guess I should be used to that," Anna replied. "I'm not lily white enough for you?"

"No, that isn't it at all. We want to be friends with you because of who you are," she explained.

"Oh, I see. You want to be friends with a token Native American. That's *sooo* much better."

"No, not that, well yeah, that too—I guess." Bridget's face flushed.

Anna scratched her head, then turned to leave.

"Anna, wait, please," she said. "Give us two minutes, and if you want nothing to do with us then, we'll never bother you again. Fair?"

Anna hesitated, but then she tossed back her hair and turned to face Lenore. Her eyebrows knitted together as she stared into her eyes. She squirmed under the intensity of Anna's gaze. It seemed almost intimate.

"Talk to me then, white witch," Anna whispered.

"We've heard gossip about you. I don't know how much, if any of it, is true. What we've heard made us want to get to know you. Not to make fun of you, but because we think we're kindred spirits. Even if none of it is true, we'd still be glad to call you friend because we think you're our kind of people. Do you think we could sit by the fire and talk?"

"Kindred spirit, huh? That sounds so California, Lenore. So what gossip did you hear that gave you this impression?"

Bridget jumped in. "Well, we heard you're some kind of witch...or something. We heard you were Indian, sure, but also that you knew stuff about the earth. They say you know about magic and that you do séances...just so much cool stuff! And of course, we heard your beliefs got you kicked out of St. Catherine's High."

"Hmm, heard all that, huh? It seems you ladies know a lot more about me than I do about you."

"Is it all true then?" Bridget charged on.

"Let's see: Indian? Yes, I am part Native American, actually only about one-fourth. Pure bloods wouldn't claim me, but whites don't either. My grandfather does though, and that's enough for me, but a witch or magic? The only magic I know is what's inside, and that's in everyone—even you, Bridget." Anna smiled. "Some call what I do...what I am, a spiritualist. After my grandmother passed on to the next world, her spirit guide began to appear to me in my dreams."

"Bridget and I want to know what you know, Anna. I've always enjoyed reading about Earth religions, even when I was little. Everyone I've tried talking to about it—except Bridget—thinks I'm a joke. Brodie Caine called me a white witch, and he didn't know me much. Am I making you uncomfortable?" She noticed Anna's eyes darken.

"Look, my thoughts and beliefs are just that—mine. Many Native Americans feel native beliefs and magic shouldn't be mixed with that of other cultures, or with the new age pagans. Again, my beliefs are my beliefs. I am also of Celtic descent and there is even some Romani, or what you call gypsy, in there somewhere...or so I've been told. All of my ancestors influence me. They are all part of me, and where I'm going, but you're asking me to trust you with my personal beliefs? I don't consider this a joke or a party game; it's who I am. It's a very personal and private part of me. You think you have been maligned? That you are judged? Walk a mile in this Injun's Chuck Taylor moccasins!"

She was at a loss for words, and now realized how much they were asking of Anna—a much maligned young woman with no reason to trust them. Anna implied she'd known much ridicule in her life, and she felt ashamed and brutish to open old wounds.

Anna stood up, and walked around the fire, stopping in front of her. Placing both hands on her shoulders, Anna stared into her eyes again. She began to fidget uncomfortably, and pulled away.

"How do you feel when I do this, Lenore?" Anna demanded.

"Ummm, kind of violated actually."

"Do you see things, Lenore?"

"See things?"

"Figures, people at the edge of your vision, especially when you're close to sleep? Do you see flecks or clouds of light when you look at someone? Do you dream things, find out they really happened, and assume someone must have already told you about it?"

She twisted her shoulders away, but Anna's hands maintained their grip.

"Have you ever daydreamed of places you've never been, and of people you've never met? What do you see, Lenore? What demons or terrors latch on when your head hits the pillow at night?" The questions were fired with machine gun rapidity and accuracy.

Anna released her from the grip of her hands and of her stare. Stiff-backed and feeling lost, she dropped her head and stared at the ground, trembling.

Bridget ran to her side. "Lenore, are you okay?"

She lifted her head. "How do you know that, Anna? Am I so easy to read? Am I crazy?"

"No, you're not, Lenore, though some might say so. Those not touched by the other side, or afraid to be, open their eyes and hearts to their gifts. I'm sorry. I really am, but you asked a lot. I needed to see your heart."

Bridget stared open-mouthed at them. "What did you do to her, Anna? Did you read her mind?"

"No, no one can do that. I get impressions, and feel emotions. We all do that, but most of the time we're too self-absorbed to concentrate on anyone else, or we don't trust our hearts. I can feel her truth, and fairness. Her life force is strong, her empathy real. I know you've heard the old saying that the eyes are the windows of the soul? It's true, you know, if you open your eyes to see, and if you aren't afraid."

She lifted her head and faced Anna. She felt a heat creeping back into her eyes. "Don't ever do that to me again," she warned.

Anna lowered her eyes. "Most people are so blind to their own spirit they don't even know when I look. If I'd thought...but I swear to you, I will not...no wait."

Anna dropped to one knee and solemnly—if teasingly—proclaimed, "I swear before all that is holy to always respect the privacy of my friends. I vow eternal allegiance to the White Witch Lenore, for evermore."

Anna stood and hugged her. "I am sorry," she whispered, "friends?"

She returned the embrace.

"So what they say about you is true?" Bridget interrupted.

"Their truth I guess, I believe in things that can't be touched, just as they do. I follow ways that've been with Man since crawling out of the muck, but my path is my own. I believe in the divinity of nature, and the presence of the creator in every aspect of her creation, including each of us, no, especially each of us. Lenore spoke of Earth religions. If you look at any of the belief systems, or philosophies from early man, you will see how similar they are at their roots. They hold to the universal truths. I believe there is one God and she has shown her face to many people in many ways, sometimes showing many faces. Whatever face she has shown, that is the face that particular people needed to see...to find their own way. No 'religion' has it right; they all do, assuming they help people find their way." Anna smiled. "Is that deep enough for you, Bridget?"

"Will you teach us some of these things that you know?" she asked.

"No."

"But, I thought…"

"I can't teach you. I seek my truth, my path—just like you. I'm not a teacher. Even if I was, I could only help you see what's in your own hearts. You can see the bounty of all creation, in nature and in your own souls without me. You can choose your own path, and find your own magic, if you want to call it that."

"So help us find that path, Anna. Help us with what you've learned."

Anna dropped her eyes to the fire and continued to stare as she responded.

"Lenore, because of what I've seen in your heart, we will be seekers together."

"Cool, I'm ready. I mean me too, right?" Bridget blurted.

"Yes, but not tonight," she and Anna said at the same instant.

"Let's just enjoy the fire, and chat about simpler things," she suggested.

"I know," Anna said. "Tell me about the boys at school, especially that Brodie Caine guy."

She and Bridget filled Anna in about Brodie's exploits since they'd known him, and the fact that he was blessedly out of their lives.

"The bastard threw a black snake in the girls' shower. I was livid," she said.

"He's sort of a teenage rebel. If it was anyone besides Brodie Caine…"

"Don't even go there, Bridget. You wouldn't feel that way if you'd been there. As self-conscious as you are? You'd pluck his eyes out and feed them to your cat! Anyway, then the shit sends me flowers with a note apologizing and asking me to give him a chance to make up for it."

"Well, maybe he really was sorry…" Bridget's lips pulled down into a frown.

"I guess I should explain, Anna. You see our little Bridget here got the hots for Brodie as soon as he showed his face in school, so just ignore anything she says on the subject of Brodie Caine."

"No Lenore, I don't, not any more. Believe me I am not defending Brodie Caine."

"Well, that's something new. What's up with that?"

"Lenore, I didn't tell you about this, because I wasn't really sure. I told you Brodie was hanging out with my neighbor, George Ferris, after school. But I didn't mention Brodie found my lost cat Tabitha. She was missing for three days and I thought she'd died, run over or something. She'd never ran off before and I thought I'd never see her again. A lot of animals had disappeared in the neighborhood since Brodie showed up—both cats and dogs. Anyway, Brodie found my kitty and brought her home to me. At first, I felt so grateful I would have done anything for him."

"Anything, Bridget?" she teased.

"Well, no, not *anything*, anything. Besides, another boy was there. Brodie said he was his cousin, but I don't remember his name. The other boy, the cousin, kept looking at Brodie like something that smelled bad. I gave Brodie a big thank you hug, but he held on…like way too long. Maybe it was me, but I was uncomfortable. We were right in front of my parents' trailer too! Maybe he was showing off. I looked at his cousin and he looked uncomfortable too, like he wasn't sure what to do. I knew what my mom told me to do in uncomfortable situations. I threw a knee into him, right where she'd taught me.

"After Brodie stopped rolling around on the ground, he said he'd been kidding around, but he had a tear in his eye so I think he knew I was on to him. That's when I started doing the math—adding up the animals disappearing and the timeframe. I can't say for sure, but I don't need proof to form my opinion. As far as I'm concerned, Brodie Caine is a jerk."

"Oh damn, Brie, I'm sorry. I didn't know, and you should have told me!" She took her friend's hand. Anna put her hand on Bridget's shoulder and squeezed gently.

"That's not all though. Brodie claimed he found Tabitha caught in some brush. How does a cat get caught in brush? After that day, whenever Brodie got close to Tabitha she would snarl and take off running. You know her, Lenore, she never acts like that. I think Brodie might be why Tabitha disappeared in the first place. Maybe he staged the whole thing just to get with me. Do you think anyone could be that self-centered… that hateful?" Bridget sniffed.

"He's a perv, Bridget, and that was awful," Anna said.

Bridget gazed at the flames in the pit, seeking solace in its depths, she thought, and noticed her eyes. For a moment, they seemed to be the source of the flame rather than its reflection. Silence prevailed for several heartbeats, no one knowing what to say.

"Brodie's a jerk. I hate him," Bridget declared. "I'm glad he's gone." She paused for a moment. "That's enough about Brodie Caine, ladies. I'm done thinking about him. So Lenore, why don't you tell Anna about that boy you've been dreaming about?"

"Okay, now we are getting somewhere. Something you want to share, Lenore?" Anna smiled.

"He sounds like a real hunk, Anna. She says she dreams about him every week or so and she talks about him all the time. Who knows how often he really invades her dreams," Bridget confided.

"No, he's really not. A hunk I mean, I never see his face, but I don't think he's what you'd call handsome. He's tall, and thin, but not like a beanpole or anything. His hair is blonde and straight. I get the impression of incredibly dark blue eyes, almost violet."

"It sounds to me like you're seeing him pretty well. Do you feel him?" Anna asked.

"What? No, it's not that kind of dream, Anna."

"No, do you feel what he's like, the kind of person he is?"

"I feel pain. He carries a lot of pain, other people's and his own. He feels guilty about something, but I don't think it was anything he did. He wants something from me, but I don't know what it might be. Can you interpret dreams too, Anna?" she asked.

"No, mostly I just fear my own and what Moll will reveal. I don't think it's entirely a dream you're having though, not a dream as most people would define one. I bet there's a real guy out there who will become important in your life, or you in his, and maybe soon."

"Moll?"

"Ah, that's a story for another time."

Despite the revelations of the night, or because of them, the young women grew tired, their eyes heavy. Bridget curled up on a rock by the fire pit and fell asleep as the other girls watched the dying embers. Lenore shook her awake gently, afraid her hair would singe. The party broke up soon thereafter.

Anna stood up. "I'm beat. Would you guys want to come over tomorrow? I have the place all to myself. My grandfather is off hunting and playing camp chef. The only fire pit we have is a small one to heat the rocks for Grandfather's sweat lodge. The sweat helps cleanse the body and spirit. If you're interested, fast tomorrow, and we'll see where we go from there…"

"We're in," Bridget answered.

Chapter Eight

Deer Camp, Nathaniel Mountain, WV
Brodie

He tossed back and forth on the thin mattress of the camp cot.

"Why did you come? They don't want you here. Don't trust any...they're laughing at you. Hate you...mock you...they'll kill *you..."*

"Who are you?" his dream-self asked.

"A friend. A brother."

"Are you with the woman? The woman by the creek?"

The clatter of pans in the kitchen jolted him awake. His clothes were soaked from the nightmarish dream, the chill of the room seeped into the pores of his damp skin. His brain in a fog, he tried to recall the disturbing dream, but there were only snippets. His first rational thought was of Jim's innuendo the night before. What was Jim insinuating during the card game? Was Jim hiding something from him...from both of the cousins?

He ran it through his mind, over and over throughout the night, and reached a few possible conclusions. First, Garren was more than just his cousin, perhaps a half-brother? Throughout his life, his mother told him how close his Aunt Diana and Uncle Adam were, and how inseparable—even hunting together. That was a doubtful connection though. Lily called theirs a match made in heaven, and bemoaned the fact she never had a relationship like theirs. His mother had a hard life.

There was another way Garren could be his 'almost brother.' He thought of the many times Jim—'Uncle'

Jim—stopped to visit when he was growing up. Jim came to his ball games to watch him play, and teased him about his first crush. He remembered his mother's continual insistence that he refer to him as Uncle. Jim lent money to his mother, and he doubted it was ever repaid. He'd just thought Jim was a nice guy, looking out for his almost family members.

Guess he should have, he thought. *Reckon it was his way to sooth his conscience. Son of a bitch knocks up my mother, doesn't marry her, and then makes out like he's doing me a favor letting me come up here to cook for him. Please to meet you, dear old Uncle-Dad Jim.*

Mika tiptoed over to his bed and gently shook his shoulder, interrupting his inner tirade.

"Hey Brodie, ready to do some cooking?"

"Ready as I'm going to get." He yawned.

In minutes, bacon, sausage, eggs, and home fries were sizzling on the stove. Mika worked quietly to allow his employers to sleep as long as possible. Brodie, however, repeatedly banged the pots together and slammed the refrigerator door closed.

"Why don't you go rouse our charges, Brodie, grub is about ready."

He went to the bunkroom door, swung it open and yelled inside.

"Breakfast in five minutes, men. Rise and shine."

The men grumbled at the callous extraction from their dreams, but soon the small cabin was filled with the excited bantering of men on a mission. Today was opening day, and after Mika's strong coffee washed the overnight cobwebs from their minds, they couldn't wait to get in the woods.

The men did little justice to Mika's repast, shoveling it down as if they hadn't eaten in days. The food wasn't in their mouths long enough for their taste buds to kick in before being washed down by their second and third cups of coffee.

Long johns, wool shirts, thick socks, gloves, and insulated boots were pulled on, tucked in, buttoned and tied. Coat pockets bulged with snacks, deer calls, and extra cartridges for their rifles. Flashlights in hand, the men hurried from the cabin, barely speaking, intent on getting in the stands before first light. Deer season had begun.

Brodie and Mika were scurrying about, trying to finish cleanup and get to their own stands. Four hands made for quick work.

"What's eating your shorts?" Mika asked.

"Nothing, I guess."

"Okay, works for me." Mika shrugged, washing the last dish.

"Doesn't it bother you? Busting your hump while these fellows, who mostly haven't worked a real job in their lives, get to go off to play?"

"I play the cards I'm dealt, Brodie. It doesn't do a man any good to worry over the fairness of it all. Maybe we are where we are for a reason. Now get your gear on, daylight is going to break over the mountain soon."

They grabbed the essentials from under their bunks and quickly dressed. Slinging their rifles over their shoulders, they hustled outside and headed down the trail toward opening day's destiny. Mika gave Brodie choice of the two stands and he picked the second stand from the cabin.

"Don't forget, back at the cabin by ten o'clock to throw lunch together." Mika stopped at the base of his tree and gave Brodie a thumbs up.

He nodded, and continued the last two hundred yards alone. Dawn was breaking over the mountain when he reached his stand. Deer snorted and ran crashing through the brush at his approach.

"Damn. I'm late, and now they're spooked." His nostrils flared and he shook his head, then climbed the ladder to his stand. "Nothing to do now but kill time and hope something else comes along."

Less than a minute passed and he heard a shot from the next stand up, and then another from below him. He bet those shots were taken at the deer he'd run off—chased them right to the lucky bastards. At least one of the hunters on this side of the property got some action. He hoped it was Mika or even Henry. He sure didn't want to hear any crap from the smart-aleck Chris.

After the early flurry of shooting, he heard few shots the rest of the morning. He tried to pinpoint their origin with little success. Some might've been close enough to be from his group. Most were faint echoes carried across the valley from other camps, perhaps from the public hunting area on the other side of Nathaniel Mountain.

Time passed slowly. He tried to entertain himself by watching the squirrels and chipmunks, but they didn't hold his interest. He began to fidget, waiting for the morning to pass. He'd missed his chance; he was sure of that now.

Feeling the grip of the cold, he rubbed his hands together. Whatever heat his system sponged up from the cabin dissipated long ago. The sky turned overcast and gray, appearing too thin to hold the sun's warmth, but pulling heat away from him. He'd had enough. He forced himself to stay on stand until 9:30 before heading back to camp.

As his feet touched the ground at the base of the stand—a soft crackle of leaves below him in the ravine. Turning, he tucked the rifle's butt into his shoulder. He looked down the hill and froze...listening, waiting. Noisy birds made it difficult to zero in on the sound. Squirrels too hopped around in the leaves to distract him. He waited—his hunter's instinct intent on his quarry's movements.

Behind a beech tree, he picked out the object of his quest. The reflection off a section of antler teased his eyes...the flicker of an ear curled towards him like a radar dish. He stared, willing the deer to take another step. The brush in the ravine was thick, nearly impenetrable, but with just one more step, he could make the shot. The antlers turned downward. The deer was feeding, its senses failing to recognize the danger. He could see its entire rack now. Its impressive spread was as wide as the ones in the hunting magazines. He sighted down the barrel, lining up his sights to prepare for the shot...one more step...

The deer threw its head up in alarm, at full alert when a rifle's thunderous crack sounded from the valley below. He waited, his index finger wrapped around the trigger guard, his thumb massaging the hammer...he shifted his weight for a steadier stance. The dried branch under his boot snapped like a firecracker in the quiet fall woods.

In a single frame of time, the shot was there. He took aim and squeezed the trigger, but the hammer was at half-cock. The deer snorted its fear for all the woods to hear, and nearly turned itself inside out to escape. The old buck didn't get big by being stupid, and he slid through the dense green briar and mountain laurel thicket like a greased pig at the county fair.

He pulled back the hammer, but it was too late. Second chances seldom came his way. He considered throwing some lead at the deer as it ran, but reconsidered. He knew the buck would be back if it wasn't too spooked. He didn't waste a moment thinking of other possibilities...the buck belonged to him.

A magical moment twisted into disappointment. What should've been a triumph devolved into a memorial to failure. He glanced at his watch. Mika would be leaving to start lunch. He slung his gun over his shoulder, and walked down to meet him.

When he reached the turn in the road above Mika's stand, he looked for any sight of him, but the stand appeared empty. He continued down the trail and rounding the bend, saw Mika dragging a doe toward the cabin.

"Looks like you had a good morning," he yelled.

"I didn't even get in my stand before she came running right up to me," Mika said. "Back straps for dinner tonight."

"Now that sounds promising. Hey, I put a pint of fresh oysters in the fridge from home. Fry 'em up for an appetizer?"

"Excellent idea, Brodie. How about you? See anything?" Mika asked.

"I jumped a couple of little ones when I first got to the stand, but didn't want to shoot them. Didn't see anything else all morning."

He grabbed a stout stick and lashed the drag rope to it. Together they pulled the deer down the mountain road to camp.

He saw the deer hanging from the game pole as soon as they were in sight of camp and wondered who the lucky hunter was. Approaching closer, he saw not one, but two deer hanging.

"It looks like it is going to be a good year for us." Mika said.

"Yeah, already is—for some of us anyway."

The cabin door flew open, and Chris and his father bolted outside.

"Need some help with that fat doe, Mika?" the older man asked.

Mika dropped the drag rope and pointed at the game pole.

"Does that mean we have a new hunter in camp, one with a first kill?"

Chris's face lit up like a Christmas tree. "Yes sir, my first one!"

Mika followed Chris as he admired his deer. Chris rubbed the hair on the button buck's neck. Mika reached down and picked a piece of honeysuckle and placed it with care between the small deer's teeth. Mika's doe also had salad fixings in her mouth.

"Forgive us little brother. Thank you for giving all that we may live," Mika whispered.

"What was that?" he asked.

"A gesture of respect and appreciation for what the deer and the creator gave us."

Henry probed the deer's wound where the bullet entered. "Come here Chris." He rubbed his blood covered finger over Chris' cheeks.

"First blood. I don't know how many generations ago this tradition started, but my father marked me, as his father did before him, in honor of a first kill."

"Traditions are important. They remind us who we are and where we come from," Mika said.

He smiled to himself. The others were still making a fuss over Chris and his button buck. Maybe he shouldn't be so hard on him. Same age or not—Chris was still a kid, but that wasn't his fault. He was enjoying himself, and proud of his first kill. But he couldn't wait to see what they'd do when they saw the deer he was going to bring back. He'd show them after the evening's hunt.

Chapter Nine

Deer Camp, Nathaniel Mountain, WV
Garren

He settled into his stand before first light, relishing the thought that his mother and father built this stand together. Although repairs were made over the ensuing years, he sat in the exact spot his father picked out, and in a stand he built. Looking around from his vantage point, he thought his father chose well. The stand commanded a great view with three well-worn deer trails merging together within shooting distance.

There were spots here and there in the shadier areas of the woods where snow still blanketed the leaves with white, the last remnants of an unseasonably early storm the week before. The morning was crisp, but he was dressed in several layers of clothes and his thickest socks. Diana would be pleased.

"You can always take some off if need be, but you won't see any deer if you are wiggling around in the tree stand because you're freezing your butt off," she'd said.

He practiced moving his eyes without rotating his head—surveying his area. He spotted a squirrel leaping from tree to tree before scurrying down a nearby oak intent on finding breakfast. Garren watched it scramble about in the leaves, amazed at how loud the small animal was and how brazen. Squirrels were a favorite meal for a lot of predators.

He continued scanning his hunting area for movement. He heard crows leave their roost but they were too far away to see. He glanced back at the squirrel and enjoyed its antics for a while. The little animal froze like a statue, and he concentrated—his eyes squinted—to find it amidst the leaves. One moment it was a blur of fur, poetry in motion; the next moment it was a stealth figure, a ghost invisible to his eyes. After a moment or two, hunger or impatience stirred the rodent to action, and he spotted it again.

A putting, scratching sound caught his attention, and he turned slowly to see a small flock of turkeys weaving their way down the mountain.

A flurry of wings whisked by him so close he heard the whoosh of their passing. Involuntarily he ducked his head. His gaze followed the flight of the red-tailed hawk as it dove for the squirrel. The small animal barked loudly, alerting the neighborhood. It scooted around to the opposite side of the tree. The hawk tried to adjust, and landed, but this time the squirrel won the deadly duel. The raptor hopped after the squirrel, but although graceful in flight, it was awkward on land. Up the side of the tree the squirrel ran, stopping to bark, teasing the bird. Spreading its wings, the hawk again took flight, soaring again in seconds. He heard its screech of frustration before it glided silently from view.

He felt in awe of both animals, and honored to have witnessed the spectacle—silently cheering for the squirrel during the showdown. Eat or be eaten. As for the squirrel, it seemed to have a short memory, as it already found its way back to the forest floor, searching.

Time passed quickly, as he sat musing over the encounter, the chill of the day ignored or forgotten. A sound, perhaps—or some intuition—alerted him to movement on the opposite hillside. Two deer! Slowly he brought the rifle to his shoulder, and looked for them in his rifle's scope.

He spotted the doe with her fawn of the year. They were legal game, and the fawn was old enough to take care of itself by now, but he hesitated, unable to find a good shot through the brush. He placed the crosshairs on the doe's shoulder, branches partially obscuring his shot. He began to squeeze the trigger when he heard a voice. *"Is it a good humane shot?"*

"I don't know, the brush is very thick," he whispered. He could swear the voice was his mother's, and actually turned his head to see.

All in your head. The deer remained in the thickets. Did they know they were safe there? He caught glimpses of their grey fur and an occasional flip of a white tail as they faded from his sight.

Odd, but he felt contented. He'd had some close encounters with nature, animals big and small, and he'd made the right decision. A shot through the brush could easily wound the deer, and he'd rather go back to camp empty handed than to have that on his conscience.

He relaxed in the stand thinking about all that happened this hunting trip. One thing he'd learned was his Uncle Jim couldn't hold his bourbon. His comment the night before still weighed heavily on his mind. What was Jim referring to, or was he just reading something into an inebriated man's foolishness? Perhaps he and Brodie did look alike, they were cousins after all. He wouldn't have given it a second thought if Uncle Jim hadn't thrown the wink across the table. Was there something about his lineage and birth that everyone knew except him?

He reached for the crucifix dangling from its chain. He rubbed it gently and absentmindedly through his coat. What had his father done? Was he Brodie's father as well? That was insane. He knew how close his mother and father were, but then too, for as long as he remembered, there was tension between his mother and Aunt Lily.

Was his father so upset at his son's conception that he'd sought solace from his own wife's sister? Did he cause his own death rather than face that stigma? He wished his father was here to ask. He couldn't understand missing someone so badly...someone he'd never even known.

He wasn't going to dwell on the question. Nothing he could do about it anyway. All he ever heard of his father indicated he was an honorable man, a pillar of the church and credit to his family and community. He would not soil his father's memory. He did not...would not believe in such things. His face reddened for allowing the thought to manifest itself. His father was a good man and he was proud of his memory. He was proud to be his son.

He drew in a heavy breath smelling the autumn woods. The sweet smell of rotting leaves and the scent of pine and cedar filled his nostrils, and soothed his soul. Another squirrel in the distance barked a warning to its companions. He looked around to see if he could see where his little friend was. He did not spot the furry tailed critter, but he did spot movement from the brush where the deer found refuge. The rabbit took a few hops and then stopped to sniff the air. This little one is even more nervous than the squirrel.

A soft breeze stirred the leaves, and a brief shiver ran down his back—a shiver from the morning's excitement rather than the air's chill. He pulled his camouflage facemask over his eyes and pulled down his hat's ear flaps in anticipation of whatever the weather might bring.

The rabbit moved toward him never getting more than a jump or two away from the thicket. He'd take a nibble of browse, and then smell something tempting and hop over to it, unaware of the watchers.

A red furred blur burst from the underbrush snapping quickly at the rabbit. Horror stricken, the rabbit leapt in a mad dash for freedom and for life. It was too late, as the fox grabbed a hind foot, and the rabbit squealed in fear and pain. A flurry of teeth, and blood stained the purity of the snow. Death sustained life.

He stood to get a better view of the confrontation, and without warning, began to shake with small rapid convulsions. A flood of awareness jolted his consciousness almost costing his balance. As if he was the one attacked, he braced himself. He felt the rabbit's pain, and embraced the fox's hunger. He empathized with them both, condemned neither. The world around him seemed to brighten as his perception grew.

Knowledge filled his body, flowing through him like warm blood through his veins. He knew. He was a part of it all, and all of creation was a part of him. He belonged, not just here in this place but wherever a creek bubbled, grass grew, rabbits played and deer ran. He was Man, and the entire universe beat in his chest. He felt a fullness of spirit he'd never dreamed of. He was fully alive.

He sat on the tree stand bench, collecting his thoughts and enjoying the solitude. His school friends teased him about his love of the outdoors, of nature and animals. He thought of Henry David Thoreau and Walden's pond. He responded to his friends' jokes by saying he was corrupted at a young age by reading Thoreau's work. Now, for the first time, he really understood where the man was coming from. All seemed right in his world. It was a good day.

When Uncle Jim whistled for him from the trail, he could not believe lunchtime arrived so quickly. A quick glance at his watch confirmed it. He still felt light on his feet and full of a childish joy from his experience. He knew he couldn't explain it, and decided he wouldn't try.

He hurried down the tree and walked toward his uncle. Jim said he saw a small buck but claimed to be holding out for the 'big boy' this year; at least until the end of the week, he'd added with a grin. Garren told him about spotting the deer and explained why he hadn't shot.

"You ain't going to tag a deer you don't shoot at, boy. Get them in the sights and spray and pray. That's what I say."

"Maybe, but I agree with Mom on this one," Garren said with feeling. "I don't want to make a bad shot and cause any undue suffering."

"Uh oh, you've been taking instruction from the goddess of hunting herself? Well, I won't tell you to do anything against what your mother's said. She is one of the best hunters I've ever met, male or female. You take that deer on your terms. We have a whole week stretching out in front of us. Let's get us some lunch and see how the other fellows did."

Chapter Ten

Deer Camp, Nathaniel Mountain, WV
Brodie

He thought lunch would never end. He tried to listen patiently to everyone's deer stories, but his patience was short. Maybe it would be different if he'd made meat or if some of his mother's famous crab cakes decorated his plate. But after striking out in the woods, the bologna sandwiches didn't do it for him.

If they'd get going, he could get his chores done and get back out there. There were dishes to clean and dinner to start before the two cooks could return to their own hunting stands. He hadn't mentioned the huge buck to anyone. He knew they'd horn in on his territory if they knew, and that just wouldn't do.

Instead of the hunters leaving, he heard Chris begin his fourth retelling of spotting and shooting the tiny buck. If he had to hear his story one more time, he'd puke. He got up from the table and began clearing off the dishes.

"You guys going out this afternoon?"

"We've got plenty of time, Brodie," Jim said. "Now you know that it just ain't good etiquette to interrupt a good hunting story. Go ahead, Chris. Finish your tale."

Chris was happy to oblige, elaborating in more detail with each retelling. He looked over at Garren, hanging on every word, pretending to enjoy the story. The other hunters were all humoring Chris too. He thought they must be as tired of hearing it as he was. He wanted to go shoot his buck!

Oh well, he thought, let Chris enjoy his five minutes of fame. Tonight, it was going to be all about him. He grabbed the stack of dishes and took them to the kitchen. He was scrubbing them when Mika joined him in the kitchen. Mika pulled out a dishtowel and began to dry. They worked together until finished—without a word spoken. Everything was dried and put away when the first of the hunters left the cabin.

"They're hitting the woods," Mika said.

"About time."

"I did notice you seem to be in a bit of a hurry."

"Guess so, I came up here to cook and hunt, not for any male bonding. Not with a bunch of guys who can't stand me."

He saw Mika shrug his shoulders. "Don't know where that's coming from, but it's like some smart fellow said, 'your perception is your reality.' Hope I'm not among those you think are against you?" Mika held out his hand and he shook it—grasping the man's hand as if it was a lifeline.

"Sorry about mouthing off, Mika. You're one of the best and I have a bad habit of feeling sorry for myself."

"I think tonight might be a good time to break out the slow cooker." Mika smiled. "We can toss all of the fixings in there, put it on low and then hit the woods ourselves. How's that for a plan?"

He smiled back; a slow cooker meal was like they were beating the system. They peeled vegetables, added some of Mika's favorite spices, and then threw in chunks of back-straps from Mika's deer.

"Using the loin for stew meat, Mika?"

"Nothing but the best for us and the boys, right?"

"Yes, sir, and don't forget fried oysters."

"Yes indeed, a quickie dinner, and we'll still feast like kings," Mika said. "If you think you'd have better luck at my stand, Brodie, I can trade off with you tonight? There were several other does running with the one I shot."

"Thanks Mika, but I'm good, maybe I'll see something up there tonight."

They dressed in a hurry. He remembered the lesson of the morning, and put on several extra layers of clothing. He didn't wait for Mika, but yelled, "Good luck," as he hurried from the cabin toward his stand.

Tonight was his night. He'd show them. He wouldn't let the events of the morning ruin his hunt. As he climbed into his tree stand, the sound of Chris' voice echoed in his head. *Where's your deer, Brodie? I'm one up on you now. Were you sitting real still so they wouldn't spot you?* He knew the only way to shut him up would be to do him one better. He propped his rifle on the stand's rail and leaned back against the tree trunk, prepared to wait for however long it took. Patience was not a virtue he'd spent much time cultivating. Determination, however, he possessed abundantly.

He concentrated on his hunting area taking note of every odd shaped tree stump, rock, or cluster of leaves that might fool him into thinking it was a deer. He hadn't spent his money on tags, and wasted some of his most persuasive lines on his mother, not to mention deserting her, just to admire the scenery. He could envision his mother's smile if he came home with boxes of venison meat for the freezer. He didn't get to see her smile very often.

He had a little trouble getting around the image of Uncle Jim with her. He didn't think either of them would own up to it, and no doubt it would shame her to know he knew. But it might help him to talk her into visiting a clinic. Remind her of the crazy things she'd done while under the influence of…whatever. People often needed persuading he'd discovered, even when it was for their own good, maybe especially then. Maybe they didn't think things through and needed a push to see commonsense.

Lenore Bauer was a perfect example. He could not fathom why she'd been so reluctant about his advances. He sure wasn't going to chase after her though. He had too much pride for that, but after his conversation with the vice-principal, it was too late anyway. It was a mystery to him why she didn't see they made a perfect match. He figured Lenore was the finest looking girl in school, and he knew he had no worries in the looks department.

She was more intelligent than the girls he'd grown accustomed to, a little too smart maybe by his way of thinking, and why his conquest of her became such a personal challenge. In time she would've come around—if he'd stayed in the mountains. He knew she wanted to. She had to. He wasn't thinking of her as a feather in his cap. True, it was a fine red-haired feather she'd be, but after months away from her, he still couldn't get her out of his mind. Crazy he knew.

He tried to wipe those thoughts from his head and concentrate on hunting. It would be easier if he could get the vision of her out of his head, but she was a distracting image.

He shook his head to clear it and willed himself back to the here and now. He looked to the left and right, then up to the peak of the hill to identify any movement. A small flock of geese flew over his head, honking in rhythm to their wing beats on their way to warmer climes.

A song about country roads in West Virginia popped into his head unbidden. Secretly he admired the way the singer could describe his feelings about the beauty of nature. Not that he would ever try to do so. It would destroy his image. He couldn't openly display such a weakness. That would give his enemies a weapon to use against him. It would be sweet to be able to carry a tune though! The girls would be lining up then—he'd be a regular Casanova!

He heard a puzzling scratching sound close by, and the sound of falling bark gave the squirrel's location away.

He watched as it ran down the tree trunk closest to him. It gave him a quick glance and continued to the ground.

I'm still and focused enough to fool a tree rat anyway. Bring on the buck. He smiled.

Time passed—all too slowly for him. Boredom settled in and he felt more than ready for something, anything to happen. For the first time, he became aware of the beauty of the woods, and the colors of the changing leaves.

Bet I could get lucky if I had a girl up here with me now. Hell, Garren or Chris might even have a chance.

He glanced at his watch and realized it was only three hours into the hunt. There were two and a half hours yet to kill. His eyes were burning and tired, and he closed them briefly. Couldn't hurt considering how little action he'd been having over this very long day.

Chapter Eleven

Hampshire County, WV
Lenore

"Look, she has the fire going, Lenore." Bridget pointed through the trees at the end of Anna's driveway.

"I love that smell. I'll bet she's burning pine. A good hot fire for the sweat lodge."

"Nervous at all?"

"No, not nervous. Tense maybe? A little…I have no idea what to expect but I trust Anna. But like I said on the phone, we can always back out, Brie."

"Oh no, I'm not going to miss out on this. Besides, what would Anna think of me?"

"I get the impression Anna wouldn't be overly concerned. In fact, I think she's a little reluctant to include us."

"I don't think it's like that. I think she takes being a spiritualist very seriously. I imagine it's a very personal and private thing for her. You know? And we're invading that privacy."

"True, and we're asking her to open herself up to ridicule—to two girls she barely knows."

"Yeah, I can relate to that," Bridget admitted.

The drive turned slightly and she got her first look at the house, a small log cabin set in a cluster of tall oaks. There was no lawn to speak of, but rather a thick carpet of leaves surrounded the cabin and cushioned their steps. Smoke curled up from a central stone chimney. It hung in the air around the trees like some ghostly entity preparing to pounce. The two girls circled the home toward the fire. A small creek wandered through the property, gurgling over rocks and miniature waterfalls. Lenore loved it immediately and intensely.

"Oh my God, this is beautiful, huh?"

"Thanks, I'm pleased you like it." Anna stepped from the woods with a bundle of small dried branches. "Would you like the grand tour inside?"

Bridget tripped backwards on a root and caught Lenore's arm to keep from falling. "You have got to stop sneaking up on us like that!"

Anna dropped the load of firewood. "Sorry, but it wouldn't be much of a sweat without heat, now, would it? So anyway, you guys want that tour now? I love the place already, but it will be even better. Grandfather is going to add on a bathroom just for me."

Anna guided her and Bridget through the small cabin pointing out the hand-hewn logs, and proudly displaying each room.

"Who won all the trophies? Are they yours, Anna?" she asked.

"Oh no, I wish I had such a talent." She laughed. "The ribbons and trophies are from my grandfather's wood carving competitions."

She admired the stitching on a quilt wall hanging. Several more were displayed around the room. "Are those handmade, Anna?"

"They are, Lenore. The quilts and baskets were all made by my grandmother."

"The 'House Beautiful' magazines would say it's warm, cozy, and simple with a charming rustic elegance. I just say I love it. Do you think your grandfather will adopt me?"

"You can ask, Lenore, but I bet he'd say one teenage girl in the house is more than enough. But I know he'd love you to visit whenever you want. You too, Bridget."

"It's truly a work of art—the whole house is." She glanced out of the window at the structure by the fire pit.

"Impressed or not, I get the impression you're more interested in the sweat lodge than the cabin, Lenore?" She and Bridget shrugged their shoulders as if choreographed and smiled. Anna led the way outside.

They walked to the backyard of the house and Anna dropped more wood in the pile by the fire. The grey skeletal carcasses of burnt wood indicated the fire had burned for a while creating red-hot coals. Large river rocks were heating on the edges of the pit.

"What can we do to help?" she asked.

"It's just about hot enough. Not much else to do. I guess you could fill up a couple of buckets with water from the creek though."

When she returned with the water, Anna led them to the sweat lodge, a dome shaped outbuilding covered with a heavy tarp. A short, ground-level flap provided the only entryway; Anna pulled it back.

"Shall we go in?"

"Wait a sec."

Anna picked up a pitchfork, walked to the fire and started moving the hot rocks into the sweat lodge, and then handed each of the girls a piece of sage.

Anna carried the two buckets of water to the lodge opening, stopped, unbuttoned her shirt and tossed it over the lodge, exposing a daisy-patterned bikini top.

"Ready?"

"We aren't...I'm not...we don't have to get undressed do we?" Bridget started. "I didn't, I don't..."

"Of course not, but it's just us three. Leave on whatever you like, ladies, but I promise the heat is intense in here. I've never quite gotten used to it. C'mon." Anna grabbed the water and entered the lodge.

She shrugged her shoulders, pulled her shirt off over her head and followed Anna. Bridget untucked her shirt and unbuttoned it, then crossed her arms over her chest and ducked in behind them. When everyone found a seat, Anna slowly poured the water over the heated rocks. A sharp hissing blocked out all other sound. The steam gave the air a presence and weight that settled over her.

She surveyed her surroundings in the dim light. A willow pole framework supported the canvas, and the dirt floor had a shallow depression dug out for the rocks. When Anna dropped the flap behind them, the world went black.

"Wow," Bridget said. "It's like midnight in the final act of a horror movie in here."

"Before we start, I only promise a sweat, spiritual I hope, but there are no other guarantees expressed or implied." Anna laughed.

"What does that mean?"

"I'm just saying I can't promise everything will be traditional, Lenore. I'm no teacher and I do not wish to dishonor our traditions. I believe my ancestors will see we're venerating the Earth, and our belief in the commonality of creation. In this way, we honor them also—as it should be. Speech done...ready?"

"Let's do it."

"Okay, we'll go slow and easy. I'll bring some heated rocks inside, add water and we steam. Remember the whole point is to cleanse your spirit, clear your mind and make yourselves open. Sweats were used by both my Native American and my Celtic ancestors. I'll do my best—with the help of my spirit guide. I pray she honors us with her presence. But remember, you came to me."

She exchanged a quick glance with Bridget as Anna dropped handfuls of dried leaves in the water buckets.

"What's that?" she asked.

"This is sage, red osier bark, hazelnut leaves, pine needles, and cedar. No Jimsonweed, Lenore. I promise."

"There's no what?" Bridget asked.

"You know, Datura...? Never mind, there's nothing in here to hurt you."

Anna pulled a pack of cigarettes from her pockets. "Take one."

"No thanks..." Bridget started.

"Look, I won't do anything to hurt either of you, but tonight, when I ask you to do something? Do it. Be open, suspend disbelief, and know that anything is possible. Can you do that?" Anna asked.

Anna pulled a cigarette from the pack, and passed it around. She reached out and took one and passed another to Bridget.

"Pinch the tobacco off and sprinkle it around in the fire. It's to show our gratitude to the Earth.

"Okay, let's just relax. Practice being meditative; pray to your ancestors, but most of all, clear your minds."

Anna added more water increasing the steam. "Concentrate on your breathing, slow and steady."

The intensity of the heat drew a trickle of sweat over her brow. Anna tapped something against a hollowed-out log. The rhythm matched her heartbeat, and the steady thump, thump, thump continued until the steam began to thin.

She began to hum in time, and felt Bridget rocking back and forth in place beside her. Anna rubbed something over her arms and face.

"What is it?" she asked.

"Just sage, Lenore." She nodded her assent as Anna brushed the residue on her jeans. She wiggled around trying to settle into a more comfortable spot.

"I'm soaking wet." Bridget sucked in a noisy gulp of air, sighed and yanked off her shirt.

"Concentrate on your breathing, and nothing else. Allow the steam to cleanse you." She heard the voice as if from far away, but knew it was Anna speaking the words.

She heard water spilling onto the rocks but they'd lost their power and put forth only an anemic veil of steam.

"Never mind, ladies. I think you've been in here long enough. I don't want to push you too hard on your first time. Lenore? Lenore?"

She nodded as the voice went on in reverential tone, like Reverend Stewart's when he was really feeling the spirit. "Earth Mother, guide us as true human beings along your sacred path, for now we are pure."

"Come on," she heard and followed the tug on her elbow out of the shelter and on to the creek. Through a mental fog she saw Anna and Bridget splashing water on their faces. She reached down, cupped water in her hands and gratefully did the same.

"Don't soak yourselves; it is cold out here though I know you don't feel it yet," Anna warned them. "Now tell me, what did you think, how do you feel?"

"Hot." Bridget giggled. "It seemed to clear my mind and heart though. Is that right?"

"Yes, that's exactly it. Lenore, what about you? Are you okay?"

"I'm sorry…so drained. Cleansed? Yeah, but it was like it must be in the womb, pitch black, wet, and the only sounds, your voice, the drum, and our breathing. Then we came out, left the womb, reborn in the sun's dying light. It was awesome. Weird when I say it out loud, but my spirit…soared. I felt like I was floating up and away. I believe for a moment I was seeing through your eyes. Is that how you feel with your spirit guide?"

"No, it's more like she tells me things—shows me things. I've had that floating feeling, especially when she shows me something far away, but I'm always me. I feel through no other senses but my own."

"Guess I am more open to most anything after last night. I'm ready for anything."

She saw the question in Anna's eyes. "Last night?"

"Just another dream, but it was so real. I dreamt about that guy again, and I think he's in some kind of trouble or something. Maybe something bad is going to happen to him? I don't know. I just felt this very real spiritual connection with him."

"Where was he in your dream, and why do you think he's in trouble?" Bridget asked.

"This will sound silly, but in the dream he was in the mountains hunting. I felt danger surrounded him. I remembered hearing that Brodie Caine came back up to hunt the mountains. Didn't you tell me that, Brie?"

"That's what I heard anyway."

"Where does Brodie Caine go when he's hunting?" Anna asked and she shrugged in answer.

"I think he went somewhere with his uncle, Jim Doyle, but I don't know where they go," Bridget said.

Her eyebrows lifted and her jaw dropped. "Wait a minute. My step-father and step-brother are at deer camp on the mountain. I don't know where for sure, but I heard Henry, my step-dad, talking about a Jim Doyle also."

"Jim Doyle is Garren's uncle, Lenore," Anna said. "My grandfather is the cook at their camp."

"Who's Garren?" Bridget asked.

"A friend from my last school—the only one I had there. You'd like him. Can't imagine he could be related to the Brodie guy you've been telling me about though."

She smiled. "Well, you can pick your friends, Anna, but not your family. Still, if he is related to Brodie Caine then your taste in friends has improved dramatically."

"I can't imagine, unless one of them is adopted? Garren is what you'd call a 'kindred spirit,' Lenore. He just doesn't know it yet."

She turned at the sound of splashing water.

"Cooling off yet, Brie?"

Bridget didn't answer as her eyes widened and moved to the forest's edge.

"Look." She pointed to the woods.

A doe entered the clearing and stared nervously at the three girls, her ears upright and focused like a satellite dish. Lenore stared back and felt her spirit drift toward the deer "It's okay. You're safe. We aren't danger." The doe dropped her guard and began to drink from the creek until she had her fill.

She pulled her thoughts back to herself and the doe lifted her head and trotted back to the full safety of the thick woods. She felt Anna's eyes on her.

"You did that, didn't you? You…you calmed her."

"I don't know. It's happened a few times before. I think animals can sense that I mean them no harm. Maybe I'm a calming influence."

"Yeah, but I believe a bit more than that." Anna grabbed her arm and pulled her closer to whisper, "You've given me an idea." Bridget leaned in closer to hear.

"Do you believe in werewolves?" Anna smiled.

Chapter Twelve

Deer Camp, Nathaniel Mountain, WV
Garren

He knew it wasn't safe to run with a firearm, still his trek down the mountain trail was faster than a walk even if not yet a full-on trot. He couldn't wait to get back in his tree stand. Maybe this evening would be his chance to harvest a deer and maybe not…somehow, it wasn't as important as before. When he reached the stand and climbed in, he remembered the morning hunt. He smiled, and goose bumps rose at the memory.

He wanted to retrieve that feeling, that life altering, priority changing epiphany of spirit. Even better than having venison in the freezer. But he was still in predator mode however, and waited—still and silent as a cat—and observed.

Life teemed around him, not so much a distraction now, but perhaps the main event. He followed every movement, absorbed every detail. A squirrel, perhaps the same one as before, barked its annoyance at his intrusion. Shadows from a pair of vultures crisscrossed the leaf bed on the ground below his stand. A lone titmouse landed on a branch near his head and tried to determine if he was friend, foe, or an odd shaped lump in the tree. Garren was a statue with the exception of his eyes. The small bird alternated between watching him and grooming its feathers and when satisfied, flew off with a song.

He'd learned more about nature on this trip than in all of his woodland explorations of the past, and more of himself as well. He relaxed his lanky frame, and allowed the sights, smells, and sounds of the woods to absorb him, and pull him along where they would.

Gradually he came to a place of calm and peace. Anna had suggested that he try meditation—many times. She said that it would expand his horizons or something. Maybe he'd been too quick to dismiss it? Perhaps this feeling he'd experienced was like that?

Anna was a good friend with a giving heart, but not many at his school would know it. Her attendance there was brief and they were quick to judge her for her differences. Anna didn't try to dissuade them of their opinion. She displayed her ancestry for all to see but shared nothing of herself. Years of whispered conversations when she entered a room and even physical attacks in deserted hallways taught her that being a silent pariah was preferable to confrontation—at least in defense of herself. But only a fool would make the mistake of taunting one of her friends or disparaging her family. Her friendships were rare but her loyalty was absolute once given.

He thought about Anna's last day at school. They were always able to sense when the other was troubled. She said they had a spiritual connection, and that her dreams conveyed his concerns to her. He never believed in all that, but still somehow, she always seemed to know. He felt equally protective towards her, a sister he'd never had. Then there was the fateful lunch on her last day. Their conversation devolved into forced snippets of polite discussion, and he knew something was on her mind. After lunch, they had a private moment walking between buildings toward their next class.

"Okay, give it up Anna. What's bugging you?"

"Are you sure you're up to it, Garren? It's okay, really."

"I think I can handle it. We're friends, so we're here for each other, right?"

"All right, it's about my mom. I guess I do need to talk to someone and my grandfather has too much on his plate, so that leaves you buddy." Her smile was pressed into her cheeks with apparent effort and didn't reflect in her eyes.

Anna opened her heart and hurt to him, describing the events of the past month. He listened with a caring ear to troubles beyond his experience, and in so doing, provided her with exactly what she needed.

He held her as her eyes poured out her sorrow. With no warning, his sister of the spirit, if not of the blood, lifted her face to him and brushed her lips into his. Pulling her in to him, he tasted her mouth with an unknown hunger. His hands caressed and explored, embracing her trembling body. She drew away, and he couldn't read the look in her averted eyes. He was shocked at his response to her need, and shamed by his betrayal. He turned away in disgrace. He'd never been more ashamed to be male.

They walked in awkward silence to class. He didn't know what to say, or where to go from there. Arriving at class, they discovered Mr. Simmons in his usual argumentative mood. The trouble began as he concluded his lecture on the historical evidence of the biblical account of Noah's ark.

"Time and again, our Christian faith has been ridiculed by non-believers. Science has continually tested the tenets of our beliefs and questioned the holiest words from the one true God—the Bible. As science advances however, more discoveries are made that reinforce the stories and timelines from our sacred book. Yet again, science shows that we possess the one true faith."

The teacher paused for emphasis, then bored holes into Anna with his eyes, and continued.

"Why is it, Ms. Hirsch, that a young woman of superior intellect, like yourself, a young woman well exposed to the teachings of the Bible, would instead choose a path of ignorance? Why would such a young woman wear the trappings of a dead pagan faith?" He pointed in turn at Anna's dark attire and the antler pendant around her neck. "Is this a bizarre quest for attention, or are you being deliberately obtuse?"

"Mr. Simmons, this amulet belonged to my great-grandmother, and my grandfather passed it on to me. Respectfully, I'm sorry it threatens you, but my grandfather says there are many righteous paths."

He smiled with pride at her answer. It was unlikely that Simmons could find fault with that. Then Frank Morgan, the class troublemaker and son of the school's biggest contributor, cleared his throat and raised his hand.

"Mr. Simmons, aren't we a Christian school? Maybe the new girl didn't know? Maybe her grandfather brainwashed her with the pagan stuff?"

From across the room, he could see his friend's blood pressure rise, the situation made worse by his betrayal.

"I didn't realize this school practices religious tolerance only in cases where everyone agrees. Perhaps you should study that book a bit more?" Anna said.

"Are you mocking the Holy Bible, young woman?"

"No sir, I don't mock any faith or belief that helps us to find our path, but if I'm honest, my bible is written on the windblown grass, and in a gurgling brook."

"That may be, but you will be graded on your understanding of the true faith."

"Indeed, we will be graded on your truth, Mr. Simmons."

By this point, the entire class was giggling behind their hands, and whispers filled the room. He saw Anna's head held high, seeming to be above the barely heard taunts. Mr. Simmons's veins were protruding from his neck, and his face took on a purplish hue.

Hoping to diffuse the tension, he waved his hand vigorously. "Sir, I am having trouble with chapter 15. What chapters will be covered in the test tomorrow?"

"What, oh, chapters 10 through 15 will be covered, Garren." Simmons cut his eyes at Anna a final time. "And I'm available after school for tutoring." The teacher returned to his desk, closed his eyes and took several deep breaths. Slowly the blood left Simmons's face and the whispers subsided. When the bell rang, Simmons asked Anna to stay behind. She never returned to school. He didn't know if she just had enough, or if she had been asked to leave.

He was proud of how she'd stood up to Simmons but knew what it must have cost her. He tried calling her that afternoon and several times the following day to see what happened after class, but her phone went unanswered. Several more days passed with the same result. On his last attempt, a robotic voice informed him that the phone was disconnected.

Her grandfather lived somewhere close—perhaps he knew what was going on? Where she was? But he'd never visited her in her grandfather's house. He couldn't recall the man's name—if Anna had mentioned it to him. She referred to him only as Grandfather. That's when he should've found out, but the wave of guilt held him in check. She wouldn't want anything to do with him after he'd nearly forced himself on her! At a time of weakness, he'd taken advantage of the affections of the best friend he'd ever had! Anna didn't try to contact him either, reinforcing his belief that he was persona non grata in her life, but he couldn't get her out of his mind. His life was diminished without Anna in it. When he returned home from hunting camp, clearing the air with her would be his number one priority.

Anna told him he was different than the others, and he should explore those differences, but he never wanted to be different. He wanted to stay under the radar, to be like everyone else, to fit in. Now he felt changed inside from his experience of the morning. He wondered if anyone looking at him could tell. His teachers would call his experience an epiphany, but it was an invisible door that opened for him. He wished he could tell Anna; she'd be proud and excited for him.

Enough of that, you're thinking too much. Just feel this place. Again his eyes embraced the woods, his ears alert for any movement. He allowed his mind to follow a buzzard as it soared overhead. For a moment, he felt he could see through its eyes, the vast expanses of the mountain, and the coolness of the wind currents beneath his arms...rather wings.

When the four deer appeared, he swore he saw them from directly above.

Chapter Thirteen

Hampshire County, WV
Anna

Bridget and Lenore's eyes opened like saucers as they stared open-mouthed at her. With no word spoken, they waited. Anna just smiled at them.

"Come on Anna, werewolves? Really?" Lenore asked. "What the hell are you talking about?"

"Easy witch," she teased. "Humor me—what do you know about them?"

"I don't know anything about them. They're mythical creatures, men that become wolf-like whenever the moon is full. Stories some parent made up a million years ago as a cautionary tale for their misbehaving children."

She bit her lip to restrain a smile. "Don't you roll your eyes at me white witch." She pointed at the sky. "It will be full tonight you know."

"Okay, so the moon will be full. Are you really trying to get us to believe in werewolves?" Bridget asked. "Cause I can tell you, I am not drinking blood, eating raw meat, or howling at the moon. A girl has to draw the line somewhere."

The three of them broke into laughter. She hoped Bridget's joke would relieve the tension she read in her new friends' faces.

"I believe the werewolf legends are based on the same concept as the Native American skin walkers and there are similar myths from many other cultures."

"So, it's just another fairytale, right?" Lenore asked. "You're not saying you believe them?"

"Not exactly, I believe I am in the woods and the woods are in me. Did you feel anything like that when you came out of the sweat?"

She noted nodding as Lenore stared at the creek's flow, waiting.

Anna continued. "Well, if you've felt that, isn't it a natural extension that all creatures of creation are a part of us and us of them?"

"I guess so." Bridget nodded again and Lenore remained lost in the water's flow.

"Bridget, remember I told you everyone has magic or personal power? I want to try something to tap into that resource. It's only worked once for me—right after a sweat and I think Moll was helping. I want to try it again."

"Moll? You never said, but she's your spirit guide, right? Will she help us do whatever this is? Help all of us?"

"I can't speak for the spirits, but I hope so."

"What is it you want to do?" Bridget asked.

"To go with the animals, *in* the animals, up to that camp."

"Huh? How do you plan to do that?" Lenore asked.

"I think you know, don't you, Lenore? Once after a sweat, I felt so in touch with nature that I went into…well, not a trance exactly, because I knew everything that was happening around me. I visualized a raccoon and there one was. It approached close enough I could've scratched behind its ears. I imagined its thoughts, and its sense of self. Well, I thought I was imagining it…until now. Now I'm not so sure. Lenore, this talent is strong in you. You may not believe this, but I saw as the animal did, as if through its eyes. I went where it went for a few minutes. I don't know if it's real, or a personal hypnosis brought on by the sweat, but it felt real. I think that's how the skin-walker and werewolf legends started," she claimed.

"What would we have to do?" Lenore asked.

"Follow my lead, if you are game."

"We're game!" Bridget answered for them.

She sat cross-legged in front of the diminished fire and motioned for them to join her. She noted the position of the sun, its globe appeared captured in the low branches of mountain laurel, and frowned. An hour of daylight wouldn't give them much time. She wanted them to be 'back' before dark.

"Get as comfortable as you can, ladies." She handed them each a piece of brain tanned deer hide and grasped the carved antler pendant hanging from her neck.

"These are to help us find our way back, to ground us," she explained.

Lenore leaned back against a fallen log. Bridget sat cross-legged but propped her back against a tree.

"Try to get back to that place where you were during the sweat. Clear your mind of thought. Just relax and breathe."

She stood and threw small pieces of wood on the coals of the fire. They were very dry, and quickly caught fire. She reached over to one of the unused buckets of water and dipped in her finger. She then touched Lenore and Bridget in the center of their foreheads just above the level of their eyes, lightly tracing a small circle.

"Focus your energy there," she whispered. "Try to visualize the mountains—the meadows on Nathaniel Mountain. Can you see the peaks blanketed with trees, the fertile river valley? Can you smell the freshness of the air, and the pines? The breeze is feathering through my hair; can you feel it too? It's cool and tingly, but not cold yet."

She opened her eyes to see Lenore and Bridget nod, their own eyes closed.

"The meadow—it's so beautiful. The grasses are so green; can you feel how soft it is under your feet? I see some brave flowers still have their heads peeking through. Oh look! Three deer in the meadow; do you see them? There is a doe with her yearling fawns."

Smiling, the girls followed Anna's vision. They rubbed their fingers in the deer hide Anna had given them, caressing it; and moved their heads in unison.

Moll, can you hear me? Will you help us to commune with their spirits?

"They appear to be nervous; they know we're here! They're staring at me," Lenore said.

Moll, will you help us? Join me and guide us? An electric current ran down her spine.

"*I'm with you, sweet girl,*" she heard Moll's answer in her mind. "*I'll help you get there but hold fast to Lenore. You're right about her.*"

She shivered, smiled and spoke in a new voice...Moll's voice.

"Slowly, gently move toward them. Don't scare them."

"Anna, are you okay? Your voice...?" Brie asked.

"I'm fine, Brie. We're fine, Moll and I. Trust us. Reach out to our gentle friends...see them, feel them? See how their chests swell and fall with each breath. They're wondering about us, curious but ready to spring away. Can you feel that? I'm closest to the small fawn now...reaching out to touch her. *Easy, easy there, little sister, I'll not harm you.* She's quivering at my touch, but standing firm. She is so soft! Reach out now; touch the deer nearest you. Feel them tremble at your touch?"

"I can," Bridget whispered. "He feels like rough cotton and smells of the land, like crisp apples mixed with the scent that hits your nose when you jump in a pile of leaves."

She looked at Lenore, saw her wide smile even as tears streamed down her friend's face.

"It's magic, it truly is," Lenore said. "The mother's eyes are deep chestnut colored pools."

"Yes, Lenore, Brie, let yourself go there. Let their eyes draw you in, do you feel the pull? Now look…look through their eyes. I see you both as you are bonding."

***

Lenore

I see as she sees. I can smell the grass like never before. It is rich, alluring. The mother is thirsty I think. I am thirsty.

"*Then we should go with them,*" Anna whispered.

The three deer ran across the meadow and into the woods on the other side. As she and her deer entered the stand of trees a voice called out from behind her. "*Wait!*"

She turned her head and through her new eyes, saw the other two deer trailing her.

"*Anna?*" she asked.

"*I'm still with you Lenore, but your doe runs faster than my little one can. I could feel her heart pounding in her chest as we ran. She thought her mother was fleeing danger,*" Anna answered.

"*Brie, where are you?*" she asked, but there was no response.

"*Stay here, Anna,*" she said, and ran back through the field. At its edge she smelled the air currents, tasting smells for the first time. She sucked in the scents of the wild grasses, herbs, and flowers. There was something else though also. She turned her ears and nose toward this unpleasant odor and located its source. There stood Bridget—dressed in her human skin—alone and appearing lost. There was a strong smell of what she now recognized as human. A convulsion shook her body as the deer registered its dread.

"*Bridget, go home now. Calm your mind, relax your spirit and you will drift back there.*"

"*Lenore? How do you know? Are you sure?*"

"I don't know how I know, but I do. Trust me, old friend. Think of the cabin, concentrate on the fire. My doe is afraid. She won't let me come closer. But I think I can hold her here. I'll wait to see you return. We are not done here."

She stood by as Bridget curled up on the ground. She could hear her breathing slow, then her image faded…faded…and was no more. Her deer had enough and trotted back to her fawns. They were safe, frozen in position, just as they'd been taught.

She knew Bridget was safe, there was nowhere else for her friend to go but back to her waiting and unconscious body. She concentrated on finding the other humans and asked her host in a manner she'd understand. They needed to find her new family members and Anna's grandfather.

Bridget's fawn seemed confused without the comfort and guidance that Bridget had provided. She thought the young buck fawn couldn't understand its mother and sister's behavior.

"My old girl knows where they are and will show us—unless fear overcomes her. Ready?"

"This is your show, your talent. I'm following you now," Anna replied.

She reveled in the sensory perception of her animal host. Sounds that she'd miss or ignore with human senses now received her full attention. The deer knew the sounds that belonged and which were out of place in her woods. She jerked to attention, then dropped her guard as she spotted the source of the sound. A raccoon was washing its dinner—a small frog—in the tiny brook at the wood's edge. The doe knew this was a safe animal that meant her no harm. Lenore, however, was entranced with the raccoon's behavior, clownish in his antics. Why would it wash a freshly caught frog in the water anyway?

Her doe tensed, and turned its ears directionally like radar, frozen in a stare at a rhododendron bush on the trail ahead. The two fawns stood like statues behind her, waiting for their mother to decide if they should flee. Their muscles bunched up in knots ready to leap.

She stared at the bush as a branch moved in a direction opposite the wind. She waited for the animal to reveal itself, but whatever stirred the branch, now remained still. She dropped her head as if to feed and then threw her head back up—hoping to catch the animal's next move. She tasted the air, but the scent blew away from her and provided no clues. She stomped her front hoof, then stomped again, hoping to scare it? She wasn't sure.

"What is it?" Anna asked from behind.

She stomped her hoof again and a small gray furred creature darted from the bush and scurried up the side of a tree. It barked at the three deer in annoyance.

Squirrel. She felt the doe relax and turn back to the trail. Her young ones fell in line, their noses now at rest.

A ten-point buck stepped onto the trail, his antlers polished and his fur sleek. The buck stared at her and she smiled feeling a quick spasm of recognition. She ignored it and felt foolish. It was a deer like any other, but she knew the buck made her deer nervous. She turned away from him, walking swiftly. The buck followed at a distance, not entering their safe space. *Perhaps he senses one of the females will be in rut soon*, she thought.

Through the trees and down the trail she accompanied her host. She wondered if the deer were aware of their presence. Time slipped away like a roller coaster ride due to her newly enhanced senses. She saw the sun dip behind the mountain.

"It's getting late, Anna. We must go back. Not enough time to find them."

"Not yet," Anna pleaded.

The male fawn snatched his head upright, ears at attention. She and Anna did likewise but saw nothing. The trailing ten point snorted a warning and jumped from the trail. The does tensed, about to follow his lead when they heard an odd metallic tap. She knew that sound, *what...*

The silence of the woods was ripped apart by a roar. The deer knew this sound, but not its source, but they knew it as a sound to fear. In a panic, they fled the awful thing that reached out to them from far away.

"Lenore!" The scream assaulted her mind from behind.

She glanced behind her. Anna's fawn stumbled, but jumped back up. It ran with a slight limp.

"Anna?"

The three deer ran toward a thicket and stopped, eyes and ears tuned in the direction of the dreaded explosions, in the direction of danger.

"Anna?" she repeated.

"We have to go back now," Anna answered.

"Okay, that's the easy part. Relax your mind and think yourself back. Down the trails we walked with cloven feet, across the meadow and toward home. See it Anna? See the embers of the fire burning low? Can you see the sweat lodge? Relax; I can see Bridget and both of us there."

"Yes, I see us, Anna. Okay, I'm..."

"Why the hell did you two leave me?" Bridget snapped as they opened their eyes.

"Oh my God, Anna! Your shoulder's bleeding!"

Chapter Fourteen

Nathaniel Mountain Hunting Camp
Brodie

His head bolted upright. Some unexpected noise woke him from a pleasant dream. His head filled with cobwebs, he looked around the woods trying to determine the source of the sound, but there was nothing to be seen. Even the squirrels ceased their continual chattering and food gathering. He took note of the position of the sun and figured 45 minutes until legal hunting hours ended.

Then, a noise to his left, the soft sound of crushing leaves. Deer, he thought. He wiped his eyes to clear out the vestiges of sleep, then drew the rifle to his shoulder to wait.

Then he saw her—a fat and sleek doe, a couple of years old. Two smaller deer, her fawns he thought, followed closely behind. He watched them walk towards him oblivious of danger. He drew back the rifle's hammer. He wouldn't forget that again! The button-buck fawn froze in place, pointing his ears directly at Brodie. No, not directly, he thought. The deer stared at the base of the tree his stand was in. The little buck was unsure what he'd heard, and more importantly, where it came from.

The other two deer followed the little one's line of sight, ears erect—scanning the area around them for movement or sound. He focused on the older doe. If any of them spotted him, she'd be the one. Slowly, he turned the rifle placing his sights on her shoulder. Squeeze the trigger, don't pull, he reminded himself.

A sharp snort sounded from behind the deer. A noise like a great expulsion of air—a steroidal giant blowing his nose. Leaving the gun in position, he moved his head slightly and spotted him—a buck—no, a huge buck. He was certain it was the same one he'd encountered earlier in the day. He was determined not to mess it up this time. The buck was on red alert—warned of possible danger by the little button buck. It stared at the does, and then towards his ambush tree. It was now or never. There'd be a different story in camp tonight when he dragged this monster in.

Shifting his shoulders slightly, he adjusted the gun's position to make the shot. The buck sensed his intent and didn't hesitate. He leapt from the trail and bounded away. His tail displayed its white flag in warning to all forest dwellers. It felt like the glove slap that southern gents employed in the days of old to challenge another to a duel.

He swung his gun and squeezed off a hasty shot at the running deer, but it was safely ensconced in the brush. Before he could shoot again, it was gone. He swept the rifle back towards the other three deer. They were running and he shot at the last deer, the small doe fawn. He knew his sights weren't aligned, but he shot again. The small doe staggered slightly and ran toward the others into the safety of the thicket. The intensity of his woodland encounter faded back to solitude and peace. In five minutes, the squirrels had forgotten the cause for their alarm and scurried about in the leaves sniffing for some tasty tidbit. In ten minutes, vultures circled overhead hoping for a fallen meal. Their winged grace belied their horrific countenance and morbid bill of fare.

Shaking from the adrenaline download, he breathed deeply and willed himself to be still. His watch indicated thirty more minutes until full darkness seeped over the mountain. He waited with as much patience as he could muster. The deer needed time to settle down before he could take up the blood trail. That's what all of the hunting magazines said. He'd hit the small doe, but he'd check for blood spoor where he shot at the buck as well. If he'd hit that big boy, he wouldn't bother tracking the doe. The buzzards needed to eat too. Time and daylight were getting short.

From the vantage point of his stand, he picked out landmarks where each deer stood when he shot. He knew the terrain would look different from the ground. He stretched and climbed down from his stand—hoping for the best.

Though he felt more confident about his shot at the doe, he decided to look for the buck first. If he saw no sign there, he'd have time to get on the doe's trail before full dark. He spotted the gnarled wild cherry tree he picked out while in his stand. The buck was running past the tree when he shot. He soon found the deer's tracks in a small patch of snow, but no trace of blood. He followed the disturbed leaves up to the cherry tree, but saw no blood. Stopping to look around the thicket for any other sign, he noticed a white splotch on a tree and investigated. It was a fresh bullet hole; the damn pine tree was the only trophy he'd connected with.

So much for going back to the cabin a hero—with the big buck in tow. Maybe he'd have better luck with the doe. Any deer taken was better than going back empty handed. He walked toward his other landmark—the fallen tree covered with fox grapevines.

He felt a moment of alarm when he saw no blood, and began walking in a zig-zag pattern in the area the deer was last seen in. There was nothing, but he was certain he'd hit her! There had to be something. Leaves were disturbed under his feet and he wondered if he did it wandering around, or if it was the deer. A small red dot hidden in the leaves…dogwood berry? He reached down to touch it and his finger came away wet and red. He did hit her! But the sunlight was fading, and he hurried to find the next drop.

The blood was dark red. The outdoor magazines said that meant a flesh wound. That would be his luck. He continued looking in the direction of the deer's escape, another drop on the leaves there? No, this time it was a fallen holly berry. He worked his way down the trail, sometimes on his hands and knees looking for sign. Then he spotted it…another drop of blood, and then another, but after an hour searching, no more were to be seen. The little doe made good her escape. He guessed the bullet had only grazed her, but he hated to think of the teasing in camp over this.

A huge hollowed out oak towered above him, its branches arching upward as if in prayer. He stood and stretched, looking around. Pointing his flashlight in every direction, he tried to get his bearings. He hadn't walked far. Where was that fallen tree? He tried retracing his steps. He decided to walk straight up the mountain to get his bearings.

After an hour, he continued to hunt for something familiar, a landmark or any sign of his prior passage. The clump of mountain laurel ahead, was it the same patch he spotted on the way down the mountain? He hurried toward it, hopeful. It looked the same…he quickened his pace, safe in the knowledge he was on the right track.

Tripping on an unseen rock, he rolled down the hill. His hand hit a tree, scraping and twisting his wrist. He grimaced with pain. Great, a sprained wrist. He looked closer at the tree. It was the same hollow oak he passed an hour before. He was walking in circles! His heart rate accelerated, realizing he was very lost.

He sat on a rock outcropping to consider his predicament. The rock felt warmer than the outside air. Perhaps it absorbed the heat of the day? He placed his injured hand palm down on the rock and rubbed his wrist. *This is gonna mess up my shooting.* The rock was extremely smooth and flat but he felt irregular notches as he rubbed its surface. Years of erosion cut lines into the rock, both vertical and horizontal lines.

He slid off his perch, kneeling and shining his flashlight across the face of the stone. With a bit of imagination, it looked like letters carved there by some long dead stonemason. He looked closer. They were letters! After all the years, he could still make out some of the words. Some were vague in the dim light, but by shining the flashlight at just the right angle, he could read them. The engraving read 'Zachary Dyer.' Other letters followed the name. Brodie assumed it was a date, but he could only discern the final year, 1869. He stood up abruptly and hit his head on a low tree branch and fell back to the rock.

You realize you're sitting on some dude's tombstone, Brodie? He felt a spasm of revulsion and slid off the rock again. He rubbed his head and decided to try and read the rest. It was some sort of epitaph, the lettering in better shape than the dates were. In fact, they were still sharp and legible, hardly worn at all. 'Zachary Dyer, The black man's friend,' the carved words read. He noticed the mark at the end of the word 'friend.' It looked like a comma, but just as likely a slip of the stone worker's chisel. He pulled away the leaves and soil at the base of the stone and wiped it clean as best he could with his gloves. There were additional letters there. The full inscription now read 'Zachary Dyer, The black man's friend. Bound in hell for his sins.'

"Great, I'm in the middle of a damn racist graveyard," he yelled, bolstering his courage. He shined his light around the forest floor, but saw no other markers.

"Well Zach, I guess they buried you all alone out here in the middle of nowhere. Don't think you were very well liked, old boy. I know what that's like," he said, feeling sorry for himself and a bit for old Zach as well.

He thought of what he'd face when he got back to camp. He knew no one in the group liked him very much. Growing up poor and fatherless, he was used to people looking down their noses at him. His mother was a drunk and loose as a goose, but at least she was there. He knew the tricks to get people to like him and show them the version of Brodie that they wanted to see. But he seldom felt the inclination to do so.

He'd shown Bridget a little of that Brodie. It wasn't as if he meant to hurt the damn thing. He was trying to get her to like him. He knew what Garren thought he'd done, and he let him think it. Garren would think the worst of him anyway and sometimes that was best. He'd found the cat the night before on the side of the road and in pretty bad shape—hit by a car or some kid's lucky rock throw—he didn't know. It had blood in its ears, and couldn't even stand. He wasn't taking it to Bridget just so she could watch the damn thing die. He'd felt close to her in the little time he'd known her—like a kid sister, someone he needed to protect. So he played nursemaid to a cat for a couple of days. He didn't understand her reaction though, but guessed it was his reputation or Garren whispering in her ear that turned her sour against him.

He looked at the stone again. Little wonder he didn't recognize it as a tombstone at first glance. The carved rock was fully seven feet long and at least three feet wide. It rose from the ground to the height of his knees. Surely they'd used stone that was already here, but they had to move it to place it over the grave—somehow. Was the rock placed there to keep the wild animals out, or to keep something in? God, Brodie—get spooked much? But it was a spooky place...

A shiver ran up his back as a light drizzle began to fall, misting his face. The wind picked up and leaves swirled from the woodland floor. A long cold night loomed ahead. He grabbed at his hat—too late—as a strong gust of wind snatched it from his head.

"Brodie, hey Brodie!" The voice echoed through the hills.

He jumped up and shined his light to the left and to the right. Get a grip, Brodie. Are you hearing the ghosts of this place? Imagining voices?

He did hear a voice, though, and it sounded close. He listened carefully to see if it would repeat again. A distant screech owl emitted its eerie warbling call. Again shivers crept up his spine, settling for a moment at the nape of his neck, and his hairs stood at attention. The branches that creaked in discomfort from the wind's assault created the only other sound.

He shook his head and walked away from the stone. Once, twice, he glanced back to ensure nothing followed him. The wind's tempo increased, and he walked with no destination known, trying to put distance between himself and Zach's final resting place. He'd never admit it to anyone else, but the whole thing gave him the jitters. On he walked, hoping to find a rock outcropping or some brush to hide under to get out of the rain. Come morning, he'd get his bearings and find his way to camp. He might even jump his buck on the way.

A large square shape loomed ahead, captured in his flashlight's beam. It looked to be an abandoned shed or perhaps a small homesteader's shack. He climbed onto the weather-beaten porch bypassing the rotten steps. The front door hung from one rusted hinge and he pulled it aside to enter the building. There were gaps in the ceiling and holes through the walls, but large sections of the interior remained dry. Broken glass littered the floor showing the effects of years of vandalism. It was likely a teen hang out at one time. He waved the flashlight from one revelation to another investigating his surroundings.

"What the hell?" He dropped his light and the room succumbed to total darkness. He searched sightless where he'd heard the light land, and his fingers closed over it. Tapping the head of the light, the bulb flickered, and then stayed on. Again he moved the beam around inside. On every wall, six-foot-tall hand-hewn crosses hung. They looked new, or at least freshly painted. Strange for someone to hang them here, he thought, but country folks did like their religion. Despite this overture to Christianity however, nature was well on its way to reclaiming the old building. He didn't care one way or another, as long as it stood for one more night. He curled up in the center of the floor and fell into a fitful sleep.

Chapter Fifteen

Nathaniel Mountain, WV hunt camp
Garren

He woke with her name on his lips. "Anna?"

He shook his head to clear his mind. Must've dozed off, just a dream. He rubbed his eyes remembering the four deer, but little else. He'd dreamt of a doe with her two young of the year on a trail just out of his shooting range. Maybe there really was a trail there, but he didn't know. He would be sure to check it out later though. He'd had the strange feeling of floating above them as they stared at a fourth deer, a buck. In his dream, he became the buck and followed them until he sensed danger. He ran, but watched them until they were beyond his view and then…?

He checked his watch and realized he'd lost a lot of time and felt disappointed with himself. An entire herd of deer could've walked by his stand and he would've slept through it. He smiled. That wouldn't be a piece of information he'd share with his camp mates.

Maybe the other guys in camp had some luck. Maybe they were disciplined enough to stay awake—much better odds of seeing deer with your eyes open. The sun set a good hour before and shooting light was long gone. That's a wrap for tonight. He descended the ladder from his perch.

His dreams were strange, and shadowy fingers of them clawed at his mind. He remembered the fragment of another dream. He was somewhere with Anna and two other girls he never met before. What he most remembered, though, was an overpowering sense of impending disaster. Someone or something was pursuing them and they were running through the trees to escape. Weird, but he was thinking about Anna just before the weight of his eyelids betrayed him. Perhaps that made it natural to weave her into his dream.

He enjoyed the late-night woods and found the walk back to the cabin relaxing. The woods, although quiet, were alive with a myriad of sounds—if one listened—but the solitude with nature filled his spirit. Uncle Jim didn't share this sentiment. He'd confided that when the sun went down, he was out of there. He said he didn't want to take any chances walking up on a black bear at night. He had a friend, who had a friend, who'd been mauled by a bear late at night. He suspected Jim's story was another often repeated urban legend.

Besides the possible physical threats waiting for him in the dark, his semi-inebriated uncle once confided there were things in the night woods that would make a man soil his long johns. But the next morning he feigned no knowledge of the conversation.

He was surprised Uncle Jim didn't yell or at least signal him as he passed his stand on the way back to the cabin. Maybe Jim got a shot at that big buck he was waiting for.

The metal roof of the cabin reflected the moon's light. He saw that it was almost full as he shined his flashlight toward the back of the building. There were no additions to the meat pole. The wind was brisk and he felt a chill run up his backbone. Welcoming smoke curled up from the chimney—that wood stove was sure going to feel good! The back door of the cabin creaked open.

"Garren, is that you? Brodie?" Chris yelled.

"It is I, the noble hero back from the Trojan wars!"

"Man, I'm glad to see you. Mika just got back in and he couldn't find Brodie. We're going back up to his stand and see if we can find him."

"Maybe he got a deer?"

"I don't know. Mika said there were some empty cartridges on the ground under his stand and he thinks Brodie got turned around while he was tracking one."

Jim, Mika, and Henry Gale filed from the cabin as he reached the door.

"Where have you been, Garren? I yelled and yelled from the trail and never heard any answer from you. Thought maybe you had a deer under your stand, or maybe you were already back at camp. When neither one of you was here, I was ready to call out the National Guard for the two of you! You know your momma will kick my butt if anything happens to you, and I don't figure on taking an ass whipping for you, boy," Jim scolded.

"Sorry, I was trying to get every minute in the stand I could."

He felt Mika's eyes on him and turned to see the old man's smile. He ducked his head to avoid the man's gaze.

"You have some of those new night vision goggles? That's what you'd need to harvest a deer at this time of night." No trace of a smile touched Jim's face.

"Well, let's go see if we can find the other rookie," Henry Gale joked. "Bertram and Frank say they're too worn out to go traipsing through the woods in the middle of the night. Nice fellows, those two. Where did you find them, Jim?"

"Come on, Henry, don't start with that again. We both know why the members voted him in, even you." Jim rubbed his thumb and index finger together. "Money talks, as they say."

"Maybe it is has more to do with the sort of fellow we're looking for, rather than the type of men they are," Chris said.

"Don't judge too harshly," Mika said. "I've known Bertram for several years. He made his choices, but remember, sometimes good fortune is an affliction. As for

Brodie, he's still young. The wolves are still nipping at his spirit, trying to get a piece."

"Wolves? I didn't know there are still wolves in these woods." Chris shined his light back and forth to cover the woods in front of them.

"Not that kind." Mika laughed. "It is a story my father told when he caught me in some mischief as a young boy. He said his father told it to him, but I don't know for sure. The story's been around for years and many lay claim to originating it. I cannot say, but it is a good story.

"He said a young man approached an elder of his tribe. He was twisted inside from the many bad things he'd done in his short life and sought the old man's counsel. He was afraid he'd lost his path.

"The elder explained to him that like all men, he had two wolves warring inside him. One wolf was the good part of a man. He lives in harmony with the world and only fights when he has to. The other is the evil side of a man. This wolf is always angry and full of hate. He sees the good in nothing. He is envious and greedy. These two wolves split a man in two trying to dominate his spirit. This is the fight that is going on in you, the elder told him.

"The young man was anxious, and asked, 'Tell me, grandfather, which wolf will win?'

"The old man replied, 'Whichever one you feed.'"

"Mika, I think what you are trying to tell us in your subtle way is that Brodie and Bertram fed all their Alpo to the wrong wolf," Henry concluded.

Chapter Sixteen

Hampshire County, WV
Anna

"Sit up, Anna; let me see your shoulder."

"That's okay; I'm fine Lenore, honest. I can't even feel it anymore," she said.

"That's wonderful news that I'm delighted to hear, now let me see." Lenore pulled up the back of Anna's shirt.

Lenore and Bridget examined her wound closely.

She followed Bridget's pointing finger to the log she'd leaned against. "Weird, but it just looks like you jammed your back into the broken branch on that log. Luckily, it's not very deep."

"Good, I'm not sure I can handle Dr. Lenore and Nurse Bridget operating on me! It was strange though, it really felt like I'd been shot." She pulled down the back of her shirt. "I assume the examination is over? Guess I got into our 'trip' a little bit too much. Not that I could keep up with you, Lenore. It was all I could do to keep a grip on my little fawn. If not for Moll...but I think you could have done a waltz with that mature doe that you latched on to."

"I know what you mean, Anna. Now, as for your condition, take two aspirins and call us in the morning, but all kidding aside, I still want to know why you two left me high and dry."

"I am sorry, Brie, but somehow I knew your spirit would return here," Lenore said.

"That's what I mean. This is definitely your gig, White Witch. I'm sorry too, Brie. It had to be scary for you, but we hadn't found anyone yet, and there is danger there. I don't mean just from our deer's point of view either."

"Not just danger, there's evil." Lenore stared off into the woods. "We still didn't find them either. Someone started shooting at us."

"Not a good start, huh, ladies? Guess I owe everyone an apology."

"Like hell you do, Anna. It was the greatest thing ever. I could do without the gunplay, but what a rush! I've never felt anything like it before."

"I agree with Lenore, just make sure I'm with you all the way next time. Now please excuse me while I try out the cabin's facilities." She watched her until she entered the cabin.

"Evil, Lenore? Care to explain?"

Lenore shrugged her shoulders. "Just a feeling I guess, nothing I could put my finger on. I felt we were being watched long before the shooting started. You know how it is when someone is staring at you and you just know it?"

"I do. The buck that followed us, did you think he was, I don't know…familiar somehow?"

"You've got me on that one, I haven't been up close and personal with many deer, until tonight anyway, but you know a lot more about it than I do."

"Maybe on an academic level, but I can't do what you can—not with skin walking. Reading about it is one thing but experiencing it? That's new ground for me too, way out of my depth. It was pretty amazing though. Still, I'm telling you—there was something about that buck."

"Are you sure your doe wasn't in heat? Just how familiar was he?" Lenore elbowed her in the side.

Before she could respond, the screen door of the cabin slammed shut and Bridget raced over to join them by the fire.

"Okay, what did I miss? Oh Anna, I really do love your cabin! I didn't notice before, but what a great view of the creek from the bathroom window."

"Thanks, I'll tell my grandfather, he did most of the work on it. But we were discussing maybe trying this again tomorrow, but earlier in the day. Your folks will think I'm a bad influence if I keep you out all hours of the night. What do you say, Brie?"

"Promise I go where you go?" Bridget's lips formed a pout.

"I can't promise that," Lenore said. "I don't know enough to promise that, but we'll keep you closer, right Anna?"

"Yes, and worst-case scenario—you know your way home now."

"Anna is right though, Bridget. We better get our backsides back home before the parents call us in as missing persons."

The two girls gave her a quick hug and left with the promise of meeting the following evening. She sat at the fire tending her own thoughts and watched the light from their flashlights disappear in the distance.

"I wish you were here, Grandfather," she said to the night sky. "I am puzzled and afraid."

She thought of the buck and how familiar he seemed to her—despite the doe's nervousness. *Garren, was it you? It felt like you, but I don't know how, unless you…if so, thanks for the warning. Maybe I'm the one going crazy.*

She pulled at her antler amulet. She wasn't sure how to proceed with her new friends, or even if there was anything to proceed with. She hung her head realizing something about herself. Until tonight, her spiritualism was basically an intellectual query, a way to please her grandfather, and a means of establishing an identity outside of the norm. It was a connection with her ancestors she shared with her grandfather. It wasn't that she didn't believe, but her belief was tempered with logic. What was logical about this evening? What was logical about what Lenore could do?

Anna wrote a school paper once on mass hypnosis, and she knew the phenomenon was real. Is that what the three of them experienced? A short circuit in (or an overactive) amygdala?

Did anything happen that couldn't be explained rationally, scientifically? She remembered running across the meadow, as she often did in real life. How hard then to imagine doing so in the guise of an animal she was so familiar with? What of the wound to her shoulder? Was it a strange coincidence that she bled in the same spot where the young doe was shot? Even with the sense of freedom the experience afforded them, the resultant stress couldn't be denied. What she couldn't explain was the sense of inherent danger from the moment she was with the deer. There was a blackness she and Lenore both sensed. She knew this was the least tangible evidence of all, but to her, it felt the most real.

Bridget and Lenore seemed to accept it at face value—without question, though that might change in retrospect. Was it possible that by joining their spirits together, they harvested an untapped energy that allowed them to go so far?

If evil stalked Nathaniel Mountain, there was one mistake she couldn't afford to make again. She needed to keep her new friends safe—especially Brie. Bridget did not have family in those hills she needed to protect—nor any to protect *her*.

Part II

Chapter Seventeen

The haunted call of a whippoorwill echoed through the woods, hoping, searching. A pause but none answered: a silence not born of peace, but of mourning, despair. His vision blurred. "Please dear God, I don't deserve your mercy, but take this cross from me or bring me home! Forgive me, my love."

Nathaniel Mountain Hunting Camp, WV
Brodie

He woke to the sound of creaking floorboards.

"Who is there? Hey!" He rubbed his eyes and looked around the dark room...absolute darkness...*the darkness of the womb.* The walls glistened with a dull light and he squeezed his eyes open and closed. No, it wasn't the walls. Four wooden crosses glowed as if lit by lightning bugs! They swelled and contracted in size, pulsing like beating alien hearts. *Thump...thump. Thump...thump...*

He rubbed his palms into his eye sockets to remove the filmy sediment from his eyes, shook his head and looked back. The huge hand-cobbled crosses hung crookedly on the wall. They were odd enough to be sure, but there was nothing stranger here.

A glance at his watch—he'd slept for three hours and was chilled to the bone. He did recall waking to noises he couldn't explain—voices he could almost, but not quite, hear. He would be glad to see the morning. He wouldn't get much sleep in this creepy, creaky old place anyway.

His dreams were littered with shadowy, half remembered images that faded like a mist when his conscious mind regained a foothold. The only constant in these dreams was his father. He wondered how a man he'd never met could haunt his dreams. But he'd inhabited every nightmare of this night. The man's face and figure were a blur, but not his voice. He would always remember that voice! It spoke to him as if from some faraway place. *Yeah, it is a long-distance call from hell.*

He didn't discount the possibility that his real father might in fact be toasting his toes by the woodstove and sipping bourbon at camp. He didn't know, nor particularly care. There was a time in his life it would've mattered, but that time and feeling faded away long before. He was his own man now. All that mattered was here and now.

Exhaustion crept in on him, massaging his mind with its tendrils of fog. He closed his eyes, listening for hints of anything or anyone passing in the night. His head nodded, nodded again, and then rested on the floor quietly.

"They are looking in the woods for you," the voice whispered.

"Who is?"

"They call themselves your friends."

"No. I have no friends."

"No, but we know what to do. Listen..."

He sat upright and twisted around on the rotting floorboards. Shaking his nightmare, trying to force himself awake. Was the sun up? No, he could see stars through the cracked window. The light? Where did it come from then? With closed eyes, its glow still seeped through. It was inside the shack. A soothing voice called to him, drew him into its warm embrace. Mesmerized, he listened to what it had to say.

"No, I can't do that..." He shook his head.

"It needs to be done. I am the only one you can count on. We are true brothers. You will see."

"But why, it doesn't seem right?"

"You will see, but you'll need my help. Bring her to me and she will love you always."

"Who are you?" No answer reached through to his dreams.

"Brodie," a new voice said.

"Who are you?" He jerked himself from his semi-conscious dream state and forced his eyes wide open.

"Hell, it's us, boy. Cold done numbed your brain or something?" Jim shined his flashlight in Brodie's eyes. "You're lucky Mika remembered this old place or it would be a long night for you."

He looked around the dimly lit interior and met Mika's eyes. The old man looked happy to see him. *He must be cold and wants to get back to the cabin.*

"I appreciate you guys coming to look for me. I'll admit it got a bit chillish in here—as my old gym teacher used to say. I was going to hole up here and find my way out at first light."

"Couldn't leave a greenhorn out alone on a night like this now, could we?" Mika smiled. "Not to mention I need help feeding this pack of wolves in the morning."

"We saw the empty cartridges." Garren stepped in from the open doorway. "Did you have some luck?"

"No, but I think I winged one. I was looking for blood sign and ended up here." He squinted his eyes and sucked in his top lip. He heard the snicker from behind Garren and Chris stepped inside.

"How in the world did you find this God forsaken place?" Chris asked.

"Good choice of words." Jim rubbed the whiskers on his cheeks. "Let's just cut the chit-chat and get back to camp. What the hell is up with the crosses anyway? This place gives me the creeps."

"It should, Jim. Do you remember the stories about this place?" Mika asked.

"I do, not something you're likely to forget. First time it's been my misfortune to see it from the inside though. I'm not a superstitious man, but it isn't just bears I'm worried about running into in this part of the woods. Let's get a move on now."

He smiled at the 'not a superstitious man' remark and had to know more.

"What are the stories, Mika?"

"It can wait until we get back to the cabin, Brodie. Right, Mika?" Jim asked.

He noticed Garren and Chris' faces break into grins at Jim's discomfiture, but also noticed that Mika didn't share their mirth.

Henry poked his head inside. "Let's hit it, men. A warm spot by the fire sure sounds good, doesn't it?"

"Yes indeedy, Henry. The thermometer 'sposed to drop down into the knothole tonight." Jim followed Mika outside, but when they stepped out, Mika's flashlight flew across the porch. A rotted floorboard couldn't handle the activity of the night and gave way. Like a trapdoor in some haunted mansion, it dropped Mika like a trapped animal. He saw Jim catch his balance a moment before following Mika's descent.

"Ouch, damn it! Watch it—that first step's a doozy!" Mika moaned.

He rushed past Jim and knelt to the side of the broken flooring, helping Mika extract himself from the hole.

"Mika, are you okay?" he asked.

"Tell you in a minute, Brodie." Mika stood gingerly on his right foot.

"It's just a slight sprain I think."

"C'mon boys, let's see if we can find a branch he can use for a walking stick," Henry suggested.

"No, I'm fine. It won't hurt much until it stiffens up. That'll be a while. It's a long walk back to the cabin."

He held Mika's elbow as they descended the steps, and glanced over his shoulder at the dilapidated old shack.

"Something in there never did like me," Mika said.

"Don't start that story again, Mika. We had a deal," Jim said.

"We'll wait on that story then, Jim. How about a hunting story, Brodie? Yours—a sad tale of innocence lost and predatory ineptitude?" Chris asked.

His jaw muscles seized and his hands drew into fists. This time it was Mika holding his elbow.

Henry grabbed his son's shoulder. "Chris, any man tells you he's never missed either just started hunting or is a damn liar. It sucks, but it happens. And don't pretend you've never made a bad shot."

He saw the boy drop his head and kick at the leaves. "Sorry, man," Chris mumbled.

He nodded his head and took a few deep breaths.

"I'd still like to hear about it, Brodie. What all did you see tonight?" Jim asked.

He felt his blood pressure lowering as he recounted all he'd experienced...all the deer hunting parts. He explained how the blood trail ended, and that while circling around trying to find it, he ended up at the shack. He frowned at the furtive glances exchanged between Garren and Chris. *The bastards are enjoying this.* He waited for some more digs about his shooting. He really wasn't in the mood.

"Not much chance of finding the blood trail now either. Rain will have washed it away," Garren commented.

"Did you get the jitters with a big buck like that in front of you, Brodie?" Chris asked.

"No, just a quick shot at him through the brush. No time to get buck fever."

"Didn't get a good shot at the does either, huh?"

"No, they were running too."

"You must be confident. I don't think I'd take a shot like that," Chris said.

"Look, if you had a shot at that big boy, you'd take it. Don't bullshit me."

"Mika, I think we have some tired hunters on our hands tonight. Squabbling like a couple of old women, wouldn't you say?" Henry glared in Chris' direction.

"Let's just get to the cabin. We'll all feel better then," Jim concluded.

Chapter Eighteen

Nathaniel Mountain Hunt Camp, WV
Garren

Uncle Jim jabbed him in the ribs and pointed out an ancient hickory tree. "Know where we are now, don't you, Garren?"

"Yes sir, that front yard looks as fine as any I've seen. Looks like the fire is about out though."

"We'll soon fix that," Mika promised. "These old bones took on a chill."

"How old are you anyway, Mika? I don't mean any harm, but I swear you look the same as when I first started coming here—every bit of twenty years ago," Henry said. "You haven't gotten any older looking, but you haven't gotten any better looking either so I guess it balances out."

"I guess it's all in the genes on both counts. Last time I checked, though, I was 74 years old."

He followed the hunters single file into the cabin. Though the fire was low, it was a lot warmer than outside. Enough embers remained to make it easy to catch the fire back up.

"Guess those two trifling bastards assumed we'd be back to keep them nice, warm, and cozy," Henry muttered under his breath.

He heard Henry, but decided it best not to comment. The night had generated enough tension. The two bastards in question—Bertram and Frank—were already sound asleep in their racks. The newly arrived hunters stripped off their wet clothes and boots and clustered around the fire to warm up.

They sipped on Mika's stew, hot from the slow cooker, all commenting it was the best they'd ever eaten. When they ate their full and then some, he watched Brodie gather the bowls and take them to the kitchen.

"Mika, I sure would like to hear about that shack up there. What kind of tales do they tell about it?" he asked.

"Lordy, boy, let the man digest his food won't you."

"That's all right, Jim. You know I like to talk whenever I can get someone to listen," Mika said.

"I reckon…well I hate to leave good company and all, but I think I'm going to have to call it a night," Jim said. "So excuse me, fellers, but I'm sure Mika can tell the story just fine without me."

"I reckon so Jim, but sometime you should tell the boys about your own experiences up at that cabin?" Mika winked at him.

"Maybe so, but not tonight, bad memories." Jim shook his head.

Brodie came in with a smile on his lips and joined the others waiting to hear Mika's story.

"Hey, you didn't see anything strange up there did you, Brodie?" Jim stood up, his knees creaking audibly.

"Those life-sized crosses hanging all over the place were strange enough for me. Never saw anything like it before."

Mika took a long drink of water. "Well, if you fellows want to hear the story, we'd better do it now. It's getting late."

"You have our undivided attention, Mika," he said and heads nodded in agreement.

"Well, the story starts in the early 1800s, but you know how a story changes with each retelling. This one is no different, I'd guarantee—but what I'm going to tell you is just the way my granddaddy told it to me. Now Henry, you feel free to jump in there with anything you remember hearing about the whole sordid affair.

"Anyway, there was a fellow moved up here by the name of John Dyer. Folks said he had to leave from wherever he lived before. They say he was about to get himself strung up, but you know how people like to talk. They claimed his family's history included witchcraft, and that a few of them were even put to death for it. Well, he bought this small parcel of rocky land on the side of the mountain up there and called it a farm. He'd got it cheap enough, because the folks hereabouts said it wouldn't grow nothing but weeds. The Conoy tribe claimed it was a bad place, tainted with blood. They said Okeus, their mischievous and destructive god, called it home. But that might be going back too far for this story and this audience.

"So, Dyer kept some pigs, a couple of goats, and did some vegetable farming—all for his own use or for trade like folks did back then. The other settlers took to him after a while seeing how well he did with the place. I heard the ladies were lining up to spend time with him too. Then out of the blue, he up and married this itinerant preacher's daughter by the name of Ava Hartman. Beautiful woman she was too, by all accounts."

"My granddaddy said she was as pretty as a steamboat painted red." Henry laughed.

"That's good, Henry. Think your grandfather will mind if I borrow it?"

"I suspect he'd be pleased, Mika."

Mika nodded his head and continued. "Well the preacher wasn't too happy about it, as he never saw our Mr. Dyer attending his services, and of course, he was a half-breed too. Preacher Hartman wasn't about to leave his daughter alone in the mountains with the heathens either. The daughter being a grown woman though, there wasn't much he could do about it except make himself miserable, so that's what he did. Soon after, it came to everyone's attention that the new Mrs. Dyer had put on weight pretty quick, if you young fellows know what I mean?"

Chris glanced over at Garren, stifled a giggle, and Mika continued.

"Folks started doing the math and things weren't adding up just right. You boys can smile, but this was a time when you just didn't do that. At least, not so folks would know." Mika winked at him and took a sip of his water.

"Then things went downright tragic. John Dyer just up and left the mountain for a long while. People talked about the situation behind the Dyers' backs, as they do. Folks said he'd deserted his pregnant wife, and wasn't coming back. Ava got depressed over the shame and heartbreak. She wouldn't eat, couldn't sleep. Remember, this woman's father was a preacher. She started dropping weight and doing poorly. Some say her hair even started falling out. By the time the poor woman was due to have her baby she looked like a swollen-bellied stick figure, a husk of the woman she'd been. My grandfather said it would hurt your eyes just to look at her. That's about the time John Dyer returned, though only God knows where he'd been.

"Having a baby is never a picnic, but in those days, it was damn scary. There was no real doctor for forty miles, so William Jordan's wife Kate got called in. The Jordans were close with the Dyers anyway. My grandfather said Kate had some Shawnee blood and knew the medicinal herbs. She'd acted as a midwife a time or two, but things went bad, and she couldn't do anything for Ada Dyer.

"I guess you've figured out by now, Ada died giving birth. My granddaddy said sure as hell, the settlers' intolerance had murdered her. Now the baby, amazingly, lived through it all, and turned out to be a strong healthy boy. John Dyer named his only son Zachary after one of his ancestors, his granddaddy I believe."

He looked up from the fire when Mika cleared his throat. He started to stand, but Brodie pushed past him on his way to retrieve Mika's glass.

"Here Mika, let me get you some more water," Brodie said. "Hit the pause button until I get back?"

The old cook waited for Brodie's return and he noticed the man grimace when propping his foot on a table.

He grabbed a pillow. "Here, Mika." He lifted the man's foot and placed the cushion under his ankle.

"Thanks, Garren."

"This is a sad story, but I thought we were in for a good scary campfire kind of tale? You know—ghosts, witches, demons, and things that go bump in the night," Chris said.

"I'm not done yet," Mika said.

Brodie returned, placed the full glass of water at Mika's side and dropped back in his seat on the floor.

"Okay, men. So, as the story goes, I reckon being a single father was too much for John Dyer to handle. He paid little attention to Zachary's raising and the boy grew up a little wild, sort of the Huckleberry Finn type. John paid him little mind. Don't get me wrong, there isn't a thing wrong with living in the outdoors, but Zachary spent more time alone than he ever did with people and he never learned how to act around them. The only contact the boy had with any sort of human society was when he ran afoul of it.

"Then it would be all hell to pay. That being the only time the father would give the lad any attention at all. Then, they say, Dyer would all but peel the hide off him. You could hear the boy scream in Romney the beating was so bad. I guess he blamed the child for his wife's passing.

"Well, the people around here started feeling a little guilty over how they'd treated the mother. They didn't want another tragedy on their consciences. After all, they were civilized Christian folk, but they didn't know what to do. It didn't seem right to take the boy from his father. But the preacher grandfather had his thoughts on the matter. He riled the people up, quoting Scripture every which way to incite them to take action.

"One day, one of the settlers spotted young Zachary snatching up a neighbor's chicken. That was a pretty bad offense in those days, and the settler told the preacher what he'd seen. Of course, the preacher blamed Zachary's father John for the thieving. He claimed the man never fed the boy and that he'd seen the boy outside his house digging for scraps, too proud to ask for a handout. Something had to be done according to the preacher. It was their responsibility as Christians. That got the people motivated. They remembered how fast the boy's mother had wasted away.

"So up the mountain this crazed mob went, Preacher Hartman at the head of the pack. John Dyer had to realize he couldn't fight the whole bunch of 'em and he fled through the woods. He was never seen in these mountains again. Though some say different." Mika took a long pull on his water, swished it around in his mouth and swallowed.

"Go ahead, Garren. I see the wheels turning in your head."

"What is it that some say that's different about John Dyer's departure? Seemed there might be a story there? And what happened to the boy? Zachary isn't it?"

"John's is a story onto itself, more urban legend really and better suited to another night. But Zachary, he was taken in by his grandfather, the preacher. Probably wasn't much of a change for Zachary. The preacher believed if you spare the rod, you spoil the child.

"Now remember that the Jordans had been good friends with John and Ada Dyer. They tried to take Zachary under their wing and see to his care, but the preacher wouldn't allow them much interaction with the boy. He said they were mollycoddling the lad and what he needed was discipline—him being the spawn of evil or some such nonsense.

"After a couple of years though, the preacher's new wife took ill and he had to take her back to the city. Zachary was near grown then anyway, and didn't want any parts of city life. He fixed up his father's old place and moved in. They said Zachary learned a lot living with the preacher. He had the finest manners you can imagine, and just like his old man before him, he was something else with the ladies. He had a green thumb with the land too. Somehow his crops were bigger and better than any of the farmers in the valley, even though that soil up there was tissue thin, and covered with rocks.

"After a time, Zachary got involved with the Underground Railroad. Some of the settlers knew, and most were in sympathy with the anti-slavery cause anyway. Still, none of them wanted to know too much about the goings on up the mountain. They figured Zachary didn't like the idea of people being treated like he'd been treated, so they just played ignorant.

"This went on for some time, Zachary making Saturday night runs up to Harper's Ferry helping people to freedom. He chased the girls most every other night, and worked hard at farming during the days. It seemed like Zachary turned out all right despite his upbringing.

"When he was around thirty years old, a young woman named Leigh Parsons caught his eye. Just like his daddy, Zachary fell head over heels overnight. The girl's father, James Parsons, was with the Hudson Bay Company and made a stack of money off trappers. Her mother was called Elizabeth because nobody could pronounce her Mingo name. Her tribe moved inland after the Seven Years War, but I imagine the move back here was a bit of a homecoming for her. This Leigh Parsons—the apple of Zachary Dyer's eye—was my maternal grandmother."

"Oh, it makes sense now how you know this story so well," Henry said. "Hell, it's your family history."

"Not really my family's story. There's this small entwined part that starts here, and soon ends. I do know it pretty well though from stories I've been told and journals I've read from some of the folks involved. I'm no relation to Zachary Dyer, although I suspect some of us here are."

"Who?" Brodie asked.

"I shouldn't have mentioned it and I apologize for that. If they don't know, it's not my place to tell them." Mika looked at him, then Chris, finally resting his eyes on Brodie for a moment, then continued his story.

"When it looked like things might be getting serious with those two, my great-grandfather put his foot down. Even though my research shows he was half Conoy, he looked as white as Chris, but he was intent on hiding that part of his heritage—that's what folks did who could get away with it. Zachary, on the other hand, was copper skinned with hair as black as coal. My great-grandfather said no child of his would live in a shack with a womanizing half-breed who consorted with the coloreds, and violated the law. And unlike the preacher, there *was* something he could do about it. Leigh was 16 years old and he could still tell her what to do. So, he married her off to one of his business associate's son in Romney. He never gave the girl any choice in the matter. Like I said, times were different then.

"Zachary Dyer was devastated. People said he moped about and paced the floor of his shack and not much else. Months passed and Zachary decided to pack a bag and go get Leigh, said he would bring her back or die trying. The story goes that he found her but despite all of his pleading, she rejected him. Whether she was content with her new husband, or if she just wanted to honor her father's wishes, my grandmother never said, but Zachary came home empty handed.

"Zachary started to turn mean after that. Some say Leigh was the one true love of his life and he never got over her. Months passed by before any of the settlers saw him. He'd turned hermit and never roamed far from his shack. Those that did catch a glimpse of him said he changed. The man reverted back to his boyhood ways. People who knew him for years wouldn't even recognize him at first glance. Zachary's hair grew long and unkempt. He looked dirty and unshaven and his beard turned white as cotton.

"His preacher grandfather came back for a visit about then. His wife passed on to her maker that year and he thought it time to follow up with the only family he had—his grandson. Fifteen years had passed since they exchanged more than an occasional letter, and even then, most of the writing was done by the preacher's wife.

"The grandfather arrived at Zachary's shack the early part of a Sunday evening. Before Monday noon, he headed out of there as fast as his horse would carry him. Some folks asked him to stay and preach some on the good book, but he wouldn't have it. He said there was evil on the mountain and if they were smart they'd pack up and get out too before it consumed the whole valley. That was all he'd say on the subject. After that, the only visitors Zachary had were the runaway slaves he helped. Yes, he still made his clandestine runs for the Underground Railroad.

"Things settled down some until one morning, a young boy was by the creek drawing some water. As he dipped in his bucket, he heard a horrible moaning coming from the bushes. His daddy wounded a bear the night before, so he ran like the devil was chasing him—all the way back to his house. His father grabbed his gun, hollered for his neighbor to do the same, and followed his son back to the creek. The two men heard the moaning, and instructed the boy to stand back out of the way. The men tried yelling, and throwing rocks, but nothing was bringing that wounded bear out into the open. They had a great deal of respect for a wounded bear.

"Finally, the boy's father crept forward, gun held out in front of him and loaded with buckshot. The neighbor stood behind him with his rifle shouldered, and his finger on the trigger. The lead man used his gun barrel to push aside some of the brush to peer inside. A blood curdling scream knocked the man off his feet just as the gun behind him went off.

"'Sweet Jesus,' he said, and turned to the boy. 'Get up to the Jordans' place. Tell Kate that someone's in a bad way and in need of her healing. Get a move on boy or it will be too late.'"

"Who was it? Man or beast?" Chris asked.

"There in the bushes was a young black woman no more than sixteen. She didn't have a stitch of clothes on and with just a glance the men knew she'd been beaten. Thank God the neighbor's bullet didn't hit her, but it was late October and the girl was near frozen. The men tried to cover her with their own coats, but she screamed bloody murder and crawled away from them.

"'Devil!' she screamed at the men, waving them away with a bloodied hand. With the terror they saw on her face, they thought she might die of fright as quick as from the cold. They backed away from her, leaving their coats on the ground beside her.

"Kate Jordan arrived, and had almost as much trouble as the men, but she did manage to get through to her that she didn't mean her harm. The two men, Kate, and the boy half carried and half dragged the girl back to the Jordans' place. All the while, she babbled feverishly about the dark-eyed white devil.

"Kate placed the girl in her own bed, and learned her name was Sarah. The poor girl had been whipped with switches until stripes marked most of her skin. Her buttocks and upper thighs had taken the brunt of the punishment.

What appeared to be feces was rubbed into the wounds. One finger from her right hand was chopped off between the hand and first knuckle. Burn marks covered her skin and pieces of adhered wax testified to the additional torments she'd suffered.

"Kate cleaned off the blood with warm water and white wood ash. She applied oak bark powder to stem the bleeding, and bandaged her up as best she could. Herbal teas were brewed and salves administered. She found clothes that almost fit the girl from her own younger days. Kate feared the girl was raped as well, but Sarah never became coherent enough to speak for herself, or to accuse her attacker. For two days and three nights, Kate administered to the young woman before she succumbed to her wounds and a bout of pneumonia.

"Kate told anyone who'd listen about the girl's suffering, as well as her own suspicions about the crazy white man on the mountain. There wasn't any law around here then, but some of the men got together to hash it out to see what steps were to be taken. Of course, Zachary Dyer was everyone's number one suspect. He kept to himself and was rarely seen. He was even stranger since the incident with Leigh Parsons and he had access to unfamiliar black women, ostensibly to help them. The problem the men had was they had no real evidence. Kate could tell them little. She'd repeatedly asked Sarah who'd tortured her, but the girl either didn't know the man's name or was silenced by her fear. Kate recited from memory Sarah's last words to her.

"'Misses, he be a white bearded devil. His eyes are death. They're vulture eyes wanting to feed. Strong man…evil…dark…must get away now.' With that, the girl left the physical world and her torments behind her. Kate didn't know if the girl's last words were meant as a warning for her or if, in her fevered state, she imagined herself back with her tormentor.

"If it had been Sarah's destiny to be born a white woman, more would've been done. The feverish dying words of a black woman, as tragic as it all was, only inspired the men to keep a closer watch on the safety of their own women, and a closer watch on Dyer's farm."

"Was nothing done then?" Chris asked.

"Zachary was never arrested. Hell, he was never even questioned. More years passed, but not much changed that you could tell in these parts. People in the city were talking of revolution and freeing the slaves, and next thing anyone knew there was a war. West Virginia was born shortly thereafter.

"Anyway, Zachary's story became more legend than a history. On the rare occasion that anyone saw Zachary in the woods, they'd speak of him as if they'd seen a ghost, but Zachary Dyer wasn't done yet.

"One moonlit summer night a pair of young women, best friends, snuck out of their homes to meet with the boyfriends their parents didn't approve of. There was some drinking and the boyfriends were full of the false bravado that accompanies youth and alcohol. It took some convincing and a few double dog dares, but the foursome decided to pay a visit to our Mr. Dyer and see if any of the stories were true. It may seem foolish now, but there were four of them and just one old man up on the mountain. What could happen? But don't discount the power of white lightning.

"So up the mountain they went singing and dancing and making a party out of their adventure. Boozed up enough they couldn't walk a straight line, one of the boys tripped over a rock and fell off the edge of a cliff. The young fool broke his leg and messed himself up pretty bad in general. The fun was over for him, but now they had a problem. They didn't want to leave the boy alone out there, and both of the girls were adamant they weren't going to stay up there—so near Zachary's cabin—all by themselves.

So after a lot of arguing, it was decided that the boys would stay there while the girls went down the mountain toward safety and help.

"When the sun came up hours later, the two young men were still waiting for the girls' return. They knew in their hearts that something went very wrong. The one able bodied boy decided to go down to see what had happened to them, and get his friend some help while he was at it.

"The first cabin the lad reached belonged to the Jordans, and he soon discovered that the girls never made it home. The alarm was raised and once again, as in years past, a mob ascended the mountain to Dyer's farm.

"As they approached Zachary's shack, the mob fell silent. Even those too young to remember knew the stories of Sarah, of John Dyer's disappearance and the rumors of the Dyer name being synonymous with witchcraft. Three of the bravest (or most foolish) men volunteered to go in front of the rest, armed and ready for anything that might spring out of the shack's door.

"They stepped onto the porch and yelled a warning, 'Zachary Dyer, we're coming in.' Pounding on the door, a moan was heard inside, and that was enough.

"One man's shoulder hit the door as a shot went off behind him. Then another shot boomed across the mountains. The mob of men flooded inside. Several of them immediately lost their dinner on the floor of the shack. The more stoic among them merely gagged and tasted throw-up in their mouths, but choked it back. Before them, the two young women were gagged with their arms outstretched and bound to rings in the walls. Like Sarah, they were beaten across the breasts and buttocks with switches, but they were lucky. Dyer liked to take his time with torture.

"As the men cut the girls loose, another shot rang out. They covered the girls as best they could and removed the gags. Immediately they screamed.

"'Stop it. I'm not Leigh! I don't even know her.' one sobbed.

"'Don't look at me, Devil! Don't touch me!' the other moaned, staring without seeing.

"The sound of their horror filled the air as more men rushed in to help. Again, Kate Jordan tended to wounded flesh and tried to soothe tortured minds.

"'What was the shooting we heard?' one man asked.

"'My husband saw Dyer running through the woods and he shot twice. He said he put a couple of good shots on him, one in the hand and one in the leg,' Kate answered.

"'But we heard three shots…' another man said.

"'James Parsons thinks he finished him off, sent a bullet his way, and over the cliff he went,' Kate said."

Mika paused, took a deep breath and finished off his water.

"The boy with the broken leg was forgotten until the excitement was over. They recovered him, scared to death, but otherwise okay. Considering everything, he was the luckiest one. His girlfriend committed suicide before year's end, jumped from a cliff—the same cliff that broke his leg. The other two lovebirds moved away in the fall, hopefully they were able to forget, but I have my doubts."

"Man, did any of that really happen?" Chris asked. "It's pretty disturbing."

"Well, that's the way it was told to me anyway," Mika responded. "There were a few other incidentals to the story."

"Incidentals?" Brodie asked.

"Yes. The shack was filled with books on the black arts, as well as herbs and potions. Body parts from dozens of different people were buried around the place. Symbols were painted everywhere, palms drawn with eyes in the center of them, pentagrams, snakes, and what Kate said was a carved head representing the Native American god

Okeus. Knives, whips, and pliers were stored in the drawers like silverware. The rings on the walls were placed to simulate the Christian crucifixion. It wasn't the first time they'd been used. They found thorns woven into crowns, just waiting."

"Gross," Chris said.

"Well, yes and there's more. There are two stories on what happened after that. The first version says Zachary was buried up there somewhere, but he wouldn't stay buried."

"I don't recall this part," Henry said. "Wouldn't stay buried?"

"The pine box they buried him in kept rising up out of the ground, not something that usually happens in rocky soil like that. So they reburied him, only deeper. Again Zachary came floating out of the ground; even Mother Earth wouldn't accept him. Finally, the men got together and brought their horses with them. They buried him yet again and harnessed up the horses and dragged a huge rock over the burial mound. A priest came in and blessed the place. Someone hung the crosses on the walls where Zachary had tied up his victims for torture, marking the end of the Dyer family legacy."

"You said there was a second version?" Brodie asked.

"The second version says Zachary's belongings were buried in that grave to ease people's fears, but ol' Zach's body was never found. You okay, Garren?"

"Sure," he said but a shiver ran up his back at the thought. "So what happened to your grandmother, the woman that Zachary was into? Was it Leigh?"

"Yes, Leigh. She stayed in Romney and never returned, raising four beautiful daughters. One of the four, Agatha, met a young man from here when he was in town for supplies. Fell in love with him and moved back here with him. His name was Richard Pritchard, my father."

Chapter Nineteen

Nathaniel Mountain Hunting Camp, WV
Brodie

He slept well that night though his dreams transported him back to the first pages of West Virginia's history. He lived that night as a settler from the era. His dreams weren't dark as he feared after Mika's gruesome tale, not to mention his own experiences in the shack. Instead, his reveries were nearly erotic.

In the dream, Leigh Parsons was his girl. They walked hand and hand on a beautiful moonlit night. He'd presented her with a necklace he'd made for her—an arrow carved into the slice of deer antler. On the opposite side of the pendant, a triple spiral was etched. *Guess they hadn't invented diamonds back then.* Leigh was thrilled with the gift though and promised to wear it always. She rewarded him with a deep passionate kiss. He knew she wanted him.

What a drop dead gorgeous woman she is…was. I can see why old Zach was so hot after her.

His dream-self drew Leigh down with him to the soft leaves prolonging the kiss and moved his hand…

"Stop, Brodie. I'm going to be married…" she said. Did she mean it? He pulled her to himself. She twisted away and slapped him across the face—almost as hard as Lenore had.

"Enough!" Leigh warned again.

"You know we're meant to be together." He reached for her again.

She grabbed him by the shoulders, held him at arm's length, and shook him. "Brodie!"

"Brodie, wake up. Brodie!" Mika's voice. "It's time to start breakfast."

His eyes opened to see Mika limping from the room with a stiff-ankle gait. He turned in the bed, his feet hitting the cold wood floor, and reached for his clothes. Eyes closed, he pulled on his pants, then grabbed his shirt. It felt odd as he pushed his first arm through a sleeve. Slipping it off, he held it up in the low light of the bunkroom. A large chunk of it was cut away and now sported a long ragged cut from mid shoulder down. "Low life bastards!" he yelled. Pulling another shirt from his bag, he hurried down the stairs to the kitchen.

"Look at this Mika. The assholes cut up my shirt," Brodie blurted out heatedly.

Mika smiled. "They got you all right."

"What the hell is that all about?"

"It's a deer camp tradition, Brodie. When a hunter misses a deer, they cut his shirttail off. I never figured out the symbolism involved, but I've seen many a shirt cut over the years up here. Only supposed to be the tail of the shirt though…must not have known the tradition very well."

"They knew—just wanted to screw me over the best they could. That tradition doesn't play well with me, Mika."

"Tradition is important, Brodie, even when it's unpleasant. Helps you remember who you are, and where you come from."

"I don't agree there. Yesterday doesn't matter, it's ancient history. Today matters, and today I'm pissed."

He heard the sound of old mattresses creaking and boots hitting the floor announcing the hunters were rising. Bertram and Frank were the last to make it to the table. He saw Bertram staring at his ripped shirt, and the man's lip-chewing attempt to stifle a laugh.

"Somebody miss a deer last night?"

"A big one from the looks of it. Half the damn shirt is gone." Frank laughed.

He gritted his teeth. "Matter of fact, it was and for the record, I don't appreciate having my stuff ruined, but payback will be hell."

His chair grated against the floor when he jumped from the table. He took the stairs two at a time with the sound of Chris's snicker mocking him until he entered the bunkroom. He finished dressing, putting one shirt on backwards to keep the cold from creeping down his back. He heard the men leaving the cabin and went downstairs to join Mika in the kitchen. The head cook limped around the room in obvious pain.

"Mika, why don't you go and get ready? I'll take care of this. I think you need to put a tighter wrapping on that foot."

"Doubt I can climb into that stand, Brodie. I'll take care of the clean-up. Think I may stay in this morning and see if I can loosen this dang ankle up. Old age is rough my young friend. Thank you though and you're welcome to use my stand if you want."

"Are you sure?"

Mika nodded.

"Okay, I'll try to bring one back for both of us." He grabbed his rifle and headed for the door.

"Don't let the shirt thing get you down, Brodie. It's a harmless tradition, well not totally harmless, but some guys never grow up, and take things too far."

"Sure, I know."

"And that shack? Stay away from it, Brodie. It will draw you in."

"Are you superstitious, Mika? No worries, there's nothing there that I want. Get that ankle straight, old timer."

He walked to his stand, anger coloring his cheeks. Who did they think they were? Who hated him enough to humiliate him like that? He *would* figure it out, then he'd return the favor in spades. His mother loved to quote the good book when it suited her needs. What did she say about getting even with that boss of hers? Oh yes—vengeance shall be taken on him sevenfold.

He tried sitting still in Mika's stand, but anger and frustration consumed his thoughts. It was a slow morning. He heard one distant shot—far from their hunting area. As one hour dragged by…then two…he climbed down from the stand and walked to his stand of the evening before. After the rain, it might be futile to renew his search for a blood trail, but better than sitting in a tree fuming.

He began his search following the same trails as before. Images from the cabin—and of his failure with the deer—ripped away his confidence until his heart wasn't in the search. The shirttail incident was icing on the bitter cake. A missed deer, a haunted shack, Mika's story, even the pretty girl slapping him in his sleep darkened the bright day. The combination of torments fueled his anger.

He knew Garren was against him. He and his snarky buddy Chris mocked him openly when they had 'protection,' and at the edge of his hearing when no others were there. Jim, a man he once respected, lied to him for years. The man might even be his father. The rest of the hunters meant nothing to him. They were background noise in his story, but Garren and Jim were family, and his family plotted against him.

His head pounded, and he felt every beat of his heart echo inside the walls of his skull. He empathized with how that Zachary guy felt years before. Sometimes he felt the whole world conspired against him too.

Zachary Dyer—why did that name sound familiar?

His thoughts returned to his enemies in camp. At first, he'd assumed Garren and Chris were responsible for the shirt insult, but it had to occur during Mika's tale. The two of them wouldn't mess with Brodie's stuff while he was there. Who did that leave? The ones absent during Mika's story were Bertram, Frank, and Jim. He didn't think Jim would pull a stunt like that. Frank was a new guy and still feeling his way around the others, and he didn't think the man had the balls for it anyway. *That leaves Bertram. He's the one.* He didn't have his revenge plan in place yet, but he'd think of something. The story of his revenge might serve as a cautionary tale for future generations of deer camp back-stabbers. He had all week to plot it out.

He noticed the disturbance in the leaves where he left the trail the night before, and turned to follow his footsteps back toward Zachary's old shack. If he managed to find it again, would he feel its primeval pull again? In the daylight, would its dark attraction match that of the night before? The huge oak tree should be an easy landmark to spot, and forgetting the deer, he began a different hunt. It would be a lot easier finding his way by the sun's light than by flashlight.

After the challenging uphill climb, he spotted the shack, closer to his stand than he'd remembered. He found the huge grave marker, and knelt to examine it. Reading the markings was harder without the angled illumination of his flashlight, and he traced the impressions with his fingertips.

He sat beside the stone and pulled an apple from his coat pocket, peeling it with his skinning knife. *Nice and sharp.* When he finished, he slipped the blade back in its sheath, and noticed the trickle of blood.

"Damn," he shook the blood from his hand, "nicked my trigger finger." He squeezed the tip of his finger and blood seeped from the small cut. He traced his finger over the worn markings on the stone. The glistening blood made the inscription stand out. A trick of light and shadows made them seem to glow, and he read the final epitaph again:

Zachary Dyer
The black man's friend.
Bound in hell for his sins.

The words made sense after hearing Mika's story. Brodie considered the extreme lengths that people could drive a good man to.

He hopped up from the stone to look around the shack. He could see the outline of the deteriorating roof just down the hill. A small caved in shed sat behind the shack. A pile of aged lumber was stacked beside the gaping hole that served as a door. He thought someone once had plans to fix the old shack up, but then thought better of it.

He walked toward the shack, admiring the holly trees bordering both buildings. All were covered with berries like the ones at camp. An old wives' tale said when the hollies were crowded with the bright red berries, a bad winter was coming. He reached the porch and edged around the hole that Mika fell through, and stepped inside. The place gave him the creeps, even worse now—knowing the real-life horrors that occurred here. He couldn't deny another feeling as well—a sense of belonging...a sense of Deja-vu.

He reached out and touched one of the crosses. Could they be the same ones they hung a century ago? They appeared old enough and were worn smooth. Did someone keep replacing them, in an ongoing attempt to protect the present from the past?

"I'm not ashamed to call you brother," a man's voice said.

He jumped back, looked to the left and right. He was the only one there. Jim's comment about the cousins wrapped around Mika's tale and played tricks on his mind. Was his subconscious trying to tell him something? If Jim was his father, he and Garren would be like double cousins—nearly brothers. What were those odds? But he and Garren were nothing alike. They had no common ground, and no family loyalty. He cared less for Garren every moment they spent together. Garren didn't try to hide the fact that he felt the same way about him.

Brother indeed. Garren and Chris went out of their way to make him miserable. He wished someone would put them in their place too, but it wouldn't be him. No matter what, Garren was still blood.

"I'll help you."

Again Brodie swiveled his head around the shack wondering about his sanity. The voice reminded him of the Christmas when he was six years old. Helping his mother decorate, he'd picked holly, crow's foot, and running cedar from behind their trailer to use for making holiday wreaths. Together they twisted the greenery around clothes hangers, and added the berry-laden holly for color. The holly leaves repeatedly stabbed Brodie's tender young fingers.

"I'll help you, Brodie. Hold the wreaths and I'll insert the holly," Lily said.

Brodie remembered plucking one of the berries and tasting its bitterness before his mother jumped up and pounded him on the back.

"Brodie! Spit it out, they're poison." She made him drink about a gallon of milk to dilute any berry juice he might have swallowed. He was close to his mother then, before so much happened, before the world met him and did its worst. That he shared with her—the taint of being an outsider.

He pulled away from the memory, yanked open the ruined door and stared outside. A conspiracy of ravens gathered while he was inside, and now they sat in the holly trees surrounding the shack—watching him. They were strangely silent, considering their nature, as if waiting for something…but what?

"Go away! Wait all you want but nothing is dying here today." He stepped out, closing the broken door behind him, and stepped lightly around the porch boards.

The rough black birds were unfazed by his presence, and for several minutes he watched the ravens and the ravens watched him. Their countenance appeared wise and full of expectation, and they stared as if peering into his soul. *"I will help you."* Brodie wiped a tear from his eye as he picked holly berries and greenery.

Chapter Twenty

Nathaniel Mountain Hunting Camp. WV
Garren

He paused to catch his breath. The fork horn buck he was dragging was no monster, but it was certainly a trophy to him. The manner he'd taken the buck, and its being his first, made it very special.

He'd given up early in the morning and climbed down from his stand to return to camp. Walking slowly, he savored the smell of the fresh rain-washed air, and the fall woods' beauty. Then he heard it—a clacking noise from the woods below the trail. He dropped to one knee to listen. The sound repeated, followed by the pawing of leaves: a confrontation between two bucks.

He low crawled, as he'd seen soldiers in war movies do, being careful to make no sound. At the edge of the trail, he peered through the underbrush and made out their shapes below. They faced each other, a fork horn and a six point stood with lowered heads, antlers at the ready, sparring like prizefighters. One gingerly approached the other, pawed the ground and their antlers met. They twisted about for advantage and then pulled apart. Neither seemed too serious about the conflict. Rut wasn't in yet, and this was practice for what was to come.

He maneuvered to make the shot, but whenever his scope's crosshairs were on target, the deer drew back or pushed ahead. He tried to crawl closer, but the leaves were riddled with small twigs that might snap and herald his intrusion. Finally, the larger buck tired of playing. When the antlers engaged again, the six-point twisted his head and tossed the fork-horn to its knees. The smaller deer jumped up and backed away, staring. The deer turned and walked towards him, head held low down and tail tucked in defeat. He shifted his weight and waited. At twenty-five yards, the shot picture cleared and he squeezed the trigger. The buck jumped into the air and fell to the ground dead.

The buck weighed about a hundred pounds field dressed, but 15 minutes into the drag, it felt like it gained another hundred. He went over in his mind the words he'd use to tell his story that night, but it would be hard to beat Mika's tale of the night before.

The older man held them spellbound. He doubted the accuracy of the story after so many years, but not Mika's belief in it. He knew Mika recited it just the way it was told to him, and though he doubted the particulars, he had no doubt—something bad transpired in that old shack. The vibes in it were scary enough, even without the weird crosses everywhere, but legends were exaggerated over time. Still, enough people believed to continue putting up the crosses.

He remembered his mother Diana telling a tale about a family with the name of Dyer a long time ago. The kind of tale you tell your kids to get them to go to bed at night, and stay there. When Diana married, she moved from her family's home in Southern Maryland to West Virginia. Her family told a story about a witch their ancestors were related to. If he remembered correctly, the family fable started in the 1700s. In that old, but often repeated story, Diana's family—his family—might have started with the accused witch. He shrugged his shoulders. He'd try to remember to ask Mika if he thought there was any correlation between the two stories.

His mind wandered as he dragged his venison. It was funny how people acted in camp. It seemed to bring out the best in some and the worst in others. Chris was more confident and even seemed bulkier now. He stood straighter and held his head higher. Brodie, on the other hand, was even more short-tempered than usual. He hadn't been himself since Jim's reference to their being more than cousins and the shirttail cutting got blown way out of proportion.

In sight now of the cabin, he smiled seeing Chris outside admiring his deer at the meat pole.

"Hey, brother, lend a hand," he yelled.

"What did you get?"

"A nice fork horn, fat and sassy."

The cabin door opened and Mika limped out.

"Hey Mika." He tried to keep the excitement out of his voice.

Mika joined the boys and pointed to the green leafed twig protruding from the deer's mouth and smiled.

"Did you remember the words, Garren?"

"I'm not sure, Mika, at least not exactly, but I remembered the sentiment. I respected the animal, and thanked the deer's spirit for its sacrifice."

"You did me proud then. Fine crop of hunters we're breaking in this year. I think I should rustle up some grub, but you fellows are early. Chris said he saw the biggest buck ever and couldn't get a shot. That rascal wouldn't stand still for him long enough."

"A nice one, Chris?"

"A real beauty, he must be a ten pointer. Biggest I've ever seen. I saw him twice, once right after I got to my stand, and again about an hour ago. Must be a lot of doe scent around there. I think he wants to make a fawn or two." Chris winked. "I was afraid I spooked him the last time. I was trying to get a shot and he heard me or maybe smelled me. I don't know, maybe he spotted this blaze orange hat, but he tucked his tail and snuck off through the thickets."

"Probably the same deer Brodie saw last night. They don't get that big by being stupid." Mika said.

Chris pointed up the trail. "Speak of the devil, Garren, here *he* comes."

"Brodie won't be happy to hear that his big buck moved on to greener pastures."

Chapter Twenty-One

A meaningless argument with Diana and he stopped to do her *bidding. She had no one else to call. Hugging a tear-soaked pillow— anguish distorted her brow—her new love used her badly. She deserved better. Her luck in love paralleled her choice in men. But his own cousin—a man he thought decent, worthy...she confided the violent nature of the man. Hidden by his charm, his green eyes, and dark wavy hair was a violent nature, a vicious arrogance revealed. The swollen bruises on her face bore witness to the man's shame.*

Hampshire County, WV
Anna

"Are you both sure you want to do this again?" she asked.

"That's why we are here, Anna. I mean, that, *and* we enjoy your company of course." Bridget grinned.

"You know what she means, Brie. To be honest with you, I'm scared. I mean, it was the most awesome thing ever, but yeah—I'm scared. What if something goes wrong?"

"If you want to forget the whole thing, it's no problem. I'll understand. Chalk up our experience as a case of mass hysterics or something. We can cook up some hotdogs, and..."

"No Anna. That wasn't the plan. What about helping us to explore this new part of ourselves? And Lenore, what happened to the guys needing us? Was it all talk?"

"Brie, don't take this the wrong way, but you weren't there. Lenore wasn't kidding about it being frightening. We didn't even find them and still got in trouble."

"Yeah, throw that in my face. You think I didn't want to be there? I was more afraid without you than when we were together," Bridget said.

"No, you're brave, Brie," she said. "But Lenore has her new brother and father up there. I suspect one of my best friends and my grandfather is there—so we feel an obligation to our loved ones, but you? Why do you want to do this so much?"

"For the first time in my life, I'm part of something important. There's evil on the mountain. I felt it when I touched that young deer's fur. I think that's what kept me from going with you. You're my best friends. Your friends and families are there. I don't want to go. I *have* to go. What kind of friend do you think I am anyway?" Bridget's eyes watered.

"Easy, Brie. I'm not questioning your loyalty, and I understand about fitting in and being part of something. I'm just...worried—for all of us," she explained.

"I'm scared too," Lenore said. "Really though, Bridget's right, what other choice is there? I'm still wondering if it even happened, but if my new family is in trouble, I'm there. I *have* to be too."

She smiled at her friends. "I just want to make sure we're all on the same page. Hey, I saw Garren's mother in town this morning. She's a really cool lady. One of the few adults I've met that doesn't make fun of me: my beliefs, my clothing, my heritage, or my youth, you know? I asked her about Garren, and she said she was worried. She'd had a nightmare, and tried to laugh it off, but I could tell it bothered her. I think you guys are right, but I needed to make sure we all felt the same. I don't want to do this without you." She fumbled with the front of her shirt.

"What is it that you are always grabbing at anyway?" Lenore asked.

"It is my great-grandmother's antler necklace. My grandfather passed it on to me because he said I look like her. The carved arrow is an ancient protection symbol. I guess grabbing it is a bad habit I picked up from Garren. When he's nervous, he toys with a crucifix that belonged to his father."

Bridget smiled. "Hmmm, didn't you say your dream lover was always doing something like that, Lenore?"

"Yes, but it's a common enough habit."

"Oh yeah, *another* coincidence. I don't buy it. What I'd give to be a fly on the wall when you meet him and you will. A dream guy you've dreamt about…how many times? I tell ya, it's fate. But hey, maybe you can show me how to do that, Lenore? Be a fly on the wall I mean?" Bridget teased.

Lenore burst out laughing. "Sure, that's gonna happen…not!"

She smiled at their innocent banter. "Flies are nasty enough, but please promise, no rats or mice; they give me the creeps."

"Okay and no more matchmaking with phantoms, Bridget. I told you my dreams weren't that kind. Besides, ever since I was twelve, guys only wanted to get close to me for one reason," Lenore said.

"Well, two really," Bridget giggled.

She laughed, and Lenore pulled down the corners of her lips but couldn't stop herself from laughing with them.

"Your fly on the wall gives me an idea, Brie. Not a fly, but what about trying it with birds?" she suggested.

"Well, they're certainly faster than deer and we'd cover more ground looking for the guys," Lenore said.

Bridget gave her the thumbs up.

"Or maybe we'll run into the evil that lives there." she reminded them. She noticed Lenore biting her lip, and saw Bridget's unseeing stare. Was it bravery or foolishness that drove their determination despite their fear? Not something to dwell on, only time would tell.

Her smile concealed her dread. "Sooo…what kind of birds should we be?"

"With your attire, you'd have to be a crow or raven, I'll be a fly catcher, and Lenore a booby bird," Bridget joked.

"Ha ha, enough boob jokes. I get it enough from the guys. Crows maybe, Anna? They're fast and common enough that we'd not stand out," Lenore said.

"Birds of a feather, we'll flock together. But a flock of crows is a murder, right? Anyway, I'll defer to your intuition, Lenore. Crows—plenty of those around."

She added herbs to the hot stones in the sweat lodge. The girls sat together and held hands. They relaxed to explore the place in their minds discovered the night before. *The sound of feathers filled their ears as the wind raced through their hair.*

Chapter Twenty-Two

Nathaniel Mountain Hunting Camp, WV
Brodie

The entire day's hunt was a bust for him. The evening didn't produce so much as a deer sighting, much less a shot. If he was a bird watcher though, it would've been a field day. Ravens filled the sky and the trees for most of the afternoon. Not a flock but a 'conspiracy of ravens,' he recalled from some inane but mandatory class. That and a 'murder of crows,' which were also well represented on the mountain. Cousins of the bird world, he could scarcely tell them apart unless they spoke. The raven's croak sounded murderous, the voice of death—assuming death had a voice.

Shadows flitted across the ground and drew his attention to the crows—again attempting to land among the larger ravens. For the third time, the ravens rejected their company, raising the alarm and initiating aerial dogfights— although the crows fared better in the air. "Yeah, they're cousins all right," he grunted to himself. "Guess that's why they can't stand each other."

He knew the birds' reputation for discovering easy prey and carrion. He heard they led packs of wolves to their prey, hoping to steal some choice morsels of fresh flesh. *That's why they're gathered. They know that before I come off this mountain, I'm going to kill something.*

At lunch, Garren had told him how his buck had visited Chris' stand. He seemed pleased in the telling too. That limp-wristed Chris wouldn't have a chance at the big deer, he thought. He'd probably mess his drawers, and the deer deserved better. Garren and Chris took deer, even if they were small. He was determined to make the big buck his, no matter the cost.

Before full dark, he returned to camp to help with the evening meal. Mika was in a lot of pain with his ankle, and now his knee appeared to be affected also. He tried to persuade Mika to sit this meal out, but Mika insisted on cutting up the home fries while he fried up the boneless chicken and onions. Slowly the other hunters trickled in and went to change out of their hunting clothes. Jim threw a few chunks of wood in the fire.

"How long until chow's ready, Mika?" Jim asked.

"Not long now. Get yourself an apple. You'll live."

He looked out as the last two hunters, Bertram and Frank, entered the cabin—just as dinner hit the table.

"Two more deer for the pole," he heard Bertram announce.

He and Mika were closest to the back door and first to reach the game pole. A matched set of spike bucks were in a pile beneath it. They might have been brothers. The men hoisted the deer and tied them up to bleed out. Congratulations were offered all around. He felt the ache of his swollen wrist when shaking hands. *Clumsy, falling on Zachary's rock.*

"Way to go Bertram, Frank. Me, I didn't see the first deer all day," Jim confessed. "Had a couple of hen turkeys work their way through. Might be a sign of a good spring gobbler season."

"I didn't get a shot tonight either, but I saw that big bruiser again. Now that I know where he's coming from, I'm going to be ready for him tomorrow," Chris said.

"Well fellows, that makes six on the pole, great week so far," Mika said. "What say we have supper and celebrate?"

He nodded at Mika, but was the last one to go back in. He felt their eyes on him. Their heads dropped, most with smirks smeared across their faces. He glanced at the table, at his usual seat. Placed on top of his plate were his empty rifle cartridges from the night before. They were stacked in a neat pyramid with a cut off deer tail beside the plate. Across the back of his chair, someone had draped his mutilated shirt.

"The knights of the camp table reserved a place of honor for you, Sir Brodie Caine." Bertram bowed toward the chair.

Mika looked at him with a warning in his eyes. He felt the heat flash on his face, and gulped in a sharp breath of air. He realized he'd bitten his lip when he tasted the blood. But his lips twisted into a smile. He could sense the tension mounting around the table. He winked at Bertram, and slid into his chair.

"That's decent of you guys. I must really rate around here."

The room seemed to refill with air and there was laughter all around. When Bertram returned to his seat, he winked at him again and spoke, softly as if unaware his words were said aloud, "Just remember, old man, paybacks are hell."

He saw the men exchange furtive glances and supper was eaten with no further incident.

After dinner, Garren and Chris both offered to relieve Mika of his duty, but he wouldn't have it.

"That's what I came to do, and when I can't, I might as well go home. Appreciate the offer though, boys."

He and Mika made quick work of the clean up as the others gathered around the woodstove for another night of deer stories and blatant lies. When done, he and Mika joined them, Mika propping his foot on the coffee table.

"Mika says he doesn't do late night coffee, but before you fellows get all wound up lying, can I fix anyone some? Hate to make a pot just for myself," he offered.

"Thanks Brodie, but I can't stand the taste of the stuff," Garren said.

Chris, Henry, and Jim, however, all opted for the late night caffeine fix.

As he turned away, Chris asked, "What's all over your pants, Brodie? Sawdust?"

"Must be from the rotten log I sat on in the woods, but why are you staring at my butt anyway?" He shrugged his shoulders and brushed off his pants.

He continued to the kitchen, returning as Garren finished the story of his exploits with the battling bucks.

"That was a good story, Garren. Seemed to be the truth. And not one of those yarns like your father used to tell. That man could spin a tale and swear to heaven it was the gospel truth."

"I'd love to hear one of them, Mika."

"Well, there was one in particular that I enjoyed. Adam used to shoot an antique .79 caliber smoothbore muzzleloader during black powder season. One day he was in the woods and realized he was out of round balls to shoot. He was hunting an old peach orchard by an abandoned homestead and he spotted a big buck at the far end of the orchard. Not having any ammo, he spied a peach stone on the ground. Now, a white peach pit is about the size of a .79 caliber ball, but he knew how much lighter it was than lead, so he cut back on the powder charge and rammed her home."

"A peach pit, Mika?" He laughed.

"Remember, this is your Uncle Adam's story, Brodie. Anyway, he snuck up within 25 yards of that buck, took aim and squeezed the trigger. He figured he didn't cut back the powder enough because the shot went high and that deer ran like a scalded cat. He saw a couple of drops of blood, but nothing else. And never found any sign of the deer.

"The next spring, he was up on the ridge overlooking a pine knoll and looked down in the hollow. He saw a beautiful tree with peach blossoms all over it.

Now he knew that woods well, and there was never a peach tree on that stretch of the mountain. He decided to check it out—figuring some hunter had a peach for lunch and tossed the stone away.

"He climbed down the hill but when he got over to where he'd seen the tree, it had disappeared! He looked all over creation, or at least most of that bottom land, until a movement caught his eye further down the hollow. He saw that bouquet of pretty pink blossoms moving through the trees; and he was pretty sure no florists set up shop in the middle of Short Mountain. He grabbed his binoculars to have a look and there was the biggest buck he'd ever seen with a peach sapling growing out its back! Adam said he killed the buck that fall, a fat nine point and his biggest buck ever. Shot it with a .303 British rifle at 110 yards, *and* got a bushel of peaches off the tree! Diana made him a couple pies too—peach was his favorite."

The men laughed, even though Brodie knew most heard the story before. He never knew Garren's father, but figured the story brought back warm memories of their friend.

"I'm your friend…your only friend."

"Get out of my head," he said.

"What was that, Brodie?" Jim asked.

"Nothing, Jim. Just thinking about that crazy story." He laughed.

"Well, just like we did the first time I heard that story—from Adam, I think that calls for a drink," Jim said.

Bertram and Frank followed suit with their tales of success. Bertram said he'd left his stand early. He'd come down the trail past Frank's stand when he heard a shot from his friend's direction. The spike buck ran onto the trail and froze in front of him. The shot was a gimme. For Frank's part, he said both deer were together passing his stand and he only got a shot on one.

"We haven't decided for sure," Bertram added, "but we may be leaving after tomorrow morning's hunt. The weather is supposed to turn bad tomorrow night. Unless that big buck of Brodie's comes along, one deer is about all my family will eat anyway."

Mika admitted that unless his ankle and knee were miraculously healed, he'd be staying in camp the following day.

"Looks like a few of us will have the whole mountain to ourselves. I may even be able to fill my tag," he said.

Chapter Twenty-Three

Nathaniel Mountain Hunting Camp, WV
Garren

H e rolled over in bed, immersed in a deep but troubled sleep. Some small sentient corner of his mind registered the scratching, clawing sound at the window. Caught in the grasp of a grim specter, he didn't immediately recognize the sound and it fueled the fire of his dream. The sharp nailed fingers of the Dyer witch worked feverishly at the window, tapping, pawing, the glass smeared with blood wherever they touched.

"Your mother got away, Garren, but not you...oh no, my pretty...not you!" The so-called winter witch gave him one final glare and tossed herself into the darkness of the night.

He bolted upright—snapping the nightmare's tendrils from his mind. The aftermath left him shaken, his spine shivering and his senses alert. At first, he had difficulty remembering where he was and why he was here. He listened attentively, and waited for some visual clue. Awareness slowly seeped into his anxious mind.

The wind whistling through the myriad of cracks around the cabin windows brought him back to the present. Branches from the willow tree whipped at the window panes.

"So much for my witch," he said to the room. He remembered Mika's story from two nights before. He wouldn't admit to him what a lasting impression it left, but that was one campfire story Mika should be proud of.

Rain washed against the windows and fell in sheets on the metal roof. He rolled over to find the source of a repetitive plopping sound, and saw a bucket strategically placed to catch the leak from the ceiling.

The mattress nearest him was empty. *Odd for Chris to be wandering around in the middle of the night.* He listened for any sounds of movement in the cabin. There was a faint rumble coming from the restroom. Probably plumbing problems, he thought, just water in the pipes. He dropped his head back to the pillow to salvage what sleep he could. As he closed his eyes, the rumbling in the other room escalated into a low growl.

"What the hell is that?" he asked the room.

Brodie's head popped up from his bed. "What?"

He walked to the bathroom door and identified the sound. Another growl followed a splash of liquids hitting the small ceramic pool—like schools of fish surfacing.

"Chris, are you all right in there?" he asked.

"No, I'm puking my..." Another growl and more splashes hit the bowl with force.

"Ahh...my guts out," he finished.

Garren felt his own stomach heave and astringent tasting saliva burned the back of his throat. He spat in the trashcan hoping it would be all he evacuated.

"Hey man, can I get you something, a glass of water maybe...?"

"Would...just...throw it...up." Chris punctuated by hitting the commode again.

He climbed back in his bunk and pulled his blanket up to his chin. The sickening sounds upstairs began to repeat themselves in the bathroom below.

"Is that you Henry?" he heard Jim ask.

"Umm-hmm," Henry said.

"Are you all right?"

He heard the toilet flush in answer.

Upstairs, he heard the bathroom door creak open.

Hunched over, Chris walked to his bed—his face pale as a wraith.

"Damn, are you going to make it, Chris?" he asked.

Chris nodded in answer, and crawled into bed.

"Oh man, I think the chicken was bad," said Jim from the first floor. From the explosive sounds being generated, he knew Jim's symptoms manifested in a different way.

"Phew! Good God Jim, we're going to have to fumigate the place!" Bertram yelled.

"I can see there won't be any more sleeping tonight," Brodie said.

"Get what sleep you can, Brodie. It's gonna be a long night I think." As he felt the first haziness of sleep, he heard Mika's wake up call to Brodie to start breakfast. He sat up in bed, and rubbed the sleep from his eyes. He heard Brodie fumbling with his clothes.

Chris moaned beside him. "Sorry, Garren, but I don't think I'm going anywhere anytime soon."

He looked over at his friend. Chris's features stood out garishly, clown like, against the white pallor of his face.

"You look like death warmed over, my man," he said.

"That's me. Go shoot one for me, bro."

The breakfast remained largely uneaten and attended by few. Henry, Jim, and Chris remained in bed trying to sleep off the horror invading their bowels. Mika hobbled around the kitchen despite the heavy bandage support wrapped around his ankle. The hunters would be few this day.

Bertram and Frank left the cabin shortly before dawn. The slight northerly breeze promised better hunting, but both men said they doubted they'd stay for the afternoon hunt. The wind blew in a cold front predicted to hang around for the remainder of the week.

"Do you think there's anything we can do for the sick and wounded, Mika?" he asked.

"I think we're good. I reckon it will just be a sleep-in day for all of them. I'll use the time to catch up on some reading and rest my ankle. Good luck to you both."

Brodie shook Mika's hand. "The stands on our side are going to be empty. I think I'll go up a little further and hunt Henry's or Chris' stand this morning. I can use a change of scenery."

"I don't suppose they'd mind, Brodie. What do you think, Garren?" Mika asked.

He felt his face flush at the suggestion, remembering how excited Chris was over the buck he'd seen.

"I really don't think Chris would appreciate that, but it might be okay, as long as you don't shoot his buck." He stared at his cousin.

"His buck, hell! That deer practically has 'Brodie' tattooed on his side. He's mine," his cousin answered.

The two hunters left the cabin, and as they had for all of their lives, turned in opposite directions towards their stands.

Chapter Twenty-Four

Nathaniel Mountain Hunting Camp, WV
Brodie

He found Chris' stand in short order, as it was located only a few hundred yards past his own. It seemed to him that the very air smelled of deer. He knew it was only a matter of time now. It was an amazing stroke of good fortune, having everyone from his side of the hunting area laid up in bed. But it was a shame about Mika. *Their loss is my gain.*

Most of the tree leaves fell victim to the strong winds, leaving skeletal branches reaching for the sky. He could see for a country mile now. The deer's approach would stand out in the new landscape. They had no chance of slipping by him now.

He watched eagerly as the sun crept over the nearby peaks, and as the first warming rays reached him, a shot echoed across the valley. *Could it be someone from our group?*

He heard no follow up shots, a good sign for the shooter. He hoped Lady Luck smiled on Frank, and not the other two. He didn't hold anything against Frank. He couldn't help being what he was. Frank's lot in life was to be a sheep and it always would be. Frank went wherever Bertram pointed him.

"The world has no shortage of human sheep, Brodie."

They certainly weren't an endangered species. But they were born that way, they didn't ask for it. He knew how hard it was for a person to go against their nature.

It was the jackals of the world that made life difficult. The men born with silver spoons in their backsides, along with the brown-nosing yes-men. Both ascended the ranks of society through no merit of their own.

"Garren and Chris are jackals. The jury's out on Jim. You can see it, can't you, Brodie?"

Jackals line their pockets from the sweat off other men's brows because of what God gave them for free. Leeches audacious enough to look down their noses at the men enabling their parasitic lifestyle. They'd nip at the heels of people like him for personal validation.

"They'd deny a man his true love, Brodie...if it served their purposes."

He heard the rustling of leaves behind him, and turned to determine its source. Something small and white moved in the brush, a deer's throat patch. Long tines from the buck's antlers materialized from the midst of the mountain laurel thicket. The deer stepped into the open, dragging one front leg. He aimed his sights and waited for the deer's shoulder to appear, then pulled back the hammer, watching, and waiting. The buck stopped and tested the air, then turned and bedded down facing its back trail. *It's now or never.* The boom from the rifle reverberated through the hills and he recognized it as the sound of redemption. The buck did not get up, but rolled over where he sat, trembled and lay still.

He flew down from the tree stand, not even feeling the ladder rungs under his feet. He ran to the buck, grasping its massive antlers. He touched each antler tine in turn, counting eight, nine, ten points. *That will show them.*

He rubbed the fur at the base of the neck where his bullet entered. He congratulated himself on the shot, actually patting himself on the back…then he saw the other wound—the cause of the buck's limp. The other bullet was placed too far back for a quick killing shot, but would have eventually killed the majestic animal, given enough time. The buck likely bedded down to die. He pointed the rifle in the air and fired off another shot. *Insurance.*

He field dressed the deer, tied his drag rope to the antlers and started pulling him down the hill toward the trail. The deer was heavy and he considered going back to the cabin for Jim's truck.

"Hey Brodie, is that you?"

Brodie turned to see Bertram walking quickly towards him. The obese man's hurried, twisted gait reminded him of Olympic speed walkers.

"I see you finished off my buck for me, and dressed him out too. I appreciate that, young man. We make a good team you and I, the old one two punch."

"Did you shoot a deer too?" he asked.

"Yeah, and I followed the blood trail right up to the pile of guts up on the hill there and drag marks to here."

"Oh, that explains the other buck I saw with this one. He worked his way on down the other side of the hill. He didn't look hurt though. Sure you hit him?"

"Yeah, I got him all right. I thought the shot hit a bit far back, right about there, actually." Bertram pointed his gun barrel at the deer's gut shot wound.

"That's a shame. I had to shoot this one twice to bring him down," Brodie explained. "Don't give up though. When I get this one back to camp, I'll come back and help you look for your deer."

Bertram's face darkened. He opened his mouth to speak, but seemed to think better of it. Then he looked down at the ground and kicked up some leaves.

"Tell you what," Bertram said, "I'll give you a hand with *your* deer. Then we will come back together and see what we can find. Maybe have the other men follow the blood trail with us and decide. That sound fair to you?"

He shrugged his agreement. Bertram found a stout stick to weave through the drag rope so both men could pull the deer. They progressed with difficulty, the deer's antlers catching every tree and root along their route. Bertram labored for breath and sucked at the air, then stumbled on a rock and dropped the drag stick.

"Let's take a break. This deer's a monster." He gasped for air, creating a fog with every exhaled breath.

"Okay, but the main trail's just over there." He pointed. "If we can get this big boy over there, we'll be home free. I'll scoot down to camp and bring Jim's truck up here to haul him out."

Between his gasps for air, Bertram asked, "So I've been wondering, what is Jim Doyle to you anyway? Is he your real uncle, Brodie?"

His brow knitted together and his face flushed in reply. "I suppose I have uncles, cousins, and even brothers that I know nothing about. Maybe that's best, they probably wouldn't claim me anyway."

As Bertram sat resting, his eyes wandered across the trail and beyond. He knew they were close to the stand he'd hunted originally and hoped to get his bearings. *"You know what you have to do, Brodie. Listen."*

"Hey Bertram, check this out," he yelled.

Bertram stood and stretched his muscles, then walked down to where he'd entered the woods on the opposite side of the trail.

"Where are you?"

"Over here." He waved his arms. "This is pretty cool."

Bertram weaved his way through the briars and brambles to where he stood at the edge of a steep cliff.

"What do you think of this?" He threw a rock into the ravine.

Bertram turned an ear toward the cliff. "Damn, it must be deep. Took a long time for that rock to hit bottom. I don't need to get any closer to see it."

"I'll bet this is the same cliff Mika told us about in his story. I believe you slept through the whole thing though."

Bertram shrugged. "There isn't much sleeping with the chatty crew in this camp. Did I miss anything important?"

"No." He swung the rifle, butt stock first, and heard a satisfying hollow thump at impact. "Nope, didn't miss a thing."

Chapter Twenty-Five

Hampshire County, WV
Anna

She woke with the hawk's scream in her ears, and the soft whistling of air through its feathers. Lenore was beside her, shaking her head. Her fingers were extended, opening and closing, her mouth already forming the question.

"Anna? What the hell? Were those ravens protecting Brodie Caine?"

"Damn right they were," Bridget said. "I didn't spy any dead meat anywhere. Nothing anywhere in sight except Brodie."

"So I've finally met the infamous Brodie Caine. Can't say my first impressions were warm and fuzzy, nor especially generous."

"Yes, but a long-distance introduction. Just wait until you get to meet him up close and personal," Bridget said.

"What do you make of it, Anna?"

"I'm not sure, Lenore. Every time I got close to them, I felt vulnerable. Like Bridget said, I looked around for carrion or any food source and found nothing. I never saw birds act like that before. I think they were protecting him too."

"What could do something like that, harness power to control the birds?" Bridget whispered.

"Love, it's the strongest emotion, right Anna?" Lenore asked.

"Yes, but nearly as strong is revenge," she said. "All the blackness on the mountain is centered on Brodie

Caine. Why? What does it want from him? What does he want from it?"

"If you don't know, we sure don't. I'm even more worried about the men now though, if that's possible," Bridget said.

"I think we should assume revenge. It's more likely considering who it's concentrated on—Brodie Caine," Lenore said. "So that means what? Some sort of vendetta, and if so, against whom?"

"There's a place near the camp that my grandfather avoids. He's spoken of other places in the mountains that made him anxious, places where he knew terrible things happened in the past. The old shack near camp is the worst of them all. The rocks and trees around the place are saturated with this evil, and emanate a soulless stench. He thinks the darkness is waiting for something or someone. Maybe it's found what it was waiting for? Maybe something in that shack is being...I don't know—reborn?"

Lenore placed a hand on her shoulder. "I don't know, Anna. Now we're back to your area of expertise."

"Okay, enough about ancient evil and haunted woods. Let's not forget the real flesh and blood Brodie Caine is there, and he hates everyone. Well, everyone but you, Lenore," Bridget added.

"Yeah, let's not forget about him. But why would he or some...thing be after Chris or Garren? I don't know anything about my new family's past, or of any past feuds, so I can't help much with Chris or Henry. What do you know about Garren's family, Anna?"

"Garren's dad died before he was born, and I know his mom some from hanging out with him, but nothing about the extended family that would help."

"The other place we went, the other hunter? Was that Garren?" Bridget asked.

She noticed a sparkle in Bridget's eye. "Oh, yeah, sorry I didn't introduce you, Brie, but I was at a loss for words you might say."

"So Lenore...*is* he the guy?" Bridget asked.

Lenore paused. "I can't say for sure, I've never seen his face, but I'll admit he looked...familiar."

"I just bet he did. So does the real guy live up to the dream guy's billing?" Bridget pointed at Lenore. "Oh my God, you're blushing."

Lenore punched Bridget's arm. "Do something with her, will you, Anna?"

"Be nice, Brie. It must be pretty weird for Lenore. Seeing a guy that can't see you, but you've seen, but only in a dream?"

"I don't know. My mom says the best way to enjoy a man is vicariously." Bridget giggled.

"It's all weird. Anna. What did you call it, thought transference? Here we all sit, giggling and laughing about events and people we've seen through the eyes of crows, while being attacked by ravens on a mountain that's a two-hour drive from here. I'm not really sure whether the guys are in more trouble or if we are. Maybe we're mental cases. The men are probably up there having the time of their lives, and when and if I ever meet this Garren, I bet he looks totally different than any image my mind's conjured up. We don't know if any of it is real. How could it be, Anna? What do you really think? Are we wacko? You're supposed to be the expert on this...crap?" Lenore caught her breath and tossed a pinecone into the dying fire.

She felt her friend's hot stare bore into her, pleading for a reply.

"This isn't a Sunday walk in the park for me either, Lenore. It's more than I'm prepared for. You ask if it's real, and I can't answer you, but if it didn't feel real to you, you wouldn't be here. You'd be a fancy girl on the sidelines making fun of the wacky witches, yet here you are. I can't, no I *won't*, stop. My grandfather and my best friend are up there, with a guy you tell me is a scary bastard on his best day. Maybe nothing is going on, *probably* nothing is going on, and we just have overactive imaginations. *But maybe*, two people I love are in trouble and they don't know it yet. I don't see a choice, and I don't even see what difference it makes. If I'm crazy, big shit, nobody gets hurt, and everybody already thinks I am anyway. If anything happens to them because I ignore my instincts, though, I couldn't live with myself. For me it's a no-brainer, I'll do whatever I can. By the way, I never said I was an expert on any of this!"

She folded her arms across her chest and stared off toward the horizon.

Bridget glanced at her friends, then stood and found another seat, wedging herself between them.

"I'm in. I've been called worse than crazy. Maybe it's the element of danger, real or imagined, but I'm having fun. The perception is all that matters I guess." Bridget put her arms over her friends' shoulders. "What could be better than hanging out with my best buds, the White Witch Lenore, and Anna the Enchantress, as we hunt down evil-doers in our unending quest for truth, justice, and the American way?"

"Don't forget Brie the Brave. Never forget her." The corners of Lenore's lips edged upwards into the beginnings of a smile.

"I guess you guys are right. After all, what do we have to lose? That is, besides our sanity and that's overrated. So what's the plan, Anna?"

"I want to pay a visit to Mrs. Doyle to see if she knows anything about their family that might help. I think you guys should go home and get some rest. After that," she shrugged her shoulders, "who the hell knows?"

Chapter Twenty-Six

Nathaniel Mountain Hunting Camp
Garren

As the cabin came into view, Uncle Jim's truck pulled out into the dirt lane and drove away. He figured Jim must be feeling better and might be up to hunting this afternoon. There were no new additions to the meat pole, although the deer had moved well that morning. He'd spotted eight deer that morning. The abrupt drop in temperature brought with it an increased need for calories and a jolt to the breeding cycle. Despite the quantity of sightings though, the biggest deer he'd seen was a yearling spike buck. He considered taking him, but with a couple of hunting days left, he decided to let him walk...maybe another day, another hunt. He was hunting for the meat not a trophy, but with the bag limit set at two, he didn't want to end his hunt early either. Hopefully he didn't offend the gods of the hunt by passing up what they offered.

He'd stayed in the stand as long as he could, but the cold settled into his bones, and hunger began to gnaw at his guts. He couldn't keep his mind on the hunt anyway for worrying about the others back at camp. Chris looked the worst of all of the lot. So bad, he was surprised to see Henry's truck still parked in the front of camp. Maybe, like Jim, they felt a little more energetic also.

Frank Harvey came out of the front of the cabin, and waved.

"Hey Garren. Any chance you've run into Bertram this morning?"

"No sir. Didn't you go out together this morning?"

"Yes, I thought I heard him shoot earlier, but sound bounces off these hills and sometimes it's hard to tell where a shot came from. He wasn't at his stand, and Mika said he hasn't been back to camp yet. He didn't plan to stay after this morning's hunt, so I'm wondering what he got into."

Frank turned and headed away from camp.

"Where are you headed?"

"Just to the end of the drive. I want to see if his truck is still out there. Can't tell through all the honeysuckle and wild rose. Bertram wants to get some young fellows to come up and cut that mess down."

He gave Frank the thumbs up sign and went inside. Jim and Mika were on the sofa rubbing their hands together in front of the old cast iron wood stove. Jim looked up as he closed the door.

"Have you seen Bertram?" Jim asked.

"No, Frank just asked me the same thing. Why all the worry? He probably got a shot and he's tracking his deer. It isn't very late yet."

"I guess because Bertram is most always the first hunter to come back to camp in the mornings. He says the cold gets to him faster these days but I think he just can't wait to sample some more of my cooking." Mika grinned.

"Plus his dead deer's done took off. Just a chunk of rope hanging off the meat pole where it was last night. Bertram's stuff is all here, but he does that sometimes when he's coming back in a few days. You'd think he'd take his sack of dirty clothes though," Jim said.

"How's Chris and Henry? Are they recovering any yet?"

Chris stepped out from the bathroom at the mention of his name. "I don't know if I'd go quite that far, Garren, but it's getting better anyway."

He gave his friend the once-over. "You look like crap, Chris."

"Well, I'm glad to hear you say that, Garren. If you thought I looked hot, I'd be worried." Chris smiled.

Henry stepped in from the bunkroom. "Hey fellows." He held his son at arms' length, then slapped him on the shoulder. "Good to hear that Killer has his sense of humor back. What do you think, Garren?"

"Yes sir, Mr. Gale. I'm not sure he ever lost that, but it sure wasn't firing on all cylinders last night with the commode as his audience. He still looks as weak as a kitten. I'd bet his new sister could kick his butt."

"You're only saying that because you've never met Lenore. I'll bet she'd do that on my best day."

A burst of cold air washed over them as the cabin door opened. Frank walked in shaking his head.

"That ornery old you-know-what has up and left without saying a word. His truck is gone. I can't believe he'd do that. He could be laid up hurt and nobody'd even know."

"Bertram isn't known for piddling around when he's made his mind up about something," Jim said. "So what are you wanting to do, Frank? No reason you can't stay just because Bertram skipped out."

"I appreciate that, Jim, and I think I'll take you up on it. It would be nice to get in another hunt in the morning."

"Hey Uncle Jim, speaking of wayward trucks and disappearing bucks, I saw your truck pulling away when I walked up. Did Brodie get a deer, or did somebody steal your truck?"

"That'd be Brodie. He shot a nice one up at Chris' stand."

He looked at Chris to gauge his reaction, but his eyes were dark and puffy, and hard to read.

"Now Garren, you know it had to be Brodie in that truck. Who'd steal that old war wagon? Of course, the tires are good, so I guess a man could use it for emergency transportation—as long as they didn't have to be seen in it!" Henry laughed.

"Now aren't you just too damn funny, Henry. Somebody forgot to tell me to laugh." Jim smiled.

"What did Brodie shoot, Uncle Jim?"

"He wouldn't say except it was a monster and we'd just have to wait and see when he gets it here."

"He should've waited. I'd have given him a hand. My fork-horn was bad enough for one man to try and drag all the way down here."

"Brodie said he didn't want any help, not that any of us would be much good to him, but Frank at least offered to," Mika said.

"*My deer* was a ten pointer…I bet he shot him," Chris said. He rubbed the fine sparse stubble on his chin and gazed out the cabin window.

"We've done alright," he told his friend. "It's been a great week so far, and it's not over yet. The deer were really moving this morning."

"Oh, man…" Chris rushed toward the bathroom. "Here I go again."

Chapter Twenty-Seven

Nathaniel Mountain Hunting Camp, WV
Brodie

He stood at the door of the old shack. The buck had been difficult to load alone, but better that than stooping to ask for help from the bunch in camp. They'd be impressed when they saw his monster. They'd see he was a better hunter than any of them. After maneuvering the buck onto the truck, he'd decided to pay a visit to the old abandoned shack. He knew he'd forgotten something there, but couldn't quite put his finger on what that something might be. There was a sense of urgency about this perceived loss. He knew that if he didn't find it soon, it would be lost forever. His curiosity won the battle with common sense.

There was a different feeling about the old place. It didn't feel deserted, not any more. He felt as if hidden eyes observed his every move. He glanced around in an attempt to pinpoint the origin of this stealthy spying presence.

"Garren? Did you follow me?"

There was no answer and seeing no one, he decided to check out the shed in the back. The door he thought missing, was propped open from the inside. He brushed away the spider webs that clung to his face as he entered. Despite the dim light inside, he could see the back wall was covered with carpenter's tools. Saws, hammers, and two boxes full of hand tools gave the place the impression of life, or at least the memory of lives past. A five-gallon bucket filled with oily nails sat on the floor, waiting to be put into service.

The wall to his left also held tools—mostly gardening implements. A hoe, a garden rake, a scythe, two rusted axes, and a shovel hung there. He thought it amazing these tools weren't stolen long ago.

"Find Leigh."

"Man, get out of my head," he said to the walls. His series of nightmares and nightmarish daydreams…what were nightmares dreamt during the day? Whatever they were, they'd affected him more than he'd realized. He'd had enough of the shed anyway. Time to have another go at the shack. Maybe whatever he'd lost was there.

He stepped out, and glanced up at the trees. Good. No caterwauling ravens were here now. Luckily, they didn't ruin his hunt with their racket. They became eerily silent when the buck appeared, anticipating the fresh gut pile. Walking toward the shack, nothing—human, animal or otherwise—was to be seen. Satisfied he was alone, he pushed on the door. It opened smoothly. Wasn't one of the hinges broken before? But maybe the swollen wooden door gave him that impression?

He stepped in and his jaw dropped. The crosses were gone. Disappeared! Only light-colored spots on the walls indicated they'd ever existed. Why would anyone take the rustic and punky old wood? He knew people stole boards from old barns to decorate their high dollar homes. Could that be it? Rich city folks trying to create their fashionable country décor?

Was that corner cupboard there before? Was someone really intending to renovate the old dump? The thought renewed the feeling of being watched. Probably kids wanting a hang out. He walked over and opened the door to the cupboard.

"Brothers share." The odd thought popped in his head as he looked in. He doubted he'd find anything worth sharing, even if he had a brother. He hoped he hadn't stumbled into someone's dope den. The cabinet was filled with odds and ends, but mostly camping related equipment, pots, pans, and metal cups. The bottom shelf held three old-

fashioned canning jars, labeled and written on in fine script. He pulled one off the shelf. It read 'Tea Mushrooms.' The jar was filled to the top with dried mushrooms and sealed. Brodie replaced the jar and reached for the next one to see what secrets it held.

"What the hell is this?" He asked aloud. He turned the jar, and a four-inch-long stick moved inside. He thought he recognized the bark, from a cherry tree maybe? The end of the stick was scraped clean to the wood. The jar's label didn't help. Time eroded most of the writing, but a few letters remained legible. He read the partial word 'digit.' Digitalis perhaps? Brodie couldn't remember if that drug was derived from a tree. Brodie gave the jar a shake, but the wood was so soaked and swollen it made no sound against the sides of the jar.

He put his eye close to the glass to get a better view. The portion of wood with the bark removed was very smooth, as if sanded. Brodie studied it, thinking it looked familiar. He noticed the knot at the center of the stick... and then he knew.

The jar slipped from his hands and the glass shattered on impact. "Oh shit, a finger! Holy mother of God, it's a fucking finger!"

Something metallic rolled across the floor in a circle, stopping when it hit his foot. He jumped backwards away from its touch, but it was the 'stick' that kept his attention. Surely he was mistaken. He knelt and grabbed his hunting knife from its sheath. Gently, he used the blade to flip the offending object over. Most of it did look like bark: hard, dark, and wrinkled. He examined the tip, and his stomach lurched. Hot and acidic vomit caught in the back of his throat and burned with an unholy fire.

The smooth section wasn't sanded wood at all, but rather a fingernail. It stood out from the 'stick' with its dried hangnail still visible at the base. He examined the other end. The 'meat' of the finger had pulled away from the bone as it dried. One small section of bone splintered, but stayed adhered by a tiny piece of gristle.

His watering eyes wet his cheek and he rubbed a hand over his face to erase the image from his mind. He squeezed his eyes shut, but open or shut—the image remained. He'd had enough, and didn't want to be there when the people repairing the place returned.

Turning toward the door, his boot kicked the piece of metal and sent it flying. His eyes followed it across the floor until it came to rest leaning upright against the door…a ring. He pulled a splinter of wood from the floorboard and hooked it through the ring, having no desire to touch the thing. It was a flat piece of brass hammered into shape, the hammer marks were still visible. A coarsely filed cross etching was its only decoration.

He held the ring at arm's length and deposited it back into the cabinet. Using the wood splinter and his knife as tongs, he placed the severed finger beside the ring, and slammed the cabinet door.

Fear and revulsion shivered its way down his spine, and settled in his groin. Another heave and vomit shot from his mouth unhindered. He turned and ran out the door toward the truck. The weight of his slung rifle on his shoulder was a welcome comfort. Repeatedly, he swiveled his head to watch the trail behind him. As soon as he reached Jim's truck, he shoved the key in the ignition, and yanked the gearshift into drive. A trail of dust and the reflection of the moon, a sliver shy of full, followed him down the mountain.

Chapter Twenty-Eight

Out of concern, Adam hugged her close, providing a comforting shoulder while she wept. Another stiff drink to ease the pain? Together they washed away the tears and the sting born of violence and rejection. Through the fuzzy hours of the night and early morning, Lily confided her desire for a love as true as he shared with her sister. The look of pain and longing filled his heart with empathy. The night became a fog of anguish fueled by alcohol.

Diana Doyle's home, Hampshire County
Anna

She paused at the door of the Doyles' cabin, hesitating to knock. She didn't have a clue how to begin the conversation with Diana, and decided to just grab the bull by the horns. Get it over with—making it up as she went. She rapped her knuckles on the door, and waited.

"Hello, who's there?"

"Mrs. Doyle, oh sorry, I mean Diana. It's me, Anna."

The door opened a slit as Diana peeked out. She heard the chain slide off and the door flew open. Diana stood before her beaming.

"The Lady Anna, what a welcome surprise…wait, are you okay? Is Mika…?"

"No, no. We're both fine, thanks." She dropped her eyes to the ground. "No, it's just…"

"Where are my manners? Come in, Anna, please." She did a mock bow and swung her arm around in a welcoming gesture.

"Thanks, Diana.…"

"Can I get you something, sweetie? Some tea? Oh, and I made cookies…chocolate chip."

"I'm good, but thank you. They're Garren's favorite, right?"

"You've got it, Anna. I didn't think I'd see you this evening. Didn't you say you were getting together with some friends tonight?"

"Yes ma'am, and I did but we broke up early. Tomorrow's a school day and I didn't want to keep them out too late. I'm sure their parents already think I'm a bad influence."

"Oh, now I doubt that, Anna. I know some people are determined to nurture their xenophobia, but then again, I know there are some young ladies who go out of their way to shock them. Wouldn't you say, Anna?" Diana pulled her into a hug.

"I know, Mrs. Doyle. I just don't get into playing dress up any more. Guess I outgrew it. I really don't care to impress those kinds of people. You know?"

"My name's Diana, remember? And I know it's hard to be different. I imagine it's especially so when that difference is the first thing anyone sees. I don't know your mother, but I know your family must be proud of you. My Garren would walk over hot coals for you, and he's a pretty good judge of character."

"I would for him also. He's the only one I miss from that school. He's one of the few real people I know, and well…that's kind of why I came here tonight."

"What? You mean you didn't stop by to hang out with this old lady? I did mention Garren was on the mountain, didn't I?"

"I don't think the years will ever tell on you, Diana. You'll never seem old, but I did want to check on you. I don't mean any disrespect, but I thought you acted upset earlier."

"Just missing Garren I guess. I'm not used to not having him around. At least I know he'll be eating well and Mika will keep an eye on him."

"You know my grandfather, Diana?"

"Mika? Of course I do—you didn't know? We're old friends, go way back. I've shared many camps and eaten many meals prepared by that wise old gentleman."

"That's so cool, and you're right. Garren will be eating well."

"I know in my head that he'll be fine. I'm just a worrywart I guess and I've been having weird dreams that haven't helped. Anyway, Anna, what's up with you? What really brings you out so late?"

"Well, this could have waited, but I was out walking and I saw your lights on, so I knew you were still awake. I'm doing a report on paranormal activity for school. It's for extra credit that I really need in English class. I'm trying to cite some actual examples and I'm drawing a blank. Then I remembered Garren telling me something about a story you told him when he was little."

"Really?" Diana asked. "I don't remember. What was the story about? God knows I've told him plenty of stories over the years. We had a lot of time to share."

"Something about a ghost, or something happening a long time ago to your family, a curse, maybe? Does that ring any bells? He said the story started where your family lived before they moved here?"

"Oh God, you have to be talking about Moll Dyer. They call her the Winter Witch because of how she met her demise. I can't believe he remembered that. I don't even recall telling it to him. It's not a story to tell young children when you hope they'll sleep through the night. Do you think that's the story?"

"Maybe, it sounds familiar. Would you tell it to me?"

"Sure, but this is just an old family legend, a fairy tale I guess. I'm not sure how much credit you'll get for it at school."

"That's okay, I imagine that's all part of this assignment, and I promise not to cite sources." She grinned.

"Okay then. Well, my grandfather used to come to visit us when we were little—before he got sick. I think he enjoyed scaring Lily and me with his old tales. Papa said our hometown had a resident witch in the early 1700s. He said that she'd come from a noble family, and that her parents died having left her to fend for herself and her little brother. She got her witchy reputation from dealing with herbs and botanical medicines. She didn't tolerate fools and gossipmongers and in fact, cared little for so-called civilized society. If the colonists confronted her about witchcraft, she'd laugh in their faces. She wouldn't even dignify their questions with an answer. That, of course, didn't set well with them. They were very superstitious about anything they didn't understand in those days or anyone not conforming to their cookie-cutter ideal of proper behavior. Well, maybe not so different today..."

"This definitely sounds like the story."

"Good. Well, the Indians...sorry, no disrespect. The Native Americans loved her, and she could care less about racial barriers. In fact, the townspeople said she..."

Diana stopped mid-sentence and held up her hands to illustrate air quotes "...preferred the company of savages to her own people.

"I imagine that didn't set well with them either. But the story goes that around then Southern Maryland suffered through a prolonged drought. Naturally in those days, they needed someone to blame. I guess that's not so much different than today either if you think about it. Anyway, their crops failed and the people grew hungry. Moll Dyer's small homestead, by contrast, grew plenty. She shared her excess with them, but it wasn't enough—not when the settlers' children started getting sick. About that time, the colony's governor visited with his family. As luck would have it, bad luck for Moll Dyer that is, the governor's children became deathly ill.

"The governor heard repeated stories about Moll casting spells over their children and livestock and cursing their fields. The townspeople asked him to do something about their abomination...their witch, and now he believed them. He gave authority to the local constabulary to arrest Moll Dyer and try her as a witch. According to Papa, his great-great something or other, along with a group of indignant locals paid a late night midwinter visit to the Dyers' homestead. They thought the house was empty, but regardless, they were not to be denied. They set Moll's house ablaze. One of the men claimed to see her fleeing the scene through the woods—cursing them and their progeny for a hundred generations. They tried to pursue her but the hounds lost her trail. Several days later, a young boy found Moll draped over a large sandstone rock, frozen to death, by the stream that still bears her name. Imprinted in the rock that bore her anguish were the prints of her knees and one hand. Her other arm reached out to the heavens. Did the raised arm indicate the culmination of her curse or was it in supplication to a higher power during her hours of torment? I can't say, but the townspeople took it as proof of a curse, and proof they'd rid their fine God-fearing community of an accursed witch.

"Papa said the younger brother escaped detection, and none of the townspeople ever saw him again. According to Papa's research, though, the brother was the evil one. The one they should've feared. According to the legend, the curse is still on the land around Moll Dyer's home and on the descendants of all the men who were there. Some say she can still be seen flying about on moonlit nights or walking the streambed with her half-wolf companion.

"That's about all I can remember, Anna. It happened almost 300 years ago, so the fable has stood the test of time at least. Do you think my family's old wives' tale will help with your essay?" Diana grinned.

"It will work wonderfully. I'll see if I can substantiate any of it, but you've given me a great start. I really appreciate it."

"The story is real enough. Folks still repeat it back home if that's what you mean. In fact, the rock she died on is on display at the courthouse. I've seen it with my own eyes. It takes a bit of imagination to see the prints in the stone though. I'll bet there's pictures of it on the internet."

"Yes, that's the direction I want to go with my paper. I want to show how old stories and legends have fueled superstition and belief in the paranormal. Diana, if you don't mind my asking, and the teacher says this is important—do you personally believe she cursed your family?"

A tear welled up in Diana's eye and she wiped it away vigorously. "I guess everyone has curses, some self-imposed. My family's certainly had its share, but I don't attribute them to a poor misunderstood woman, dead for nearly 300 years. Besides, we may have balanced it all out when Adam and I married. I met him when I was a teenager about your age at my uncle's wedding back home. He was marrying Adam's aunt. A year later, we were both at their one-year anniversary shindig. Let me tell you the 'shine and homemade wine were flowing. I don't recall how the subject came up, but his aunt claimed Moll was their distant relative. So maybe Moll Dyer won't deliver her vengeance on the wife and son of her progeny? God I miss Adam…and Garren too."

Diana wiped at her eyes. "Lord, Anna, you must think me a simpering old fool."

"Not at all." She placed a hand on the older woman's shoulder.

"Sorry, Anna, I'm reminiscing about events beyond my control."

The two women spoke of simpler and more pleasant things. Boyfriends, school, and books they'd read were discussed before darkness fell. At the first lull in conversation, she yawned, shook her head and stood.

"Oh my, guess I better get going, Diana. I'm keeping you up and school starts early."

"Yes, it is a school night," Diana agreed. "Mika will think that I'm the bad influence. Can I give you a lift home?"

"No, but thanks. I love walking at night." She turned to leave.

"Oh, Anna…"

She raised her eyebrows. "Yes?"

"We're friends. And if something was wrong, you'd tell me if you needed my help, right? You wouldn't make up a story about being in the neighborhood when you live over a mile away, right?"

She smiled and gave Diana a hug. "Yes, I knew I could count on you."

She waved goodbye as the door closed behind her, and walked away from the house towards the road. She paused at the hedges on the edge of the property and glanced back at the house. "Are you two still awake?" she asked.

Lenore and Bridget crawled from behind the bushes and stood up.

"What did you find out?" Bridget asked.

"Is someone or *something* using Brodie to hurt the men?" Lenore added.

"I don't know. Diana spoke a name I remember from one of my grandfather's stories. I should've paid more attention, but it wasn't a happy story. And that's the kind you want to hear when you're young. You know—stories about unicorns and fairy princesses. But hearing the same name associated with Garren's family…one way or another, I'm going up to camp tomorrow."

Chapter Twenty-Nine

Nathaniel Mountain Hunting Camp, WV
Garren

"I haven't fixed much of a lunch today, fellows." Mika leaned against the dining table. "I didn't think everyone would be up to it."

"That's fine with me," Chris said, "and thanks, but I think I'll skip lunch today. I don't think Garren's appetite is affected any."

"No worries from me, Mika." He tossed another handful of potato chips in his mouth, then lifted his head at the sound of thrown gravel outside. "Brodie's back."

He stood and moved out the back door with Frank on his heels. They watched Brodie back the truck up to the game pole. Jim dragged himself out behind them.

"Damn, Brodie, way to go. He's a bruiser," Jim said.

Frank reached the driver's side door as Brodie was climbing out. "Nice buck." Frank grabbed Brodie's hand and shook it.

"I told you I was bringing home the big boy, didn't I? What do you think, Garren?"

"He is an awesome animal, Brodie. Congratulations." He slapped his cousin's back.

"Yes sir, you've done this camp proud, boy." Jim rubbed the deer's antlers. "Let's get a tag on him so we're legal."

The three able-bodied men grabbed the buck and hoisted him up while Jim tied him to the pole. Brodie pulled out his hunting tags and attached one to the antlers.

"Garren, you haven't tagged yours yet either. You boys trying to get us fined?" Jim asked.

"No sir, you're right. Meant to do it yesterday, I even had my tags out but forgot with all the excitement. I'll take care of it right now."

He went inside and told Mika and Chris about Brodie's buck.

"Well, at least somebody got him," Chris said. "It won't be a 'big one that got away' story."

"We still have a couple of days to go after them." He started looking under the couch cushions.

"Maybe I'll be up to it in the morning. Hope this isn't some flu bug. What are you looking for in the couch anyway?"

He continued his furniture treasure hunt. "My deer tag. I had it here last night when I filled it out, but I can't find it now." He ran upstairs as the other men drifted back inside. The floor boards were thin enough that he could follow the conversation below.

"Hey Brodie, I hear you had some luck," he heard Chris say, and reentered the room as Brodie gave Chris's hand a quick shake.

"Nope, not luck. I just took advantage of my opportunity."

"I'll have a look at him shortly, Brodie," Mika said. "I'm having a bit of trouble getting around just now."

"It took you a while up on the mountain, Brodie. Have any trouble dragging him out?" Jim asked.

"It was a long drag back to the trail, but I managed. Garren, what are you digging around for?"

"I didn't want to interrupt a good deer story, but has anybody seen my deer tags?"

The men shook their heads, and he continued his search in the kitchen. He remembered drinking a soda while filling out one of his tags. Maybe they stuck to the can when he tossed it in the trash? It was worth a shot. He pulled out sticky cans and bottles, oily napkins, sloppy wet paper plates, and then finally—deer tags! He put the tags on the counter, and started tossing the trash back in the can. Reaching for a used coffee filter, he hesitated. Something disgusting was growing on it. He poked at the contents with a broken plastic fork. It looked like pieces of pumpkin...no, it was orange mushrooms mixed in with the coffee grounds, along with chopped up red berries. *Must be one of Mika's secret recipes.*

Jim walked in the kitchen. "Any luck?"

"Yeah, I threw them in the trash by mistake."

"Good, I figured they'd turn up. Look Garren, would you mind taking the chicken out of the fridge and burying it out back? I think we're all a little scared of it."

"I can understand that. I know I don't want any of it."

"Hey, mind you don't bury it so close that we'll have bears crawling in bed with us tonight. Mika said he was going to do it later, but his ankle and knee are in rough shape. I told him to go home, but you know Mika...he's one stubborn somebody."

"No problem, Uncle Jim. I'm all over it."

"Thanks, Garren. Should be a shovel in the shed, but don't mention it to Mika. The man can barely stand up, but I don't want to embarrass him. He's one proud old Indian."

"Native American, Uncle Jim, but consider it done."

When Jim left to join the others, he pulled the offending poultry from the fridge. It smelled okay, but he didn't trust it. He held the plate by the edges to avoid touching the bird—just in case.

Outside, there was no shovel to be found in the shed. There were hooks for tools on the walls, but only a few actually held any. One of the camp members must have taken tools home. He did find a broken handled hoe that would work well enough.

He went uphill 75 yards and whacked away with the hoe. When the hole was twice the width of the bird's carcass, he tossed the poultry in and covered it with dirt and heavy rocks.

He washed any possible contaminants from his hands, tagged his deer, and joined the others at the table for lunch. Brodie and Mika prepared sandwiches for those capable of holding down solid food. Those with tortured digestions were satisfied with bowls of lime Jell-O.

"Brodie, you didn't see anything of Bertram did you?" Frank asked.

"No, the only company I had this morning was my ten point. Why?"

"He took off without saying anything to anybody. The truck's gone and his deer is too."

"But most of his gear is still here. Guess he had places to go—in a hurry," Jim said.

"Bertram mentioned an appointment back in town, but I don't know when it was," Brodie said. "Didn't he say he didn't want to be in camp for the full moon, Mika? Is he really superstitious or something?"

"A lot of hunters think the deer won't move during the day when the moon's full. They do seem to travel more at night then. I don't know if that's it or not, but I've noticed Bertram doesn't stay out as long as he used to," Mika said.

"I bet he's afraid of the ghost of Zachary Dyer. Right, Mika?" Henry laughed.

"Was he superstitious, Frank?" He noticed Frank's eyebrows knit together.

"Never knew him to be superstitious, Garren."

Frank shook his head and turned his eyes to Brodie. Brodie stared at his plate.

"You know, I saw his appointment book on his bed. I think I'll check it out before I head out to the woods." Frank hopped up and headed to the bunkroom.

"Well, I'm going to get ready to head out again. I have another tag to fill." He pulled on his boots as Frank returned with Bertram's book.

"No appointments today or tomorrow."

"Nothing for the next few days?" Henry asked.

"Nope." Frank tossed the book to Henry. "But maybe Brodie's right. Bertram does have the full moon marked on there and he's circled the day in red."

Henry stared at the book. "You need to put on your reading glasses, Frank. That isn't the full moon. It's a snake eating its own tail. If I remember correctly, it's called an uroboros. It's a symbol of renewal, and it's supposed to show the cycle of life, birth and death. Lots of cultures used it, even Native Americans, right Mika?"

Mika glanced at the page, and nodded.

"Dad can't help himself, guys. Once a history teacher, always a history teacher," Chris said. "Don't encourage him, Mika, or he'll never stop. Just ask Garren."

"Hey, Chris, your dad might be good entertainment for you while you're nursing your gut."

"You tell him, Garren," Henry said as Chris threw his plastic spoon at him.

He ducked, smiled and thanked Mika for the sandwiches. Getting up from the table, he grabbed his coat and rifle from the rack.

"Brodie, what happened to your rifle? The stock is cracked."

"I don't know, Garren. I noticed that too. It still shot straight though. Do you think the cold cracked it, Uncle Jim?" Brodie showed the stock to Jim.

Jim took the gun and turned the stock toward the light. "I've had that rifle a long time and taken a pile of deer with it. It sure doesn't owe me anything. I bet it has another deer or two in it though, Brodie. Go get yourself another one." Jim handed the gun back.

"That's the plan. I'm going to get dinner started here first, and go out a little later."

"Good luck, Brodie. Hope you get another, Cuz." He left the cabin looking forward to a quiet afternoon in the woods.

Chapter Thirty

Nathaniel Mountain Hunting Camp, WV
Brodie

He considered staying in camp during the afternoon hunt. The beginning of a migraine was playing taps in his head using the inside of his skull as a drum. Pain was about the only thing his mind still had room for. Thoughts of the damn dream woman Leigh filled it constantly.

If his mental bloat correlated to gastric distress, his head was as bloated as his belly was one day last October. Being a taste tester at the chili cook-off —on the same day as the national oyster shucking contest at home—bad move, Brodie. Last raw ones he'd ever eat…

He popped four aspirin from a half empty bottle. Somehow an old man's story and an erotic dream had possessed him, mind and body. Whenever his eyes closed, *she* was there. Every waking moment, indeed every thought, became about *her*, his long dead fairytale woman.

"Find Leigh!"

"Shut up!"

Maybe there was a real-life woman like her somewhere—a woman who'd appreciate him for himself. He'd hoped that person might be Lenore in a few years. There was plenty of time for finding a woman later though. Deer season needed to be his focus now.

The men in camp hadn't give him his due when they saw his buck. Nothing like the hoopla Chris received with his tiny sandwich size deer, but he'd expected no better. He knew them for what they were: jealous sheep and entitled jackals.

His hunting time was ending soon, and he had a lot to do. The moon had swelled since they arrived, and would be full when next it rose. Then...*something*...would happen. *What was it he had to do?* He could wait; the memory would come.

He wondered about Bertram. It didn't make sense for him to disappear like he did, but thinking about him made Brodie's headache worse. He'd had a lot of them since he'd been on the mountain. The altitude, maybe, or he just needed to get used to breathing the thinner, fresher air. What was it about Bertram? What couldn't he remember? He had a vague image that lingered with him after one of his migraine blackouts. Nothing important, probably...and he needed to get back in the woods, back in his tree stand... *back to the shack.*

No, not there! He'd had enough of that place. Something about it frightened him, but he couldn't quite put his finger on it. Maybe if his visit was in the daytime, and not the middle of the night? Maybe then it wouldn't seem as scary? But hadn't he been there during the day? He couldn't remember!

The shack called to Brodie, Mika was right about that. He was glad he stayed away from that place...*but had he? Didn't he head out in that direction?* He shook his head and felt a twinge of shame to realize he was letting an old dilapidated shack scare the crap out of him. He rubbed his hand over his eyes to soothe the pounding in his head.

"You're a chicken shit, Brodie. They're right about you."

He shook his head, then remembered the deer sign around the old shack. Maybe he'd walk back up there before it got dark? He needed to prove something to himself. He wasn't a coward.

He reached Chris's tree stand, intending to hunt there again. Lightning did sometimes strike in the same place twice. Wouldn't that be something, to take two monster bucks in the same day?

He climbed up the ladder to the stand. The ravens weren't roosted in the trees this afternoon; maybe the gut pile from his deer filled them up for a while. After twenty minutes of waiting, nothing moved below him. Even the squirrels had vacated. The animals must still be spooked from the morning hunt. *Come brother, it is time.*

He stretched muscles that were sore from dragging the buck. The effort aggravated his wrist and he pulled the edge of his glove back and rubbed the swelling. Dark purple discolorations led away from his wrist like tentacles. The scrape from the rock didn't look too great either. It was a dark oozing bulls-eye. Brodie pulled his glove down. *Wimp—quit feeling sorry for yourself.* He wouldn't get another deer by admiring his wounds or from reveling in past glories.

He surveyed his woods, or more accurately, Chris's woods. Not that Chris managed to do much with this prime piece of real estate. He'd shown him how to get it done though, and he planned to do so again. It was time to hunt.

Seeing movement, he sat up straighter in his seat, then craned his neck to get a better view.

"Hey! Hey, Bertram, is that you?" he shouted, but the man didn't turn around or acknowledge him in any way. The man kept walking through the woods toward where he'd dressed out his deer. It had to be Bertram. Was the old man deaf? There was no way he didn't hear his yell. *"Come now, brother, it is time!"*

His head pounded as he climbed out of the stand and followed the path to where the man disappeared. He hurried to catch up with him, but the man was nowhere to be seen.

"Bertram, wait up, where are you?" he yelled.

He continued down the path, not really sure where it went, but he had a good idea from its general direction.

Bertram was heading for the old shack. He wondered what the old fart was up to, but he'd find out soon enough. The back wall of the shack loomed dead ahead.

He circled around to the front, and went up the steps. He stuck his head in the door and called Bertram's name. He looked around the darkened room, but there was no one there. He decided to sit and wait for Bertram. He'd find out what he was up to. He propped the front door open, and rested his rifle across his thighs, still determined to get in some hunting. The shack provided excellent cover and after a hundred years, the deer were certainly used to it.

He rubbed his temples and tried to relax. Leaning his head against the doorframe, he closed his eyes. The pounding in his head and the events of the past few days took a toll on his energy. His head dropped to his chest, jerked up, and slowly slid back down, up, and in slow motion, returned to rest.

Chapter Thirty-One

Hampshire County, WV
Anna

She rolled over in her bed, a smile on her face, content in the hypnotic trance of the remembered dream. She knew her part in this play from many past repetitions. It was a vision too real to be mental theater or the mind's attempt to 'take out the trash.' She could feel the grass, smell the trees...the vivid images carried her on a familiar journey, back to the glory days of her people.

When the people in this past world spoke to her, they addressed her as Bluebird. In the dream's embrace, she recognized herself, despite the addition of small primitive tattoos on her arms and breasts. The modern corporeal Anna blushed in her sleep, realizing her partial nudity. The dream *Bluebird*, however, felt totally at ease standing at the side of the man she knew as Two Bears. She knew the peace of belonging.

Two Bears exuded the confidence of a man at home in his world: a man who'd faced many trials in life, and emerged stronger for it. Bluebird loved him completely. They stood at the edge of a wide river, long ships with tall masts anchored at rest a stone's throw away. Bluebird wiggled her toes in the sand and felt the moist coolness beneath.

She looked at Two Bears—admiring the play of his muscles along his arms and across his shoulders. He grabbed the fish trapped in their weir and tossed them to the bank. Not handsome, perhaps, but Two Bears' beauty was not unlike the deer of the woods, or a hawk in flight. A beauty found only in nature, unblemished except for the mark on his shoulder. A lightning bolt scar inflicted by one of the bears that gave him his name. He was an accomplished hunter and reveled in his knowledge and skills in the woods.

The fish cleaning went quickly with the two of them working as one. They placed the fish in a woven basket and turned away from the river, following the thin trail that snaked along the edge of a feeder creek. Bluebird knew where they were going before Two Bears pointed out the small dwelling made of stacked trees. It was the home of the woman called Moll—one of the new light-skinned people.

Bluebird beat her fists against the door, a signal the woman had shown her, and she waited. The door opened, and the woman motioned them inside. She stepped through the doorway after Two Bears. She smelled the overpowering, cloying scent of crowded humanity. The new people seemed to be afraid of bathing. Bluebird placed the basket of fish on the rough-hewn table, and waited for the bartering to begin.

The white woman motioned for them to sit beside her at the table. The door reopened and a tall dark man entered, not the woman's brother or son, but another. Moll raised her eyebrows and drew her lips in a straight tight line. Her nostrils flared.

"Why are you fouling my doorway, Laris? You're not welcome here."

"My dearest Moll. I'm here for you always. Even as you both dream."

Bluebird felt the man's dark eyes sear into her as if they could see into her soul. *"Hello, Bluebird. No…I think it's Anna now, isn't it?"* The man spoke, but his lips never moved.

Moll slid back from the table as the man drew near her. Bluebird knew this woman didn't succumb to fear. No, it was revulsion that pushed her away from the table and twisted her face into a nauseous mask. The dark man watched as Moll dumped the contents of a sack on the table before them. Dried herbs tied together, berries, medicinal bark, and various seeds spilled across the boards. The man's leering gaze never met Bluebird's eyes. Vulture-like they lingered in an indecent caress, wandering over her body. She feared the man but felt comforted to be at Two Bears' side, and under the Raven Witch Moll's protection.

With hand signs and head nods, they conducted their business with the woman. They used the hand grabbing gesture of the new people to show their friendship and agreement with the trade, then stood to leave.

Retracing their steps along the river trail, Bluebird glanced back at the woman's house. The dark one was following them! She nodded to Two Bears, but he only shrugged. He had no fear of that one, only disgust. Halfway to their village, Two Bears laughed and pulled her from the path to the shade of a giant oak—one of their favorite spots. It captured the breezes from the river and afforded protection from the noonday sun—as well as prying eyes.

He held her in his arms, his hands tenderly stroking, his lips exploring.

"Oh my God...Garren and Two Bears, you're the same." She quivered, blushing at the revelation. Both Anna and Bluebird longed for this man, as he gently lowered her to the leaf covered sand. Bluebird closed her eyes, the heat rising in her veins, and abandoned herself to his touch. Waves of pleasure coursed through her like the tides of the river. He grunted hoarsely, and slipped away from her.

It seemed that Two Bears' touch changed—no longer amorous, his attentions coarsened as he pulled her to himself, fingernails digging into the flesh of her throat. She pushed him away, and he grunted in a voice unknown to her.

Her eyes flew open in question, and saw him there. The dark man hovered over her, his bleak eyes staring into hers as he growled. "Be still, ape." He grasped her hair, hurting her, pinning her face in the sand.

"I've been waiting a long time for you, Anna…generations. You won't stop me."

"Two Bears," she pleaded, but he didn't answer. The dark man pulled a shiny knife out of his waistband and pressed it to her throat. His eyes dared her to resist. She twisted her head and stretched out her arms, reaching, willing herself away from him. She clawed at the ground, searching for a weapon.

"Your progeny will belong to me and my master."

"No, they never will."

Her fingers closed on a soft wet branch and she pulled it free. She swung the stick with Two Bear's name on her lips, and the slice of the knife cut short her scream.

"Die then," the dark one whispered.

Anna woke covered in a fevered sweat, the horror made more real by her own scream still echoing in her ears.

"*It was only a dream, Anna. Only a dream, my dearest friend Bluebird…but he's coming…*"

"Moll?"

"*Yes, my child…only a dream, but also a warning. You know where the evil lives.*"

She shook her head and folded her arms to quell the shaking. She forced her eyes open. No ghost from the other time and place whispered in her ear. Her room was empty, but the familiarity of her own bed and her own things soothed her. She got up to turn on all of the lights, and lock her bedroom door. Then she cowered in the center of her mattress, afraid to move.

Gradually, the hooked claws of the dream released their hold on her. She listened for a long while with gritted teeth and clenched fists. Hearing no sound, she leaned over the edge of her bed, afraid to look, but more frightened not to. No bloodied bodies waited there. She reached for the lamp on her nightstand, flipped off the switch and shivered in the dark.

Chapter Thirty-Two

Nathaniel Mountain Hunting Camp, WV
Garren

He opened the door to a dark and silent camp. He switched on the lights and wandered through the rooms. Everyone was sound asleep. The dinner bowls were washed and stacked beside the sink. He was glad to see the men felt well enough to eat. A good night's sleep would be the best thing for them. He pulled the lid off the slow cooker. The concoction smelled enticing and his stomach growled in anticipation. He snatched a bowl for himself and scooped up a hearty portion of the stew.

Either his cousin's cooking showed promise or Mika proved himself to be a good teacher. He wolfed down his dinner, and went back for seconds. As he ladled out another bowl, the bathroom door opened. Mika limped into the kitchen, dragging his foot behind him.

"Welcome back, Garren. Have any luck this afternoon?"

"Didn't see a thing, but what's going on? It's a ghost town in here."

"Yeah, it hasn't been good. The fellows felt a little bit better so we decided a little grub was in order. After getting some food in our bellies, everyone was so worn out we turned in early. Dinner was a mistake though. There's been a revolving door on that bathroom ever since."

"Man, you guys caught a bad case of something. What about your leg? It looks like it's worse."

"I don't know what's going on with it. Knee's swollen, ankle's black, but I'll survive. Might be a while before I go out dancing though."

"You do a lot of dancing, do you, Mika?"

"Not much to speak of. My dance card is about punched out."

They walked into the living room, as the bathroom doors on both floors opened, then closed. He shook his head in sympathy.

"How did Cuz make out? Did he see anything this afternoon?" he asked.

"I don't think he's back yet." Mika glanced at his watch. "It's getting pretty late too."

"Oh my," Mika hobbled up from the couch, walked to the closet, and pulled out a roll of toilet paper. "Excuse me, Garren. Can't put this on hold." Mika limped toward the back door.

"This is awful stuff, Garren." He heard the door close and Frank came out of the bunkroom with his packed bags in hand.

"Hey, Garren."

"Are you heading home, Frank?"

"Yeah, I've got to get out of here before I catch what the other fellows have."

"Need help loading your deer?"

"No, but thanks, we loaded him up at lunchtime. Look Garren, do any of you guys have cell phones?"

"I don't think so. I heard those things don't work up here anyway. No reception I guess? No landline here either. It's kind of an unwritten law with phones though. Uncle Jim says they defeat the purpose of getting away from it all. Why do you ask?"

Frank reached into his jacket pocket, and handed him a boxy looking phone with a retractable antenna.

"Take this. If these guys aren't coming around by tomorrow, find somewhere you can get a few bars and call me. I'll come back up here to help. They're in bad shape. Hell, they can hardly stand long enough to make it to the bathroom."

"You think it's that bad?"

"When I came in this evening, Chris was crawling down the hall to the bathroom. I mean he was literally crawling. They're pretty bad."

Frank held out his hand. "Remember, if you need me, call. Otherwise, ask Jim to drop the phone off to me on his way home."

He thanked him, shook his hand and when Frank fired up his truck, he looked the phone over to see if he'd know how to operate it. Frank's taillights flickered on and he watched until they were out of sight.

A cabin full of sick men and Brodie was still out well after legal hunting hours were past. He should've been back by now. He pulled his boots on again. It was time to go look for his cousin. He grabbed extra batteries for his flashlight and wrote a short note to the others.

He hoped Brodie had some luck, and that he'd find him dragging another deer out. Brodie seemed happier since taking his buck—another one might help even more. Maybe the outdoors brought out the best in everyone.

***

Approaching Brodie's stand, he yelled, and smiled at the echo of his voice. Would he be able to determine which direction Brodie was in if he answered? A quick look around the stand provided no clues and he walked toward the next stand. He stopped every 25 yards or so to listen and look through the woods for Brodie's light.

Chris's stand was the most likely place to find him. Brodie was impressed with it, as he should be—considering the buck he took from there. He shouted again, and the echoes were less pronounced here. He waited, listening, but heard no reply.

He circled around the area looking for any sign of Brodie's passage. He picked up an empty cartridge, and placed it in his pocket in case Brodie wanted it for a souvenir. Not far away, he located a gut pile, and picked up another fired casing. He came out of the thick woods at a different point on the trail, and spotted two sets of footprints in a muddy spot in the trail. One he knew to be Bertram's because of the unusual tread he'd bragged about on his three-hundred-dollar boots 'guaranteed not to cake with mud.'

The tracks were as fresh as the recent rainstorm, and probably made when Bertram left the woods after that morning's hunt. He knitted his brow and squatted at the edge of the trail. He spotted where a boot slipped or dragged through the mud. He shined his light on the ground in that direction, but the light shone only on air. The ground dropped away at a deep cliff.

He stood and shined the light into the darkness. The glow of hunter's safety orange reflected back to him. It was a pull over knit cap, just like the one Bertram wore. The cap did not rest at the bottom of the precipice but got snagged in some mountain laurel branches on its descent. If the rest of Bertram followed his hat, he sure hoped something broke his fall also.

He searched for the gentlest path possible to begin his descent. The rocks were loose making a steady foothold difficult. He tested a first step and small rocks flew down the embankment. He listened for how long it took them to reach the bottom. It was too long.

A branch snapped behind him, and he whirled around. His footing gave way, and falling backwards, he landed on the small of his back. The flashlight flew out of his hands as he slid toward the cliff. Grabbing at rubble and vines, he caught a tree root, and hung at the cliff's edge. He felt around with his feet trying to find traction to climb up. Footsteps approached from the shadows.

"Hello! Bertram? Brodie?"

There was no response from the cliff's edge. It had to be Brodie. The shadowy figure was Brodie's size and shape. The moon passed from behind the clouds, and he saw Brodie smiling, but the smile wasn't Brodie's. The smile held the distorted mirth of a madman.

"Brodie? This isn't funny, asshole. Help me up dammit!"

The man stepped closer and reached for his hand.

Chapter Thirty-Three

Nathaniel Mountain Hunting Camp, WV
Brodie

"*They will be coming soon, brother.*"

He shook loose the thought, and the vestiges of a blurry dream. Confused at first, he looked around until he recognized where he was. He was on the main trail, only about a hundred yards past Chris' tree stand and he had no recollection of how he got there! Was he going crazy? He looked up at the sky, and the moon stared back at him, only the tiniest sliver missing from its edge. Full darkness had fallen on the warm November night.

"*Leigh is coming… soon.*"

"Yeah right, not soon enough though," he said out loud. "I could use the help."

At the thought of her, his mind's eye conjured up Leigh's image. He visualized her as clearly as in a photograph. Had they met somewhere? A real woman that is—in a world outside his nightmares? *But are they* really *nightmares?*

He could smell her silky black hair, the sweet scent of summer rain. She carried herself as royalty might. In his image of her, she wore the necklace his dream-self gave her.

He wiped the pleasant distraction from his mind, and tried to remember how he came to be here—asleep on the trail. He remembered nothing after spotting Bertram, or the man he thought to be Bertram. He recalled following some man down the trail, but then he lost him. Did the man lead him here? Or did he just decide to take a nap in the middle of the night? His head throbbed as the rapid-fire questions raced through his mind.

He hated to admit it, but the first thing he wanted to do when he returned home was to see a doctor. The headaches were bad enough, but forgetting hour-long blocks of time? That was something that crazy people did. What could it be: insanity, some early form of dementia, or maybe a brain tumor? But it wouldn't help to worry about it now. Besides, like Mika said, "you have to play the cards you're dealt."

In the near distance, lights no brighter than candles beckoned him back to camp. Were they already in bed? From the anemic drift of smoke up the chimney, he knew the fire was reduced to embers.

He descended the trail and stared at the cabin before going in. No additional deer adorned the game pole, and this year's hunting season was all but played out. He pulled open the cabin door and savored the smell of wood smoke and his simmering stew. He threw some wood on the fire, moving with care to avoid waking the others.

Although hungry, he denied himself the home-cooked meal. Sometimes deer stew made his stomach unsettled, and he didn't want to be laid up on the last day of the hunt. He dug through the cabinets and found sardines and bread for a sandwich.

He sat at the table and a slip of paper drifted to the floor. He picked it up, and stared at the writing. Garren went looking for him? Could it have been Garren and not Bertram he saw in the woods? He puzzled over it until his headache returned. Thoughts of his cousin triggered a vague memory, one on the cusp of his mind like a dream after waking. A recollection with a stone wall around it that he couldn't reach through. He tried to concentrate and felt like a sliver of glass penetrated his skull. He'd remember eventually. Garren was probably tucked in and fast asleep by now. His cousin wouldn't waste much time looking for him. He glanced at the note again, then crumpled it up and tossed it in the trash. The empty sardine can and paper plate followed.

He yawned; the days were long in hunt camp, yet somehow they all ran together. The week passed in a moment of time. He reminisced about the week's adventures, and about the awesome buck he'd shot. It was a great week and he was in no rush to go home. Out here, everyone was equal unless they proved themselves otherwise. Here a man had his chance to prove his mettle on his own merits. Some men proved to be more equal than others. He smiled at the thought, and relaxed. He propped his feet up on a dining room chair, enjoying the heat from the stove and his eyes grew heavy…

***

The flushing of the upstairs toilet jolted him awake. None of the other members stirred from their slumbers, and he thought it was time to join them.

He wanted to be in his stand well before first light—skipping the breakfast ritual. Mika wouldn't mind, and the guys probably wouldn't be up to eating anyway. *Deer stew can put a hurting on a man.* Tomorrow promised to be a good day, and he still had a lot to do.

Part III

Chapter Thirty-Four

Exhausted physically and mentally, they passed out together. He woke on her couch abruptly aware of his nakedness and covered himself with childlike awkwardness. Had his empathy become tainted and twisted? His shame precluded conversation. The seed of corruption and doubt was sown and the darkness in his soul grew with the malevolent vigor of evil.

Hampshire County, WV
Lenore

After homeroom, she led the others through the cafeteria to the janitor's office (and the seldom-used exit door concealed there).

"Quit worrying. I'm telling you, Mr. Jameson won't say anything if he sees us. I think he likes me. He said I remind him of his daughter," Lenore said.

"Yeah, sure, that's what it is, his daughter." Bridget giggled.

"Eww, Brie, just stop! Now you've given me the creeps!"

She grabbed the exit door as the janitor entered his combination office and supply room. She turned to him and placed a finger over her pursed lips, then winked.

Jameson smiled and winked in return. "Now, don't you ladies get into any trouble." They scooted out the door to freedom.

"So what's the plan? How are we going to get there? And what are we going to do when we get there?" Bridget asked.

"Hitchhike I guess, or maybe steal a car." She smiled.

"Are you both sure you want to do this?" Anna asked.

"Would you go alone if we said no?" she asked.

"Yeah, guess so. Scared or not, alone or not, I'm going to the camp today."

"You aren't twisting our arms, Anna," she said. "Let it rest, we're going...together."

Anna reached into her backpack and pulled out a leather-strung necklace. The thong held a curved narrow bone. "In that case, take this, Lenore. Put it on, maybe it will help you."

"Thanks, Anna." She held the necklace up and examined it, puzzled. "Okay, I give up. What is this, a rib bone from a fox or something?"

Anna laughed, and shook her head. "No, not a fox and not a rib bone either. It's a baculum bone..."

"What's that?" Bridget asked.

"You don't want to know, Bridget." She held the necklace at arm's length and her mouth twisted in disgust.

"It's a penis bone, Bridget," Anna said.

"Hmm, what exactly am I supposed to do with a penis bone, Anna? No, maybe don't answer that..."

"It's okay, Lenore. A raccoon baculum bone helps to find your true love. I guess it works for dream lovers too." Anna winked at her.

"And you expect me to put that...thing around my neck? A dick bone?"

"Quit being such a prude, Lenore. Do you have something in there for me, Anna? I could use one of those too." Bridget grinned.

Anna reached back into her backpack and pulled out a cross, fashioned of reeds and square in the center, with arms that appeared to rotate. This necklace was also attached to a leather thong. "Did you think I'd forget you, Brie?"

"Oh cool, that's Brigit's cross. How do you know about that?"

"I told you I'm a hybrid or maybe just a mongrel. Isn't that where you got your name, Brie? From the goddess of fire? I've never met anyone as drawn to a campfire as you are. So even if your name was Jezebel, this would still suit you."

"Not as sexy as the sex bone, but I love it. Thank you, Anna." Bridget hugged her friend.

"Yes, thanks Anna...I think. I'll say this much, I never received a more unique gift." She pulled the necklace over her head. "So, what else do you have in there to help us? Wooden stakes, silver bullets, or maybe an inflatable car to carry us up the mountain to camp?"

Anna held up her hand with her thumb extended.

"No car, like you said—we're riding our thumbs all the way there."

"Are you sure you know the way, Anna?" Bridget asked.

"I hope so. It was a year ago that my grandfather took me up there to show me around. It's a beautiful place. I just hope I paid enough attention during the drive. Did you say there's a shortcut to the main road, Lenore?"

She led them through the woods to the road, keeping out of the view of any nosy teachers. Before they left the shelter of the trees, she felt Anna's eyes on her.

"Come here, Lenore," Anna said. "You're the one with the boobs, and they might help us get a ride." Anna reached for the buttons of her shirt, and undid the top two.

"What the hell, Anna?"

"Hey, I'm pimping you out, girlfriend. You'll give the male drivers all the reason they need to give us a lift. I wish your hair was up in pigtails and maybe if you'd worn a skirt..."

"Sorry, I thought I was going to a hunting camp, not attending a fashion show. Why don't you or Bridget do it?"

Bridget shook her head. "Anna maybe, but you're obviously the best qualified for the job."

Coming out of the woods to the main highway, they threw out their thumbs to a passing car. The driver of the green station wagon slowed considerably, staring as he passed, but didn't stop. Bridget ducked behind the other two.

"Oh shit!" Bridget said. "I think that was Mr. Snead. I know him from church. Mom's going to know I skipped."

"Chill, Brie. I doubt he recognized you," she said.

"Umm, look again, Lenore. I think maybe he did." Anna pointed at the car as it did a U turn and headed back their way. The man pulled onto the shoulder of the road beside them and lowered his window.

"Well, hello young ladies. Where are you heading to on this lovely day?" The man spoke directly to Lenore's chest.

"We're going to a hunting camp on Nathaniel Mountain. Our father and grandfather are there already, and expecting us," she said.

"Well, I'm going about half-way there anyway. I'd be glad to give you a lift as far as Morrisfield."

She nodded, and he reached over and pushed open the front passenger's door. A leering smile split his face. She glanced back at Anna and climbed in, watching as

Bridget ducked her head and pulled her hoodie down over her eyes. Then her two friends got in the back seat.

"My name is Billy Snead. My friends call me Wild Bill. Who might you ladies be?"

"We're out of school…" she started.

"…on a school break." Anna finished. "We're on a break from WVU, and staying with some friends."

"Oh, well that's interesting. Is that the story you're sticking with too, Bridget?"

"Um, yes, Mr. Snead. I don't get to see my two friends often since they went away to college, so I skipped today. Can you please keep my secret?"

Snead smiled and winked into the rearview mirror.

The four of them made small talk. Mr. Snead seemed content to talk about himself. His conversation consisted of bragging on his financial accomplishments. He spoke of wild parties and the women in his life, even as the November sun reflected off his wedding band.

Her discomfort increased with each suggestive word from the pervert's mouth. The direction of his gaze was equally divided between her chest and the road. She buttoned her blouse to the collar and scooted as far away from the man as possible, pressing herself into the vehicle's door handle. How could he drive with his attention riveted on his warped fantasy's wanderings, instead of the road ahead?

As they crossed the county line, Snead became more suggestive.

"So what are you taking in college?" He reached over and tapped her leg.

"Pre-law. I thought it would be a good fit. Most of my family is in law enforcement."

"Oh…I see."

Snead drove on in silence—at least until a mile away from his destination. He turned his head and smiled at her.

"Maybe you have the wrong impression of me, Lenore? I'm not a bad guy and I wouldn't expect something for nothing. But if you try being nice to me, I'll drive you all the way to that camp." Snead eased his hand over to her thigh.

She grabbed the offending hand, lifted it up and away from herself, and placed it back on the steering wheel.

"Please keep your hands to yourself, Mr. Snead."

"Come on, Lenore. You don't want me spilling the beans about you girls skipping class do you? Bridget wouldn't want that I'm sure."

The man's hand grabbed her leg in a painful grip.

"Let go of my leg, asshole!" she yelled and tried to wiggle out of his grip.

The sound of a metallic click from the back seat, and Wild Bill Snead's eyes bugged out.

"Are you deaf *and* a pervert, Mr. Snead? Take your filthy fucking hands off her or I'll splatter your degenerate brains all over your windshield." Anna pressed the pistol's barrel against his temple.

The car stopped abruptly and the three girls jumped out of the car. It drove away in a shower of thrown gravel, squealing tires, and shouts of 'crazy bitches.'

"Well, I doubt that Mr. Snead will be telling my mom we skipped when he sees her in church this Sunday," Bridget said. "You okay, Lenore?"

"I'm good. Thanks Anna, I owe you one."

"That was pretty awesome, but you think maybe the gun was a bit of overkill? And when were you figuring on telling us you were packing heat?"

"Packing heat? You've been binge-watching gangster movies, Brie? I am sorry, though. The whole thing unfolded like a nightmare, but he had no damn right! The pistol is my grandfather's and rest assured, I know how to use it. I thought it might come in handy at camp, not knowing what we might run into. I figured you'd call me paranoid if I told you about it."

"So, what are we going to do now?" Her body shook in a convulsion of downloaded adrenalin.

"Stick to the plan, but only if you're up to it, Lenore. Are you okay?" Anna asked.

She nodded her head. "It's our only option."

"Well, at least we know we have protection. Some sick shit cops a feel, Anna will send him to meet his maker." Bridget smiled.

The girls stuck out their thumbs as another car headed their way. The young man behind the wheel slowed down, nodded and spoke to his female companion. She looked toward them, and he rolled his eyes back in his head. He wet his lips as he stared, then waved and tooted the horn as he drove away.

"Dickhead!" She shot him the middle finger salute.

"God, what is wrong with guys? Do they really think that shit gets us all hot and bothered?" Bridget asked.

Anna shook her head and smiled. "My grandfather says they are trying to prove their manhood in some ridiculously juvenile way. Maybe they don't know any better, but it's hard to distinguish the obtuse and ignorant irritants from the true psychos."

"Or maybe they're the same? Maybe only opportunity separates them," she said.

"Lenore, I'm sorry I suggested you loosen those buttons. I didn't expect…"

"No, and don't make this about us, Anna. This is about Snead—a dirty old man looking for cheap thrills. If I was dressed in coveralls or a ball gown, it wouldn't matter. He'd still be a groping disrespectful perv."

Anna poked her with her elbow and she turned to see her smiling. "Seriously, though, Lenore, you do look like a nerd like that. At least undo the top collar button?"

"No, she's like the movie version of a spinster librarian," Bridget said.

"You are both so damn funny, I forgot to laugh." She reached behind and loosened her hair, then tied it up in a tight ponytail.

"Oh, that's so much better." Bridget giggled.

"Okay, stop it now, here comes another car."

217 • Sons and Brothers (Legends of the Family Dyer)

Chapter Thirty-Five

Nathaniel Mountain Hunting Camp, WV
Garren

With returning consciousness, his pain renewed. He didn't know, or care, where he was; his pain rendered other concerns irrelevant. His knee was the worst, feeling as if smashed by a hammer's blow. He reached out to assess the damage, but something caught at his arms. He pulled at the entangled vines, but they were coarse and tight, allowing little movement. He twisted to look at his imprisoned hands, and the pain in his head caused his vision to blur and spin.

He squinted to focus and his jaw dropped. No vines held him. His hands were tied to a tree that carved the image of its bark into his back. The early morning darkness gave few other clues about his predicament.

He remembered seeing Bertram's hat at the base of the cliff, and vividly recalled his fall. It replayed over and over in slow motion in his mind's video cassette recorder. *What the hell was wrong with Brodie? It had to be him! Why would he tie him up?*

His stomach rebelled against him, churning and nauseous. His guts felt as if he'd swallowed an appetizer of ground glass. Breaking into a cold sweat, he thought his bowels were ready to explode. He reached for the snap of his pants, grateful he wore no belt, but couldn't reach it. The phantom knife blade in his intestines continued to twist. He inched the top of his pants over the rock he was seated on. The pants moved downward slowly, until a belt loop caught on the rough edge of the rock. He arched his back and pulled, reduced to tears at the sound of the snap popping loose. When his pants reached mid-thigh, he couldn't hold back the tidal wave any longer. He turned in an attempt to evacuate the liquid fire away from himself and mostly succeeded. His nose crinkled up at the scent of his own filth, and the first rays of the new day burst over the mountain. He leaned back and closed his eyes. Something soft moved away from his head's touch, then bounced back. He craned his neck upward.

Oh, God! His stomach convulsed as the dead man's sock-covered foot swung back and slapped his cheek. He hurled violently into his lap. Forgetting the pain, he wrenched himself up and away, the rope burning the flesh from his wrists. He saw now that the tree holding him was not a tree at all, but one of the crosses from the old shack. At the cross-beam, Bertram hung, his wrists nailed to the wood in the position of a crucifixion. A crown of multiflora rose vines encircled his head. The thorns cut into Bertram's flesh, but the wounds were bloodless. He was placed there after death. Post-mortem is what they called it on the TV detective shows. He burst into a crazed laugh at the thought. His laughter echoed through the hills.

"Get a grip, Garren," he told himself and bit his lower lip. "Keep it together or you're a dead man and they'll be finding you post-mortem."

He yanked at the rope and felt some movement in the cross. He pulled at the rope, then pushed back with his shoulders, and the cross swayed. Over and over he repeated the movement, and with each attempt the cross increased its pendulum motion. The cross moved forward to its balance point, paused and then moved backwards again.

One more time. He drove his shoulders back against the wood, then pulled with everything he had against the rope. Again the cross paused, creaked and looked as if it would return. He gave an additional yank, and heard the rewarding sound of wood splintering and rocks rolling downhill. The cross with Bertram's added weight crashed toward him, twisting him forward in an unnatural position and slicing his ear as it landed over his right shoulder. He felt an alarming pop in his back, rolled his legs to the left and turned to face the ropes.

Again his stomach lurched as the cramp struck with sledgehammer force. He scooted to the side of the rock just as his intestines voided. He waited for the spell to subside, his body trembling from the exertion and pain. Sweat trickled into his eyes and he wiped at them with his sleeve. He slumped forward, feeling impotent and sorry for himself, and unwanted tears flowed.

That's not going to cut it, Doyle. You have to do better than that. He shook his head to clear it, initiating new waves of pain. But the pain provided him clarity.

Dear God, the men in camp! They were all sick, after eating the food Brodie prepared! It wasn't a virus! This infection was named Brodie! He had no illusions now; it was Brodie who tossed him down the embankment. Brodie was insane!

"What did he do to you, Bertram?" he asked, but luckily for his sanity, Bertram did not answer.

He glimpsed fur on the other side of the rocks and dragged himself toward it. Bertram's deer lay on its back with the man's boots shoved into the stomach cavity. From the deer's mouth, instead of the greens that Mika placed with tender respect, hung a severed human finger. A class ring bulged from the hacked off end of the finger, and Garren recognized the stone, but he knew Bertram wouldn't miss it.

He had to get loose and warn the others—soon! Brodie would be back, and he wanted to be long gone when he did. He craned his neck, bowed his head and started working at the knots with his teeth.

Chapter Thirty-Six

Nathaniel Mountain Hunting Camp, WV
Brodie

He woke early, too excited to sleep. It was the last day of the hunt, and tonight the full moon would shine. Again, his limited slumbers were highlighted by dreams of the beautiful and elusive Leigh. She was more real to him than the flesh and blood girls he knew. What was that other girl's name he'd been infatuated with? He couldn't remember. Something about snakes? But it didn't matter...

Other images also haunted his dreams: torture, violent death, and blood—there was lots of blood. But those imaginings already slipped away and only the visions of Leigh remained. *"We will share, brother."*

Leigh came to him as before, even more responsive this time, more *giving*. The woman felt so real, he woke feeling uncomfortable and unfulfilled. He reached for her and whispered her name over and over.

"Enough, already!" Chris shouted. "Take your fantasy girl elsewhere or shut the hell up and go to sleep, Brodie."

His eyes flickered open at the rude intrusion, and he glanced at his watch. Time to get moving. The punk kid served as a decent alarm clock, but he wasn't good for much else.

The cabin was still and dark as he dressed and tugged on his boots. The men had made a feeble attempt to clean up after themselves, but the room and the entire cabin smelled of sickness and decay. He crept downstairs avoiding the fifth stair down, the creaking one, and continued his descent. Tiptoeing into the kitchen, he

221 • Sons and Brothers (Legends of the Family Dyer)

snatched a paper towel from the roll and wrote a short note for his cabin mates.

He took the stew out of the refrigerator and placed it back in the slow cooker in case the men were hungry when they woke. The stew looked thin, so he added a couple handfuls of the mushrooms he'd collected…somewhere. *Where did he pick them?* He tossed a few pieces of wood on the dying fire before heading outside and leaving the cabin behind him.

At the first bend in the trail, he looked back. The smoke curling from the chimney took on a ghostly, ethereal feel, backlit by the nearly full moon. Something about it made him sad, as if he might never see such a beautiful sight again.

He turned back to the trail and strode toward his hunting destination. Garren somehow beat him out to the woods this morning, but he'd still make it to a stand before first light. Fewer hunters in the hills was a plus, and if he knew one thing, it was how to take advantage of opportunities. *Now is our time.*

Half way to the stand, his headache returned to stay.

Chapter Thirty-Seven

Hampshire County, WV
Anna

"Oh shit," she said as the jeep approached. "I know that car. It's Garren's mom Diana."

"Well, it's too late now, she's seen us," Lenore said. The jeep stopped beside them.

Diana rolled down the passenger's window. "Hey Anna, do you girls need a ride?"

"Hey sure, thanks Mrs...I mean thanks, Diana."

She took the front seat this time as Lenore and Bridget piled in back.

"Aren't you going to introduce me to your friends, Anna? I don't believe I've met you girls? I'm Diana Doyle. Maybe you know my son, Garren?"

"Diana Doyle? Double D might be worse than what I have to put up with," Bridget said.

"What was that?"

She cut her eyes at Bridget in the back seat. "I'm sorry, Diana. That's Bridget Braden on your side and Lenore Bauer behind me. Brie hasn't met Garren yet, but Lenore thinks she may have..."

"Where are you girls heading on this beautiful fall morning?"

"The teachers had conferences all day, so we have the day off. I forgot all about it. It's so beautiful we decided to go up to camp and visit with my grandfather and Garren."

"Oh, do you two ladies know Mika also or just out for a jaunt?" Diana glanced at them in her rearview mirror.

"No ma'am," Lenore said, "but my stepfather and step-brother are up there too."

"Are you Henry's new daughter then? I heard he'd remarried. He's a nice man your dad, and Chris is a great guy too. Anyway, I'm pleased to meet you neighbor." She offered her hand over her shoulder and Lenore shook it. Diana then turned her gaze to Bridget in the mirror.

"Oh, I guess I'm just along for the ride, Diana," Bridget answered.

"So where are you heading, Diana?"

"You're going to think I'm some stupid, over-protective mother, but after you left last night, I started worrying about Garren. I just want to see for myself that he's okay. I'll tell the men that I was *in the neighborhood*, and thought I'd stop by. That always works...right, Anna?" Diana smiled.

She felt the heat on her face. "I have a feeling you're not going to let me forget that, Diana."

"No chance. You girls won't tell on me will you?"

"Your secret is safe with us," Lenore said.

"That's my girl." Diana smiled. "Women have to stick together. Huh, Anna?"

She heard Brie whispering in Lenore's ear, less secretive than Brie imagined. Something about Garren's dream girl...she turned to see Lenore stick out her tongue at her seatmate.

"I'm sorry, what was that?"

"Some private joke they're sharing, Diana."

"Oh, like the Double D thing?" Anna smiled to see Bridget's face blush blood red, almost the shade of a child's wagon.

"I always thought you and Garren might get together, Anna. You're the only girl he's ever talked about." Diana glanced at her, then at Lenore.

"You know I love Garren, Diana, but from the moment we met, we've been like a brother and sister to each other. I tell him things I'd never tell any boyfriend, or girlfriend either for that matter. Sorry, girls."

Diana laughed. "I know what you mean. It's good to have a close friend of the opposite gender."

"So how far is it to the camp?" Bridget asked.

"Timely question." Diana switched on her turn signal. "We've arrived."

As the jeep made the turn into the drive, she noticed a metallic reflection from the ravine beside the road. "Could you hold up a second, Diana?"

She climbed out of the jeep, and walked over to the shoulder of the road. "You won't believe this, but there's a truck down there. She began descending the hill, and the other women followed.

"Nobody is in it," she yelled back, "but I hope nobody drove it down here like that. The front bumper is all smashed into a tree." She ran back up the hill.

"Someone threw branches and evergreen boughs all over the truck like they were trying to hide it or something," she huffed, catching her breath.

"Probably a drunk driver ended up there and didn't want anyone to see the evidence until they could pull it out. Come on, let's get up to the cabin and see how the men are doing," Diana said.

They pulled up to the house and parked beside Jim Doyle's old truck. Diana led the way to the door. She knocked hard, and hearing no answer, opened it slightly, stuck her head in and yelled. "Are you men decent? I'm here with three lovely young ladies for a quick visit."

"Diana? Is that you, come on in."

"Grandfather, is everyone all right?" she asked as the women filed into the cabin.

"Of course we're all right, Anna," he answered. His pronounced limp and the walking stick he leaned on indicating otherwise.

"What's wrong with your leg then?"

"Just a little sprain is all, twisted it one evening. I wish that was the biggest worry in this camp. Most of the guys have been sick as dogs for the last couple of days. You ladies might want to think twice about coming in here. The place should be quarantined."

"What's wrong with them? Oh, I'm Bridget by the way." She extended her hand.

"I'm sorry everyone, Mika, this is Bridget, and the other young woman is Lenore. Of course you know Anna. Ladies, Mika is not only Anna's grandfather, but also the finest camp cook in the country."

"I'm very pleased to meet you both." He shook each of their hands in turn, then turned his intense eyes to her. "What did you do to convince these lovely girls to skip school with you today, Anna?"

"That's my fault, Mika," Diana said. "I asked the girls to ride along with me. They had a slow day at school scheduled today, and I've been so worried about Garren. They were sweet enough to come with me and look out for an old lady. First time he's really been away from home, you know? So please don't be mad."

Mika nodded at Diana, but his eyes remained focused on her.

"So what's wrong with the guys?" Lenore asked.

"It's the worst stomach bug I've seen. Henry, Chris, and Jim have it the worst. I had a mild case, but with my bum leg, I'm not good for much either. Those three though, can hardly walk they are so weak. I've been shooting the fluids to them, so hopefully they're staying hydrated. Bertram and Frank left early. I guess he was afraid of catching it, and I don't blame him a bit. Luckily, we had some early luck with the deer, so we didn't get skunked."

"Any idea who owns a big yellow truck? It's all smashed up down in the gully," Diana asked.

"Bertram has a new yellow truck, but in the gully? Now I'm confused," Mika said. "He took off with his deer, and didn't even say goodbye. Was anyone down there or still in the truck?"

"No, Anna checked it out. No key in the ignition, either," Diana said. "Do you think Bertram might have hitched a ride to town to get help towing it out? Knowing Bertram, he'd be too embarrassed to admit he lost control before he even cleared the driveway."

"Maybe so, but it does seem strange, even for Bertram."

"What about Garren and Brodie? Are they sick too?"

"I haven't seen them this morning, Diana. I got up before daybreak, and the two of them were already in the woods. There was a note on the table from Brodie. It said they were getting an early start this morning, and hunting together. So, they're the only ones around here that aren't laid up. Did I tell you that your boy shot a nice fork-horn? Brodie took a buck too, a monster."

"Are Henry and Chris here?" Lenore asked. "I'd like to check in on them, if that's okay?"

Mika pointed across the room and upstairs toward the bunkrooms. "You help yourself young lady. Chris is up there, and Henry's in the back. Anna will show you the way. Ask them if I can fix them anything to eat."

She led Lenore to Henry's room first, with Bridget close behind. They found Henry asleep, so they moved upstairs to look in on Chris.

"Are you decent, brother mine?" Lenore asked.

"Dressed anyway, don't know about decent," Chris answered.

Chris recognized her immediately. "Hey, I know you. You're Anna, right? Garren talks about you all the time, and didn't we have Biology together before you were…? What are you doing up here?"

"Mika is my grandfather, and we decided to come up for a visit. I've been telling my friends how beautiful it is up here."

"You didn't mention the smell though. Sorry, brother," Lenore cracked open the window, "it smells like disease in here."

"Well, if nobody is going to introduce me, I guess I'll do it myself," Bridget said. She walked over to the bed and grasped Chris' hand. "Pleased to meet you, Chris. I'm Bridget."

"I'm very pleased to meet you too, Bridget."

"Think you're up for some grub, Chris?" Lenore asked. "Mika offered, but I'll be glad to rustle you up something. Henry is racked out, but he might wake up if he smells food."

"I think I might try a very little bit of something, Sis. I haven't held anything down for a while, but I think I'm coming around now."

She raised one eyebrow seeing Bridget's hand still gripped in Chris's, and he noticed her noticing.

"Oh, I'm sorry, Bridget."

She and Lenore stood to go.

"You two go ahead. I'll stay and chat with Chris for a while." Bridget winked at her.

"I think that's our cue, Lenore."

"Okay," Lenore said. "We'll give you a call when something's ready. Keep a good eye on brother for me."

She led the way to the kitchen and found the stew Brodie left on to warm. She took off the lid and sniffed. She peered inside the slow cooker, and pulled something out with a spoon.

"Oh, cool. What kind of mushrooms are those?" Lenore asked. She picked up the jar off the counter. In the muted light of the kitchen, it gave off an eerie light green glow.

"Grandfather, come here!"

Mika hurried in as fast as his ankle allowed. "What's wrong, Anna?"

"Look at these. I think they're jack 'o lantern mushrooms." She handed over the jar Lenore had admired. She lifted the lid from the slow cooker. "Look in here, they aren't glowing in the stew, but I think they're the same ones. There's a ton of them in here. Where did they come from?"

"I don't know. Brodie did up the stew for us because my ankle's been so bad. I don't know where he got them. I've never seen that jar in the cabinets before. Maybe this isn't a stomach bug then."

"What's the big deal with the mushrooms? Are they poisonous?" Lenore asked.

"They're one of the worst ones around these woods anyway," Mika answered.

"I think we'd better cook up something to absorb whatever's left in the guys' systems, Lenore. What's left, Grandfather?"

"We keep a pretty full pantry up here. Usually these men can pack away some food." Mika glanced at his watch. "Well, it is nearly lunchtime. Garren and Brodie should be back by now, Anna."

"I'll go look for them if they aren't back after lunch. Any special requests?"

"Maybe just some sandwiches. I don't think any of them will want anything too heavy on their stomachs. We have some of those pre-made gelatin cups in the fridge too. Anna, would you do a crippled old man a favor and bring in some firewood after lunch? The fire is nearly out."

229 • Sons and Brothers (Legends of the Family Dyer)

Chapter Thirty-Eight

Nathaniel Mountain Hunting Camp, WV
Brodie

As he drew near to Chris' stand, he heard a scratching, clawing noise down the hill from where he took his buck. An odd noise, as a large animal might make, perhaps an animal as large as a bear. Grunts, strangely human sounding, drifted over the cliff, and his heart skipped a beat. He'd not admit it to anyone, but the sounds frightened him. He hurried away from the path, looking over his shoulder as he went, until out of sight of both the cliff and the trail.

He assured himself he was no coward. He didn't know if the scratching and grunting got to him, or if it was just the place, but it wasn't a pleasant feeling. Like being physically attacked by unseen tormentors while his spirit was twisted by an unfounded, anonymous guilt. The combination transported him back to the third grade.

He remembered a classmate's change purse was stolen from her desk during recess. The teacher made his class wait in the hallway while she searched each student's desk. They all heard the teacher call his name, summoning him back into the classroom for questioning. He had nothing to do with the theft, but the purse was found in his desk—minus the girl's money.

Perhaps it was the bewildered look on his face when asked, but the teacher believed him. The rest of the class returned to their seats and no mention of the purse or the theft were ever made again. He didn't forget though, nor was he allowed to. He saw the accusation in everyone's eyes from that moment forward, the guarded glances, and whispered comments. On the rare occasion that he received a party invitation, they watched him, their eyes boring into him whenever he'd approach their hoard of presents.

There was nobody for Brodie to talk to about the situation. His mother was busy being a single mother and breadwinner, leaving little time for a social life, and less still for him. He tried talking to Uncle Jim, but was advised, "to hell with them, quit whining and act like a man."

The distrust of his classmates increased, and his teachers soon picked up on it. Accepting the adage that 'where there's smoke, there's fire,' their eyes soon matched the accusing looks of his peers. If a fight broke out at school, it was his fault. When the fire alarm went off, when they got back to their classrooms after the *all clear*, the school's intercom speaker would announce, "Brodie Caine, please report to the principal's office." He was cast as a villain, and in short order, his actions mirrored his reputation.

He'd learned life didn't play fair. He knew friends were hard to make, and easy to lose. The third-grade pariah still lived inside him and knew he could only count on himself.

Standing in front of Zachary Dyer's old shack, the memories flooded back with newfound clarity. He sat on the porch steps when his head swam from his migraine and memories. He forgot the bottle of aspirin at the cabin, and wondered if he could make it through the day without it.

As his vertigo eased, he stood and ventured inside, intending to stretch out on the floor for a short nap. He was home here, or it felt like home. He puttered about, checking if anything was disturbed, taking an owner's pride. He found the mushroom tea just where he left it, in the cabinet untouched. Brodie considered how relaxing a cup of tea would be, and rummaged in the cupboard until he found an old can of Sterno and a small rusty pot.

He pried off the lid with his hunting knife. The gel was thinned out and liquefied, but it might still burn. One flick of his lighter proved his theory, and he filled the pot with water from his canteen, rinsed it out and filled it again to place over the flame. The heat should sterilize any germs. He pulled a clump of mushrooms from the jar, and allowed them to steep.

When the tea turned dark enough for his liking, he went outside and sat on the porch. The tea tasted nasty, but he worked it down like medicine, knowing it would make him feel better. When he had it all down, he relaxed on the porch, letting his mind wander.

His stomach churned. Were the mushrooms bad, perhaps not dried out properly? At least his headache dissipated. He felt more relaxed than he had for many years.

He was exhausted, his life force drained. He squeezed his eyelids together, and offered a prayer to any god who might listen. Disenchanted and disenfranchised, he longed for another path to follow. With his eyelids still shut, his mind's eye visualized the fissure as it opened, a shadow butterfly emerging from a scabrous cocoon. At first manifesting itself as a pinprick absence of light, it grew in size and energy becoming a lazy, revolving vortex.

Brodie stared at it with a familiar yearning. Gazing into its depths he saw, not despair, but an odd sense of peace, a world without demands. The only admission charge was losing one's self in its consuming embrace.

It didn't require any effort on his part, only his resolution not to fight it any longer. He relaxed as the void's caress pulled him along. Mercifully and thankfully, he embraced the tranquil warmth of the abyss.

"*We are brothers, we are one.*" He accepted the surge of unexpected energy, and stood up to dance. He thought of Leigh, and smiled, as the porch floorboards began to breathe.

"That's rather unusual." He laughed.

As he spun around the porch, he noticed his surroundings as if for the first time. The homestead needed a lot of work. He needed to see to some repairs before spring planting, but that could wait. He needed to see what the hunters were up to.

He skipped along the trail, happy to be there and happy to be alive. As he passed the cliff, he remembered the noises that shook his courage. He picked up several large rocks and tossed them over the side. He wasn't afraid of the noises now. He wasn't afraid of anything. Didn't someone break their leg down there? It served them right though. Now they'd leave him alone.

Drawing within sight of the cabin, he slowed, and crept closer—ducking behind the trees. He assumed a watchful, hidden stance. The cabin wavered as if fashioned from heat waves. As he stared, the cabin walls transformed into the gaping mouth of a cave.

"Cool!" He laughed, surprised at the childish sound of his voice.

The back door of the cavern creaked half-way open and stopped.

"Come out; come out, whoever you are," he whispered, gaily misquoting.

The door opened wider, and a woman emerged. Dark of hair and skin, and lithe of body, the air around her reached out to caress her as she passed. She bent over to retrieve firewood and her breasts momentarily flared, threatening to spill out.

Someone inside the cabin-cave called to her, and she turned to respond. She smiled, and the set of her lips brought him a joy that filled his heart until he feared it would burst. Her smile evoked his most cherished memories, a smile to die for.

Oh yes, he knew her, though sadly, not in the biblical sense. Her essence consumed his every moment's rest, and preoccupied most conscious thought as well. She returned to him, this love of his life. For too long, he'd waited for the fulfillment found only in her arms. Nothing and no one dare deny him again.

Again she bent over and faced him, as he admired her from his secret spot. Maybe she knew he lurked here in the bushes? She looked directly at him! His vision blurred, swimming in and out of focus. He concentrated, trying to maintain one focal point. He stared fixedly at her left breast, and slowly his vision cleared.

As he watched, her breast jumped out of her blouse. *All* the way out, bouncing like a ball on the trail towards him, coming to rest on his boot. He looked down at it and grinned. The nipple formed into an eye, and winked suggestively at him. Come and get me, it seemed to say.

Chapter Thirty-Nine

Nathaniel Mountain Hunting Camp, WV
Garren

As he chewed away at the ropes, he wished he'd paid more attention to his dental hygienist and flossed more. His teeth and gums took a beating from the knotted hemp rope. The minimal progress was slow and tedious. His gums began to bleed, and only the first section of the knot was loosened. His position didn't allow a good grip on the rope and his teeth kept slipping off with little effect. He'd need a dental visit when this was all over. Assuming he lived that long, of course, but he allowed no other conclusion to enter his mind. Survival was the only option.

When he did get loose, he wouldn't make the climb out of the ravine without assistance. His knee was swollen to the size of a grapefruit, but he didn't think anything was broken. If he could work his hands free, help would be a phone call away. That's what he told himself, though in truth he placed little faith in the new technology. The pocket holding the phone made tinkling, metallic sounds and gave rise to additional doubt about its functionality. Still hope, any hope, is what drove him on.

The weight of the saliva-soaked rope increased the fatigue from holding his hands up for so long. The sliminess of the rope seemed to help though and another piece of the knot began to work loose. He pulled at it frantically with his teeth, as if it might tighten again if he didn't work it fast enough.

One end of the knot fell away, leaving only a loose square knot holding him bound. He worked frantically and bloodstained the fibers of the rope a dull pink. His teeth ached, but his onslaught didn't diminish. He pulled off the last coil of rope, and threw his arms up in a gesture of victory. His lungs filled with air prepared to scream out his joy. Then the sound of footfalls on the trail above silenced him. He held his breath. Was the walker friend or foe? Should he take the chance? If friend, he wouldn't know of his predicament—unless he called out. If a foe, the bastard was back to admire his handiwork anyway. He went back and forth between yelling and holding his breath when rocks began to rain down on him.

"I'm not afraid of you. They should have left you down there to die!" a voice yelled from the trail. *Brodie?* It must be him, but the voice sounded older and deeper than Brodie's. Was he masking his voice? Another avalanche of rock and stone bounced down the embankment showering him with grit. He tucked his face against the large rock for protection.

"You won't keep Leigh from me. I'll kill every one of you first," Brodie screamed.

He froze in place, not wanting any movement to betray him. He heard Brodie again...his voice now sounding like his own. "Wow, look at the rocks, Zach. Have you ever seen colors like that before? We've got to show Leigh. Come on, brother."

He heard the two voices converse with each other as they walked off down the trail, but he only heard one set of footfalls. He waited, not daring to breathe until certain they were beyond hearing. He rolled over and pulled the cell phone from his pocket, several chunks of broken plastic with colorful spider-leg like wires sticking out from them. He studied the small ripped wires to determine if repair was possible, but knew it was beyond his abilities. He rolled toward the cliff and stood gingerly. He tried reaching an outcropping or tree root that might bear his weight. Everything he grabbed pulled away from the bank, dropping gravel in his face and eyes.

Just beyond the reach of his fingers, a substantial rock jutted out from the face of the wall. He tried a one-legged jump for it, but it remained beyond his reach. The landing sent bolts of electric pain searing through his knee and up to his thigh. His head whirled and the edges of his vision darkened.

A different approach was called for. He grabbed the length of rope that once held him prisoner, but doubted it was long enough to help. He wished he'd worn a belt, but he had a pair of strong denim pants. He sat back on the large rock and gritting his teeth to help negate the pain, pulled off his boots and pants. Putting the boots back on was more difficult, and his knee throbbed from the effort.

He stood and wavered on his feet as his equilibrium slipped. He drew in a deep breath, and tied one end of the rope to a pants leg. The other end was tied in a loop, then cowboy-style, he whipped the mongrel lasso, tossing the looped end towards the extended rock. It took four tries, but desperation improved accuracy and on the fourth attempt, the loop circled the rock! He felt like he'd hit the winning three-pointer as the final buzzer rang. Now all he had to do was crawl out of there. *Yeah, that's all!*

He grabbed a pants leg and began dragging himself up the wall.

Chapter Forty

Nathaniel Mountain Hunting Camp, WV
Anna

Her eyes moved around the table. Diana sat to her left, followed by her grandfather at the head spot. Chris and Bridget sat across from her with Lenore to her right. They chatted, told jokes, and exchanged silly stories to stave off the memories of the past few days.

The offending slow cooker of stew next caught her gaze. It perched on the counter, its façade sprinkled with gay images of daisies. Harmless in and of itself, but possessed by ingredients that corrupted it into a tool of torture. She needed to dump it out—soon.

But what about the mushrooms? Were they added with the knowledge of what they'd do? Or was it a fool's mistake?

Her eyes returned to Chris. He nibbled the last of a PB&J sandwich. His face was pale with a greenish tint. Tall and skinny, and considering his current complexion, he reminded her of a green bean. She bit her lower lip too late and looked up to see her grandfather staring at her.

"Thanks for lunch, Sis," Chris said.

"You're welcome, but a half sandwich isn't much of a lunch. Are you sure you don't want something else? There's gelatin in the fridge," Lenore said.

"Believe me, that's enough. I'm scared to put any more in there yet. Hey Mika, where's Garren and Brodie? Aren't they coming in for lunch?"

"Maybe not, I get the impression they wanted to make a day of it. I can hardly imagine Brodie missing out on lunch though."

"What stands are they hunting out of?"

"Well, Brodie's note said they were going to hunt together today, if you can imagine."

"Oh no, were they trouble being here together, Mika? Tell me the truth," Diana asked.

"No big deal, Diana. Just being boys, teenage hormones, you know…but they're good boys. My guess is they'll be at two of the stands where Chris and Henry hunted, by the old cliff stand."

"Are we ready, Anna?" Lenore asked.

"Sure, let me grab up a couple of armfuls of firewood and we'll be off."

"Give me a minute to throw on my boots and I'll join you," Diana said.

"Would you stay behind, Diana, in case the men get sicker? You mind?" Mika asked.

"No, don't mind at all. I'm counting on our young ladies to 'bring 'em back alive.'" She laughed. "Sorry, I fell asleep watching an old spaghetti western last night. But Bridget and I can stay and keep an eye on you guys. Is that okay with you, Bridget?"

Bridget shrugged. "Sure, that works for me."

"Okay, Anna, I'll join you at the woodpile in two shakes," Lenore said.

***

She loaded her arms with all of the wood she could carry, making several trips to the cabin. She had a strange feeling of being watched, and glanced around to see if it was Garren. It wouldn't be the first time they'd sensed each other's presence, but she didn't spot anyone. Lenore joined her as she made her last trip inside.

"Bye, guys," she yelled to the cabin.

"Okay, which way, Anna?" Lenore asked.

She pointed down the trail towards the cliff stand. "I sure hope we can find Garren first. Then we'll decide whether we want to see Brodie or not."

Lenore's laugh gave her hope that the worst was over. With the anticipation of young people on a picnic, they skipped down the path. Their worry was over nothing after all, just bad mushrooms.

"It's beautiful up here. I think the leaves are near peak," Lenore said.

"I love the deep yellow ones on the hickory trees, but the maples are giving them a run for their money this year. This is going to be fun." She thought about her two friends meeting for the first time. *The first time when they're awake anyway.* She didn't want to play matchmaker with her friends' hearts, but she knew at the very least, the two of them would be great friends. If she and Garren weren't meant to be, then Lenore would be her second choice for him.

"Do you still have your necklace on?"

"You can really be annoying, you know that Anna?"

"You know I'm teasing, but you're both my friends, and you'd be good for each other."

"Diana sure doesn't think so. Man, the look she shot me when we were driving up here! Then Bridget with her crack about me being Garren's dream girl. I'm sure Diana heard that. Lucky for me, she didn't have your gun. I think the woman might've shot me. You're definitely her number one contender for Garren's affections, Anna."

"I don't think it was a big deal. Oh, shit!"

"What's wrong, Anna?"

"I left my backpack at the cabin."

"So, what's so important in there?" Lenore asked.

"The gun, remember the gun, Lenore?"

"You really think we need it out here?" Lenore asked.

"No, I think we were very worried about an evil on that mountain that was just evil mushrooms." She laughed. "But if my grandfather finds that gun, he'll be very upset with me."

"Mad?"

"Yeah, I'm confident about that I'm afraid. I'm going to go grab the pack. I'll say there's bottled water in it or something."

"Okay, let's go then. I don't know the way to the stands."

"No, you can go on ahead. Walk slowly, and I'll catch up. It will give me an excuse to leave in a hurry without a lot of explaining. Keep straight on this path. It's only about a hundred yards to the first stand, the one by the cliff. You'll see it from the trail on your left." She was already waving goodbye as she trotted toward the cabin.

After running halfway, she slowed to a fast walk. She could run the whole way, but didn't want to be breathing hard when she reached the cabin. Then her grandfather would really be suspicious.

She didn't like lying to him, and rarely did, regardless of the situation. She just didn't want him knowing how irresponsible she'd been. Having the care of a teenage girl thrown into his lap was hard enough at his age, without any additional reasons for concern.

She was glad to have the security of the gun in her hand when the old pervert groped Lenore, but she knew that didn't excuse her for bringing it in the first place. Even without the gun, the three of them could've taken him out. They weren't defenseless. Oh no, Snead wouldn't have gone home a happy man.

She wondered if Lenore would recognize Garren when she met him. She remembered Bridget's comment about being a fly on the wall when the two of them met. Maybe she should have waited until they found Garren before scurrying back to the cabin. She might have been a witness to posterity. She smiled, but secretly hoped she hadn't made a big mistake. She didn't have many friends and didn't want to sacrifice two, although Garren's friendship was already lost. The memory of her last day at the private school still replayed in her mind.

After burdening Garren with her troubles that day, and explaining her mother's situation, she got caught up in the moment. The reality of what he meant to her, how he was always there for her…it filled her heart. She kissed him, and not a sisterly kiss as he'd always regarded her as. In deference to their friendship, he'd responded. She was as shocked as he was with her actions, and pulled away in shame. It was obvious that his feelings were not of the romantic variety. He'd turned away from her—wouldn't even look at her! And she was too much a coward to risk further rejection. For her part, she'd always consider him her best friend. If she could win back his companionship and trust—that would be enough. Her heart would be full.

She shook the memories from her mind, and rubbed the tear from her eye. She started to jog again around the last turn in the well-worn path, and stopped flatfooted. A man stood in the middle of the trail! He looked to be her age, with dark hair and built a bit heavier than Garren. Dressed in camouflage clothes with a rifle slung over each shoulder—Rambo-like—she surmised he was the infamous Brodie Caine. She lifted her chin and continued down the trail to the cabin. As she drew even with him, she held out her hand.

"Hello, Brodie is it? I'm Anna."

The young man looked confused for a moment, as if he was puzzled by her name. His eyes lingered too long on her breasts. When his hand reached toward her chest, she instinctively recoiled and drew back her fist. The look of innocent bewilderment on the man's face stayed her hand.

He didn't speak, but held out his hands palm up, then reached out and lifted the antler necklace from her chest. His smile was innocent, child-like as he admired it.

She smiled back at him, her cheeks still flushed from her quick anger. He looked up from her necklace, and his face aged and darkened before her eyes!

Again he reached for her, catching her unprepared and pulled her towards him. "Leigh," he whispered in her ear. "You've returned to me."

Chapter Forty-One

Nathaniel Mountain Hunting Camp, WV
Zachary Dyer

He crouched in the shadows, waiting for the right moment, knowing she'd be happy to see him again. It had been too long. He watched her carrying in wood, back and forth she went. Once, she stopped to look around, focusing on the very spot where he sat. Did she spot him? But she dropped her guard and went back in. He moved closer to the cabin, ready to spring out to surprise her when she came outside again.

He heard the cabin's door open and close. She stepped out, but another woman joined her now. His Leigh pointed down the trail past him, and the two women walked toward him. They giggled over some man named Garren, a name vaguely familiar to him.

When they passed his hiding spot, the other woman changed. Her red hair burst into flames, melting her face into a jack o' lantern's head. His muscles coiled, prepared to pounce, to leap to Leigh's defense…when her scent tickled his nose. The sweet fresh fragrance of a spring rain cleared his mind, and the flame headed girl became just a girl again. He crouched down lower, waited for them to get out of sight, then stepped out on the trail and followed.

Keeping a safe distance away from them, he wanted the reunion to be a wonderful surprise. They were around a bend and out of his vision when he heard rapid footfalls running toward him. He turned to hide, but thought better of it. There wasn't time. He stood his ground. When Leigh appeared on the trail, he could've danced a little jig. Somehow she knew he was there, and came back to him.

But it was surprise he saw in her eyes when she spotted him. She moved to strike him with her hand, but instead of a blow, she wounded him much deeper. When she looked at him with the eyes of a stranger, and called him by that boy's name, it ripped the heart from his chest.

What treachery was this? She still wore his necklace, yet didn't remember his name? He dropped his head, and again, her scent filled his nostrils. With a tear in his eye, he pulled her to him, his Leigh.

She struggled to pull away from his loving embrace, but she'd remember with time. Maybe if she saw his homestead again? He'd make her some special mushroom tea. That would bring back her memories…maybe he'd show her the pretty rocks too.

His spirit split again when the touch of his lips did nothing to bring back her memories. The anguish made him careless and she smashed her knee into his groin. He fell forward in the dust of the trail, and she ran from him. He gathered himself and chased her down the path. She screamed the name of the one called Lenore.

"Don't yell, Leigh, they'll hear you," he yelled, then laughed at his own contradiction.

Was she really trying to get away from him, and not just playing hard to get?

"Wait Leigh," he yelled. Without slowing, she held up her left hand and pointed her middle finger at him.

"Lenore, help me," she screamed again, and her look was one of terror.

"Stop, Leigh," he shouted.

If she continued running, he'd never catch her and he couldn't allow that to happen. He reached down and scooped up a rock without breaking stride, and hurled it at her. The rock connected with the center of her head, and she dropped like the deer the boy shot.

He ran to her side and stood over her. Thick blood clotted in her hair. A tear cut a path over his cheek. How could she not remember him? She would. She had to. He had time. If not, his love would be enough for both of them.

He grabbed her by her waist, slung her over his shoulder, and started carrying her home. He remembered the other girl, and decided to take the long way through the woods. Leigh first, there would be time for the others later.

Chapter Forty-Two

This night, Lily tearfully announced the pregnancy and suggested he might be the father instead of his cousin...but did they...did he commit this act of betrayal? He took a final pull on his lukewarm beer and smashed the empty can against the dashboard. "Sweet Jesus!" He shook his head.

She asked that it remain their secret.

"No, but what a hypocrite I am! But there's nobody else to blame. Our lives and our family will be in disgrace. I know this town too well. What can I do?" he asked the mountain. "In God's name, what can I do?"

Nathaniel Mountain Hunting Camp, WV
Garren

Climbing to the rock proved more difficult than anticipated, but gaining a foothold there marked the worst of the ascent. After he gained this perch, the cliff was less sheer, and the footholds more regular. Shallow scratches and dark bruises covered his arms and legs as monuments to this success, but he had no awareness of them. He concentrated on the next step, the next handhold, and the prize—the top of the embankment.

He worked his way uphill with infinite care. He didn't want to take any chances for a mis-step to throw him down. His knee throbbed with every movement, and when still, pounded in rhythm to his heart's pulse.

Looking for his next handhold, he saw the root he'd first grabbed, before he was tossed into the ravine. It protruded from the ground, frustratingly close. He stretched to his full height, and managed to touch the smooth surface of the root with his fingertips. He couldn't reach any further. The root formed a perfect handle as both ends were firmly imbedded in the rocky soil. Hoping his rope would support his weight one more time, he worked it under the loop of the exposed root with his fingertips. Once started, he pushed and pulled at it with bloodied fingers, until enough rope draped down for him to grip.

As he pulled himself from his resting spot, the muscles of his arms trembled with exhaustion at the effort. Freedom was a few grunts away. He pushed at the wall with his one good leg, and his boot caught on a small stone to propel him upward. Anticipating success, hope soared and he worked on his next set of problems—how to get back to camp, and what to do about Brodie. Did he still haunt the woods? Was Brodie alone in his madness? He couldn't be sure, considering the other voice he'd heard.

He rested with his good knee in the root's opening, and leaned forward to catch his breath. He could crawl the last yard if he needed to. He'd made it!

Snap! He lifted his head at the sound. In a frozen moment of time, he stared open-mouthed at the woman. He took in her red hair and dazzling green eyes, and even the bone dangling around her neck. Then she screamed, "No!" and her kick sent him flying back over the cliff.

He landed on the rock protrusion, the same rock that only moments ago, he was ecstatic to reach. His back ached from the impact, and he twisted in pain. Forgetting for the moment where he was, he caught himself before he rolled off his perch.

"Oh shit," he moaned. He turned toward the wall, and rotated his upper body to rub his back. His knee scraped over the rock face and pain shot up his leg. His vision darkened to a blur, and the world turned black.

***

The next sound he heard was ravens flying overhead. He didn't know how much time he'd lost, but the shadows were a little longer. From his position, he couldn't see the sun in the west. He sat up, and his head swirled. He looked for his rope without success and using the rock wall for support, levered himself up. His pants, now his sole means to the top, fell away to the bottom of the crevice…thankfully without him.

He looked up to the top of the cliff to plan another climb. He grabbed his father's crucifix.

"I could sure use your help," he prayed. "I'm not sure I can do this again."

A rustling sound at the cliff's edge drew his attention, and the woman's head popped into view. "Are you Garren?"

He ducked his head and waited, anticipating a deluge of rocks from above. He cautiously lifted his head from the protection of the wall. The woman stared down at him, and he read no ill will in her expression. "Yes, I'm Garren. Who the hell are you?"

Chapter Forty-Three

Nathaniel Mountain Hunting Camp, WV
Anna

"Leigh, are you awake? I've prepared something special for us."

The voice roused her. Her head pounded, and she ran her hand over the knot forming there. Opening her eyes a slit, she was confused at her surroundings. Where was she? How did she get here? She took stock of the dark room as her eyes adjusted to the light. She was propped up in a rustic dining room chair with her hands bound in front of her. She shifted her eyes back and forth—without moving her head. She wanted to know what she faced before revealing her consciousness.

The dark-haired man sat in front of her—the man who assaulted her on the trail. Physically, the man reminded her of Garren. His hair was dark and wavy, rather than blonde, and his build was similar though stockier. But there was a definite family resemblance—they shared the same nose, cheek bones, and dimpled chins. She thought they'd pass for brothers, except for their eyes.

Garren's eyes were a deeper blue than any she'd seen. But it wasn't just that this man's eyes were green. She often teased Garren about how unguarded his eyes were, that she could tell what he was thinking with just a glance. This man's eyes, Brodie's eyes, did not evoke trust, or express empathy. His eyes were eyes of despair, and what she read in their shallow depths was soulless madness.

"Come on Leigh, have your tea. I'm sorry, but I started mine without you." He smiled and winked at her.

He drank from a dirty cup of dark liquid, and then held the cup to her lips. She shook her head.

"Leigh dearest, please don't misunderstand me. This isn't one of those optional things. It's the only way to get you to remember me…to remember us. So, you *will* drink it!"

He turned the cup up and some of the hot vile liquid flowed through her clenched lips. She tried spitting it out, but gagged as it slid down her throat. The taste was nasty, like cough medicine and kerosene. Again he turned up the cup and forced the hot tea into her mouth. She feared poison, but Brodie drank of the same concoction. He emptied his cup, and fixed her another, making sure she drank her full share.

She felt nauseous, and the room swam with colors that whirled like a kaleidoscope. Brodie stared into her eyes, but she found it difficult to focus.

"What did you give me? You've drugged me!"

He drew his chair closer to hers, reached out and caressed her neck.

"I'm helping you remember, Leigh. My brother and I share one purpose. We will be one, and you will be ours."

She moved her eyes around the room, but saw no one else.

"What brother? Who are you talking about?"

"In time." He leaned over toward her. She closed her eyes in disgust and tried to twist away as his lips touched hers. Her head was woozy and she opened her eyes—wide. Her skin was melting like superheated rubber. She felt him pull her towards him, and tried to scream, but their mouths were joined, their lips grafted together.

A slimy, slug-like protrusion entered her mouth, and she bit down at its invasion. Brodie jumped back, and she saw their mouths elongate and stretch as he pulled away like saltwater taffy. He slapped her face.

"Bitch!" he shouted. His fingers examined his bloodied tongue. Again he slapped her, and snatched the necklace from her neck.

"You are undeserving, but I will give you time to reflect on your sins. Try to remember."

He pulled at the rope binding her, then yanked her from the chair. He led her out into the night. Her legs felt like rubber as he dragged her along with the full moon lighting their way. Unnatural in its brightness, it swelled and dilated as she watched.

"It's okay, Anna—he's drugged you, sweet girl, but it will wear off."

"Moll?"

"Who?" He lifted her off her feet and shook her like a rag doll. "Never mind, there's nothing that old witch Moldy Dyer can do." He laughed and dropped her to the ground. She heard the screech of rusty hinges. A door covered a deep hole in the ground.

He tugged at her blouse, pulling her toward the hole. She pulled away and heard cloth rip and felt cool air against her exposed skin.

"No, Brodie. I am not going in there!"

"It will give you time to remember. I'll be back when you know that I'm me, Zachary Dyer, your one true love."

She fought against him, trying to kick him with rubbery knees, but he evaded her attempts with ease.

"Lenore, Brie, where are you?" she whispered.

"Oh, don't worry, I'll find them for you, Leigh."

She snapped at him with her teeth, and he shoved a piece of cloth into her mouth. He lifted her with one hand in her hair, and the other on her belt, then kicked her feet out from under her. She fell several feet before the rope jerked her to a stop.

The man crouched down and looked down into the hole at her.

"Like your new home, Leigh? I don't want you to get lonesome, so I invited guests."

The odor of urine and the dampness of mildew filled the space. Another smell caught her interest, familiar but she couldn't identify it. The man moved away from the hole, and she heard the creaking of the hinges. She bit at the gag, and the door slammed shut. She saw only blackness.

Chapter Forty-Four

Nathaniel Mountain Hunting Camp, WV
Garren

He watched as Lenore ran down the trail, admiring her form despite the circumstances. His first impression of her was that she was tough and independent—no wonder she and Anna became friends. He limped to the edge of the trail, to the spot they'd found a button. Brodie had moved off the path between there and the cliff, or Lenore would've spotted him.

The light from the full moon helped, and he spotted disturbed leaves, and a partial boot print pressed in the mud, then…drag marks. Looking in a straight line through the woods, Brodie's direction became clear. He was taking Anna to Zach Dyer's old shack.

He walked stealthily, again the hunter. He felt for twigs with the toe of his boots before committing any weight. Brodie could've stopped anywhere and set up an ambush. He wished his father's rifle was slung on his shoulder, but he'd improvise. He swung Lenore's stout walking stick left and right. It would do double duty, and a club was a better weapon than no weapon.

His progress was slow. His knee threatened to drop him in his tracks, and as he approached the shack—even greater stealth was called for. The top of the hill loomed ahead, and dim lights from the ruins of the building filtered through the woods. He stood up straight in the thicket, looking for any movement. Despite the lights, nothing moved in or around Zachary's shack.

He stepped from behind the brush, and moved toward the lights. He anticipated Brodie's ambush from behind every tree and shrub and tightened his grip on his walking stick. He held it in front of himself like a baseball bat. It seemed very thin and frail—not the best weapon for a gunfight!

His heart beat wildly in his chest and his breaths were short and rapid. Something wasn't right. He looked left, then right. Nothing moved. He looked down and a shiny object caught his attention. He picked it up and rubbed his thumb over the polished antler. Spots of blood stained the arrow engraving. "Anna," he whispered.

The leather of the pendant was twisted around a root, and he gave it a tug.

"Crap!" he yelled as rope whistled through the leaves, and a bent hickory sapling sprang up beside him. The snare's loop closed around both of his feet, and snatched him from the ground and swung him.

"The damn place is booby trapped," he said and his head hit the boulder.

Chapter Forty-Five

Zachary Dyer's Homestead, Devil's Peak, WV
Brodie

The man paced back and forth on the splintered wood floor planning his next move. He'd expended too much time and effort on Leigh and, so far, it was all for nothing. The bitch didn't even remember him. Everything they'd shared meant nothing to her.

He sat down and placed his elbows on the table, then cupped his face in his hands. He was so weary. Too exhausted to finish what needed to be done. His head pounded. How was he supposed to think his way through this? Leigh's betrayal broke his spirit, and only the thought of revenge sustained him. It was clear that her thirst for him was quenched, but he'd make sure no others drank from that well.

Now he had lover boy to take care of—Leigh's wannabe hero. He should've stayed out of it, but the Dyer family always had trouble minding their own business. He would pay the price for all of them, past, present and future, but his time was short. The others would be here soon. He didn't know if he could fight them all, even fighting dirty…fighting bloody.

A grunt from behind him signaled the beginning of playtime. He smiled, and turned to face the waking teenager. His competition…yeah sure, as if…he laughed and stepped over to him. He bent down until his nose was inches from his hostage's, and felt Garren's breath against his face. He watched him wake, his eyes opening into slits, and then flaring open as his focus cleared. The rope held him upside down from a pulley attached to a ceiling joist.

His arms flopped around the floor like a fish tossed into a boat.

"Brodie? What the hell is wrong with you? Where's Anna? What did you do with her?"

A tingling awareness scratched at the man's mind when addressed by that boy's name. His eyes rolled back in his head, and he whispered to the defeated boy inside his head. *"It's too late for regrets, boy. Retribution doesn't come cheap, Brodie. Enjoy our revenge, brother."*

He turned back to his prisoner, and watched him squirming on the rope.

"How do you feel? It's Garren, right? I can't imagine what it's like hanging upside down like that. Is it uncomfortable?"

"Where is Anna? What did you do to her?"

"Anna? Is that Leigh's nickname here? Don't worry yourself, brother, or excuse me—cousin I believe, but I think you have more pressing concerns."

The man smiled, and pulled a hunting knife from his belt. In one smooth move, the knife flashed through the air and pressed against Garren's throat.

"Any last requests?"

"Yes, let Anna go. She's done nothing to you. You don't even know her."

"Ah, still trying to play the hero? Or martyr, given the situation."

The man drew the knife's edge across his neck, piercing the outer layer of skin. He held the blade up and admired the thin smear of blood. Licking the blade clean, he looked Garren in the eye.

"Come on then, hero." He slashed the rope holding Garren's feet to the ceiling. "Let's see if you can measure up to the part."

As Garren tried to stand, the man sheathed his knife then kicked him in the knee, driving him to the ground. Garren reached for a chair to pull himself up, and the man kicked the chair away. He drove his elbow into the back of Garren's head.

"Sucker punches," Garren shouted. "You pick on women, and can't fight a man fair."

Brodie grinned widely, and bowed extravagantly. He held that pose as Garren stood on wobbly legs. Once facing him, Brodie growled and charged! Garren side-stepped and stretched out his leg, sending the man sprawling. The move proved too much for a twisted knee, and as the man fell forward, Garren followed, landing neatly in his lap.

Again the knife flashed, and the man tucked it under Garren's chin pulling his hair back to expose his neck.

"You lose, but at least you'll see Leigh soon. You can tell her Zachary said hello."

Chapter Forty-Six

Zachary Dyer's Homestead, Devil's Peak, WV
Anna

She had no way to measure the passage of time in the darkness, and she suspected she'd lost consciousness as well. Her vision slowly acclimated to her prison, and tiny laser-thin shafts of moonlight crept through the planks of the door above her. Nothing was clearly visible, but she could make out vague shapes now. It reminded Anna of her grandfather's sweat lodge, but no good memories would be made here. She continued pushing at the gag with her tongue until she gagged on her own saliva. That's when she recognized the scent filling her nostrils. But why would Brodie put peanut butter in her prison?

She shifted her weight to turn herself into a human pendulum, and lifted her legs to determine the size of the enclosure. Her knees struck rock or concrete on either side of her. She guessed the walls to be about four feet wide. Her dangling feet did not touch the ground.

A whispering, scratching noise caught her ear, the sound of small furtive creatures scurrying about, sharing her jail. Something tickled her hand as it squeaked its way to her arms and down to her shoulders. She screamed then, loud enough to render her throat raw and long enough to leave her gasping for air. Still, little sound escaped her makeshift gag. As for the mouse, her squeal sent it scurrying away in fright—for a moment. But the rodent's curiosity was piqued, and it returned to examine her mouth with its tiny paws and whiskers.

She gagged, and twisted her head from side to side. The mouse fell away, only to grip her ear firmly in its teeth.

Tears streamed down her cheeks before the mouse decided to move on to more stable footing. It ran over her chest and over her pants leg to her shoe before realizing it couldn't go further. It retraced its steps, running all the way up her body, stopping to sniff at her hands. Anna quivered with revulsion.

More scratching announced the arrival of the creature's friends. She watched transfixed as furry forms raced up and down the rope and over her body. Mice, and animals too large to be mice, met at her hands and fought at the rope for position. *Rats!* But she didn't want to look too closely.

Small fibers of rope drifted down on her. The rodents were eating their way to her freedom! Looking up, she spotted six different animals chewing away, and watched them until a filament fell into her eyes. She rubbed at the ropes, feeling a pasty substance, and suspected she knew the source of the peanut butter smell.

Brodie must have known this would happen. Why did he smear gobs of the stuff on her ropes? Did he want the mice to chew her loose? Maybe he wanted her to get away, or maybe…

"Moll, where are you? I need you…"

She kicked at the walls of her prison, sending the vermin running. The familiar splashing of disturbed water bounced off the rock walls. She kicked again, harder and listened. One second, two seconds, and plop, plop! The stones hit the water a long way below her and confirmed her suspicions. The bastard had her hanging in an abandoned well!

She hung her head praying for an answer, but only the rats seemed to hear. Bolder than the mice, they latched on to the rope and worked vigorously, ignoring every effort she made to dislodge them. Only an occasional fight among them slowed their progress, and chewed rope rained down on her.

She flipped several away with her fingertips sending them diving into the water below. Then one brash rat bit down and held on, chewing the knuckle of her index finger. The combined scents of peanuts and blood drove them into a frenzy, and brought more mice out of hiding for the feast. A strand of the rope broke free, and she dropped several inches as it stretched.

She screamed again, but the only sound was the gnawing of tiny sharp teeth.

Chapter Forty-Seven

Zachary Dyer's Homestead, Devil's Peak, WV
Garren

Every moment he could stall Brodie gave him another chance to get out of this alive. He had to delay him, then get him outside where there might be an opportunity to escape. During their short fight, he'd heard scraping outside, probably a squirrel, but *maybe* the shuffling of feet on the porch floorboards? It could be Anna or even help coming from the cabin. He needed some small fantasy, some hope to cling to! His earlier plea to Brodie worked, and was worth trying again. Whether it appealed to Brodie's sense of fairness or an overdeveloped machismo to show he was the one in charge, it was the only tactic he had.

He swallowed, and his Adam's apple moved up and down, bumping against Brodie's knife blade. "Wait," he said. "My last request. I want to see Anna. That would be the noble thing to do."

Brodie paused as if considering the request, then turned the blade and pressed the blunt edge against his throat. He reached back and grabbed the bolt-action rifle leaning against the wall.

"Local deer hunter killed with his own gun. Wouldn't that make for a great story?" Brodie smiled and pushed the rifle barrel in to his back. "Let's take a walk then."

Brodie walked behind him, poking him with the gun whenever he moved too slowly.

"Open the door slowly," Brodie said.

He crept through the door and out into the moonlight.

"Which way? Where is she?" he asked.

A bright light flashed in front of him, and blinded him. A shot echoed through the hills and instinct took over. He dropped to the porch floor.

"Get down!" a woman yelled. He rolled forward and fell from the porch to the ground. He turned toward Brodie, anticipating his attack, but Brodie just stared at his hand. The hand holding the gun was dripping blood. Brodie shook his head.

He saw Brodie's face change, the darkness gone. The years dropped away and the light returned to his eyes. He became the Brodie he knew again. The Brodie standing tall defending him in Nickel's bar. The prank pulling, joke telling Brodie of their youth.

"I'm sorry, Cuz," Brodie said. "Gotta do this now." He pulled his knife from its sheath and held it over his head poised to strike…then froze.

"Stop, Brodie, don't move!" the woman yelled.

Brodie winked at him and gestured towards him with the blade. There was another camera-like flash of light, the bark of a gun, and Brodie's knife fell to the ground. Blood spurted from his chest as he fell to his knees. He looked surprised as blood seeped through his fingers. There was pain in his face, yet it was a look of relief and peace, not agony, that settled on his face.

"Thank you, Diana." He fell to his side and looked toward the approaching footsteps.

"Mika," he said. "I made some killer stew, didn't I?"

"Where is she, Brodie? What have you done with my Anna?"

Brodie looked sad and confused at the question.

"Anna? Who's Anna? There was a Leigh…?"

Diana reached the shack, and levered another cartridge into her rifle.

"Garren, are you okay?" He nodded. His mother pulled a bandana from her pocket and bent over Brodie. She pressed the cloth against his wound.

"Oh dear God Mika, this isn't good, he needs a doctor right now."

Mika reached down and shook Brodie.

"He's going to tell me what he's done with Anna! Where is she, you son of a bitch?"

"Stop, Mika," Diana whispered. "Look."

He looked over Mika's shoulder. Brodie's eyes misted over, and rolled back in his head.

"It's too late for the doctor." Diana reached out to slide Brodie's eyelids closed.

"Dear Brodie, what have we done to you? Forgive us."

Diana turned to Garren. "Henry and Jim went for the police." She hugged him with a hunger born of a mother's despair, making no attempt to hide her tears. Garren pulled her close.

"I'm fine, Mom. Just bumps, bruises, and sprains— nothing serious. Thanks to you."

"Around here, everyone," Mika yelled. "The coast is clear!"

"Who else is up here?" he asked his mother.

"Chris, Lenore, and Bridget," Mika said, "we circled the place."

Diana held her son at arm's length, and smiled.

"I don't know what happened to him, Mom. He was like a madman. He even spoke in a different voice—like he was someone else."

Diana frowned and shook her head. "Did Brodie say anything to you about Anna? Did he say anything at all?"

"No, he said he was taking me to her when you… when we came out. I don't even know which direction to look in."

Chris and Bridget approached from behind the shack, and Lenore's flashlight bobbed toward them from the other side.

"Hey buddy, good to see you. Oh…" Chris stumbled over Brodie's body.

Lenore appeared from the other side of the shack. "Where's Anna?" she asked.

He noticed her eyes widen in shock as they discovered Brodie Caine's crumpled body, and she turned her head away. She wiped at her eyes with her shirtsleeve, and turned back to face the group.

"You okay?" he asked.

She looked him up and down. "Yeah, but man, you look like hell."

He laughed, and she gave him a quick hug.

"Anna?" she repeated.

"We don't know where she is, and we have to find her soon."

Mika took a step forward. "Let's split up in pairs and look for any sign of her, Chris and Bridget, Diana and Lenore, and Garren with me. The police will be here soon to help. Let's spread out." Diana grabbed Garren's arm and pulled him aside.

"What did you leave out? You said we have to find her 'soon.'"

"I didn't want to tell Mika, but it was something Brodie said. He was about to slit my throat. He said I'd join Leigh shortly, and to tell her hello for him."

Chapter Forty-Eight

He would tell Diana, and throw himself at her mercy. Plead for her understanding and forgiveness, and pray every day for the return of her trust and love. He knew the knowledge would wound her deeply, scar her heart permanently, but he was unable to keep this dark secret from her. Even if capable of such deception, it would ferment in his soul and poison them all. He had to be a man and face the consequences, whatever came to him. If Diana forever cast him from her life, he deserved no better.

Zachary Dyer's Homestead, Devil's Peak, WV
Anna

She feared she might never see another mountain sunrise. Far from defeated, she'd fight for her life with every breath, but as long as she gave it her best, she'd accept whatever came. A strange peace and renewed determination settled over her with that understanding.

Her teeth ached from gritting them with every renewed attack of the rodents. Blood from her chewed hands reached to her elbows, and the diminishing effects of the tea gave the blood a yellowish glow.

The gnawing nearly drove her mad before she discovered the secret. She learned if she wiggled her hands and fingers slowly, the pests avoided them. Too quickly though, and they felt threatened and became more aggressive. For now, the rodents were distracted from her hands, and nibbled at the peanut butter with renewed vigor.

She'd heard gunshots, and once thought she heard someone yell, but the sounds were distant, distorted and vague inside the hole. She didn't know if people came to help her, or if Brodie was back to hurt her. Did he kill her friends? She decided to make all the noise the gag would allow. Humming and repeated grunting was the best she could do, and her throat became raw and sore from the effort.

She kicked at the walls, but feared putting too much pressure on the rope. Another strand broke free, leaving half of the rope's original thickness. She knew the odds of surviving a plunge to the bottom weren't good. The well was very old, and she doubted it held enough water to break her fall—even without the summer's drought.

The pace of the rats' munching increased, her time was close. Something needed to be done.

"*Remember?*"

"Moll? Where have you been?

"*I'm sorry, sweet girl. I had to help him remember.*"

"Who?"

"*It doesn't matter now.*"

"Are you here to help me? They've almost chewed through the rope. He put peanut butter on it as bait, Moll."

"*I'm here to help you help yourself. Do you remember what you did with Lenore?*"

"With the deer and the birds?"

"*Yes. Think, Anna. What's the bane of a mouse's existence?*"

What would scare them off, and keep them off? If she couldn't do that, she'd fall and die. It was that simple. A snake! There was no better mouser! They were the bane of the rodent's existence!

"I can't, Moll. I don't know how without Lenore to guide me."

"*You can, but I'll hold your hand. We'll do it together.*"

She felt a light electric touch on her hand. It warmed her skin and a new peace settled over her.

With the number of rats and mice in the hole, a snake had to be lurking nearby. She reached deep within herself trying to find her spirit's essence…her soul. She felt the tug on her hand and held on, floating up and out of the well.

Chapter Forty-Nine

Zachary Dyer's Homestead, Devil's Peak, WV
Garren

Revolving red and blue lights flashed around the shack as the state troopers arrived on the scene.

"Guess I better go fill them in, Garren," Mika said. "I hope they brought the hounds. We're no closer to finding her than we were an hour ago."

He watched Mika's retreating back as he limped toward the troopers. He continued examining the forest floor for any clues while yelling Anna's name. He was careful to avoid kicking up leaves or disturbing any sign, but there were few places they hadn't checked and rechecked.

He felt a void settle in his chest that squeezed the breath from his lungs as a wave of awareness washed over him. For the first time, he realized how much Anna meant to him and he choked back a sob. The world would be dark without her and he felt ashamed he wasn't there for her—again. But he knew in his heart she was alive; she had to be. He couldn't imagine any other option. Sucking up the pain, he called her name.

Jim and Henry arrived in Jim's truck and parked behind the police vehicles. Chris headed their way to update them on the search. He could hear snippets of conversation, and heard confusion in the officers' voices.

"Have you seen Lenore?" Diana asked behind him.

"No, don't tell me she's lost too?"

"She's probably with Brie. She said she needed to ask her something. We nearly walked into a pit trap, and the bottom of it was filled with sharpened spikes. We need to be careful and watch our steps."

"Garren!" Chris yelled. "Over here."

They both ran to where Chris and the others were gathered around the shack. Diana threw her arms up in the air. "Where's Brodie?"

He bent down to inspect the ground in front of the men, and saw only spots of blood where he'd fallen.

One of the officers touched him on the shoulder. "Mr. Doyle? We'd like you to step inside with us and tell us everything that's happened."

"Yes, sir, but I want to find Anna first."

"Are you refusing to cooperate, Mr. Doyle?"

"Not at all, but…"

"We're hoping your description of the events will help lead us to her, Mr. Doyle."

"Okay, let's hurry then." He stood and stepped toward the shack. Diana followed.

"Mrs. Doyle, if you would just wait outside, please?"

"My son is a minor, and I have a right to be there during any questioning."

"Yes, ma'am, but we think it will help find the girl if we can talk to him alone."

Diana looked at Garren and he nodded. "It's okay, Mom. Anything that helps find Anna."

He followed the two policemen inside. They sat him down and asked for his version of what happened. He related everything from his fall off the cliff to Brodie getting shot outside the cabin, as well as their search parameters for Anna.

"Mr. Doyle, we understand your concern for your friend, and from everything you described, you've been through a lot. Is there anything else you would like to tell us? Anything you might not want the others to know? We can protect you."

"What? No sir, I don't think so."

The policemen snapped handcuffs on one of his wrists.

"Am I under arrest?"

"No sir, but we can't have another witness disappear; and some of your story just doesn't add up. Why would this boy…your cousin? Why would he tie you up in the ravine if he planned to kill you anyway? Then later, he could have cracked your head open when you were unconscious, and no one would be the wiser. Your body wouldn't be found for twenty years. Why go traipsing around the woods with you in tow? To show you where his other victim was hidden? When according to you, you'd already given him considerable trouble? Then he's shot, by your own mother no less, in front of all of you, and he disappears without a trace?"

"He had some kind of psychotic break, officer. He acted like someone else."

"I've got blood in the shack, blood out here on the ground, and a missing girl. As if that isn't enough, I'm told there's another body down in a ravine. I can't take any chances until we get this sorted out. Sorry, son."

The cops walked him out to the porch, and snapped the other end of the cuffs to a corner porch post. Diana hurried to her son's side.

"What the hell is going on, officers? I shot him, not Garren!"

"Yes ma'am, we know." The officer snapped Diana's left wrist in cuffs and attached the other end to an eyebolt on the porch post. "We're just taking precautions until we get this thing straightened out and find the girl. You and your boy aren't under arrest—yet. You can consider it protective custody."

Mika stepped forward. "What's going on?"

"Please back away, sir. This is a precaution for now, but Mrs. Doyle already confessed to the shooting anyway."

"Okay, so Garren had nothing to do with the shooting or Anna's kidnapping. Anna couldn't wait to see him when she got here. They were…they *are* friends, and we need all the eyes and ears we can get."

"I understand, sir. Now please back off."

A dark shadow passed over Mika's face, and he turned and stomped away.

He turned his attention to the others gathering near the porch. "Don't worry about us guys, just go find Anna, please."

He settled on the porch, and turned his awareness inward, allowing his mind to drift. He felt worthless—sitting doing nothing while Anna was out there somewhere *needing* him. The search moved away from the shack. He could still hear the searchers calling Anna's name, the beams from their flashlights worked steadily away from him.

Whispered female voices came from beyond the porch, but he couldn't see the speakers. Anna's name was spoken, but he couldn't hear the context. He listened intently, and recognized the voices belonging to Bridget and Lenore.

"Hey guys, what's going on? Has anyone found anything?"

The girl's heads popped out around from the side of the porch.

"No, nothing, no sign of Anna," Lenore said. "We don't know what to do." She looked at Bridget and when she nodded, Lenore continued. "Look, we're trying something…different. Something Anna's taught us."

"Anna and Lenore," Bridget chimed in.

"Anyway, you'll need to be quiet so we can really concentrate, okay?"

He nodded his head, and the girls moved closer and sat on the ground in front of the porch. They held each other's hands tightly and closed their eyes. He could see the intensity of their concentration. They whispered Anna's name over and over, almost as a chant.

"Where are you Anna? We're here for you," Lenore said.

"Help us to find you, Anna."

Diana twisted her head to see what was going on. "Are they trying to do what I think they are?" He pursed his lips to indicate the need for quiet, and she sat beside him.

"I guess it can't hurt."

Tears oozed from Lenore's eyes, and she shook them away in frustration.

"It's not working, Bridget. What are we doing wrong?"

"I don't know a lot about this sort of thing," Diana said, "but Mika tried to teach Adam some of the old ways. I think you're too tense. You have to relax and open your minds, and I think it works better when there's three. Come sit by me." Her left wrist in handcuffs, she held out her right and both of the young women grabbed it.

"Do you have anything belonging to her?"

They shook their heads no.

"Hey, I have something in my pocket," he said.

Lenore walked to the other end of the porch, reached into Garren's pocket, and pulled out Anna's antler amulet.

"Will this work?" She held the necklace up for Diana to see.

"Perfect. Thank you."

Lenore rejoined them, and again held their hands.

"Shall we try again?" Diana asked.

The girls nodded their heads vigorously. "Let's do it."

He saw the same look of concentration pass over their faces, but now his mother led the chant.

"Anna, where are you, girl? We're searching for you. Show us where you are." They looked lost inside their own minds, and after whispering her name for some time, the three grew silent. Bridget scrunched up her nose as if smelling something unpleasant.

"It stinks," she said. "It's old, and wet."

"Rats, oh my God, there's rats," Diana said.

Lenore broke away from their circle. "We need to find her now, she's about to fall."

"Where is she?" he shouted.

"I felt her fear. She's in a hole, a deep hole, there's blood and she's tied up and about to fall. Is there a place like that?"

"Maybe an old abandoned well? I don't remember one, but if there is one, I'll bet Mika remembers," Diana said.

"Mika, we need you!" she yelled.

He saw Mika running up the hill toward them ignoring his limp, but his flashlight swayed to and fro.

"Where is she?" Mika yelled.

"Is there an old well?"

"Yes! Dear God, yes, I remember one. We had to board it up so nothing fell in and got trapped."

"Where is it?" Diana asked, but Mika turned away and waved his flashlight for them to follow.

Chapter Fifty

Zachary Dyer's Homestead, Devil's Peak, WV
Anna

The snake curled lazily in its hole resisting her efforts to wake it. She began to doubt her ability to pull the reptile from its slumbers. Finally it responded, emerging from the deep layers of leaves and soil—lethargic, but still menacing to the denizens of the well. As the snake's head slithered through an opening in the boards above her, the rodents squealed in fear and dashed off in every direction. Her efforts were successful.

Frayed fibers of rope continued to stretch, inching her towards death, and she feared she'd only delayed the inevitable. Looking overhead, she was amazed such a small thickness of rope could hold her weight…but for how long?

The snake curled around her tightly, not threatening, but sharing her body's warmth.

She'd done everything that could be done. She couldn't think of anything that would have changed the fate waiting for her below. Some consolation.

The snake lifted its head to look at her, and then at the rope. Anna heard the sickening snap, and felt the weightless descent.

Chapter Fifty-One

Adam floored the gas pedal on the old jeep, anxious to be home. They had to get past this, somehow, whatever the cost. Neither of his children would be raised without a father.

The deer leapt from the shrouded depths of the woods into the road. Adam swung the steering wheel to avoid it, and felt the rear end sway. He sighed as the vehicle caught traction and squeezed past the animal lightly brushing its hip. He glanced in the rearview mirror to ensure it was unhurt, and heard the sickening crunch as he collided with the second unseen deer.

The jeep ricocheted down the embankment, rolling five times, coming to a rest against a giant sycamore tree at the bottom. As the sound of the crash subsided, the call of the searching whippoorwill broke the silence. Drawing his last breath, Adam heard its mate answer and a lone tear journeyed down his cheek.

Physical pain left him as he floated above his crushed and lifeless body, but his soul ached with the knowledge of all he'd miss… and for what he'd done.

**Zachary Dyer's Homestead, Devil's Peak, WV
Garren**

He tried to catch any snippets of conversation that reached him. The search moved beyond his vision, but the moving beams of light clearly defined the advance.

He'd never felt so frustrated and helpless. Days seemed to pass as he waited, and the world continued to revolve while he sat incapacitated and weary.

Mika's voice floated up to him. "I know it's in here somewhere. Spread out here and kick away the leaves, the opening is probably covered over."

"Did anyone bring rope?" Diana's voice.

"There's some in the shack up here," he yelled, but heard no answer.

The flashlights weaved back and forth aimlessly finding nothing. Mika's recollection of the well's location seemed imprecise. Lights still moved over a 75 square yard area.

He twisted against the handcuffs wanting to join the search now more than ever. His wrists were raw from his frustrated attempts to work free. It wasn't right what they were doing to him. Anna needed him. He heard footsteps in the leaves behind him, but couldn't see anyone.

"Who is it? Help me get loose." He felt a tug on his wrists.

"Look kid," the young policeman said. "Sargent Moore is a stickler for protocol. I've been collecting evidence inside, and watching you. I know you didn't have anything to do with this missing girl, and we need every set of eyes and ears we can get. I'm going to take a chance and let you out of these. You run off on me or dime me out and I will shoot you. Any part of that you don't understand?"

He shook his head vigorously, and hearing the cuffs click open, offered his thanks, leapt from the porch and hobbled toward the others. He stopped, ran back to the shack as the officer was giving the same speech to Diana. He grabbed a length of rope, and tied it around his waist as he ran. To escape the darkness closing in on his life, he ran toward the lights—towards Anna.

Chapter Fifty-Two

Zachary Dyer's Homestead, Devil's Peak, WV
Anna

Free falling, she instinctively threw out her legs, and her knees and ankles dragged at the walls of the well. Her head bounced backwards and bright flecks of multi-colored light flashed in her eyes and she fought to retain consciousness. A black out now meant death. The cloth of her jeans offered minor protection from the jagged rocks, and skin scraped away from her kneecaps. Pushing against the walls, ignoring the pain, her descent slowed and stopped abruptly when one knee slammed into a protruding rock, sucking away her breath.

Tears flowed from her eyes. She couldn't hold her position for long. She looked up and estimated she had fallen about five feet. The bottom of the well still waited for her far below.

She wondered about the others. Lenore surely found Garren, and she felt a momentary pinprick of pain in her chest at the thought, but they weren't meant to be together. He'd made it clear he thought of her as a sister, and nothing more. Bridget and Chris were probably sitting around the fire gazing deeply into each other's eyes. She smiled at the thought...then felt them!

Her grandfather, Diana, Lenore, Bridget, and Garren, she felt them all—close! They were here for her, but it was too late. She squeezed her fingers in.

"You're still here, Moll. Will you be there to meet me on the other side?"

"*I will, but that day needn't be today, child.*"

"Thank you, Moll, for all you've done. For raising the curtain and letting me see. It's been an honor."

"*My dearest friend Bluebird, my brave Ada, my strong-willed Leigh and last but never least, my sweet beloved Anna. By all those names, I've loved you since our time began.*"

The snake unwrapped itself from her shoulders and lifted its head toward the well opening, as if listening. She followed its gaze and heard the sounds. Voices calling out for her, closer now.

Rodent hairs tickled her nose, and she sneezed violently and the gag flew from her mouth!

Chapter Fifty-Three

Zachary Dyer's Homestead, Devil's Peak, WV
Garren

He kicked the leaves violently, angrily. She was near, he sensed her, could almost smell her breath, yet she eluded him. He stepped to his left to attack another section of ground cover, and heard her voice.

"Garren!"

He jumped in the direction of her voice and twisted his ankle painfully. He bent down and touched wood planks.

"Anna!"

"Yes, hurry. I can hardly hold on."

He brushed away the leaves, and pulled at the door of the well and found it locked. He beat at the boards with his fists, and yelled for the others.

"Help me! She's here!"

Splinters formed in the boards, and pierced his knuckles as he continued his assault. A piece broke away, and he inserted his fingers and pried a board loose.

"We're coming Anna. Hold on!"

He kicked at the door opening with his good leg, and grinned as another board flipped away. The sounds of the others closed in around him. He tossed the end of the rope towards them and wedged himself into the opening.

"Mika, grab the rope!" Without waiting, he levered himself down, gripping the edges of the well walls with his hands and knees, and plunged into the darkness.

"Anna?"

"Careful Garren or we'll both go down. I don't have much to cling to."

"Garren, we've got the rope," Mika yelled from above. He worked his way down the well, and slid in front of her. He felt around with his feet until he found a solid perch.

"Put your arms around my neck while I tie you on to the rope." He untied himself and tenderly worked the rope under her arms, and began to tie it behind her. He felt something brush against his neck, and moved his head and stared into reptilian eyes.

"Oh shit, a snake!" His feet slipped, and he twisted precariously in the air, holding on by his hands. He wiggled himself back into position in front of her and regained his footholds. He reached out and caught the snake behind the head, and pulled it away from her. It wrapped itself around his arm, and he shook it.

"Garren, don't hurt it, please?"

The snake draped itself over his neck. His knees quivered, but he bit back the fear, reached behind her and finished the knot.

"It's going to be okay, Anna," he said. A tear tickled his cheek, and he bent forward. Gently touching his lips to hers, her arms circled his waist. "Did I ever mention I love you?"

"It must have slipped your mind," she said.

"Pull her up, Mika!"

Her mouth soundlessly formed the words, "Me too," as she was pulled up and out of his arms.

Chapter Fifty-Four

Hampshire Memorial Hospital, WV
Anna

She moved her eyes around the room, savoring the presence of her friends. They looked like a pack of refugees from a war zone. Parents and guardians waited in the hallway engrossed in different interpretations of everything that happened, and trying to piece it all together. Her arms were attached to the emergency room wall by tubes running to IV bags. Both her dehydration and the mushroom tea needed to be alleviated. Garren sat in the bed beside her, his knee swollen to an unnatural size. The dried crusty blood traversing his neck marked the trail of Brodie's blade. It looked worse than it was, he'd assured her. Chris had the coloring of a ghost, the lingering remnant of his experience with Brodie's stew. Bridget's eyelids grew heavier with every blink, but she discovered that the more exhausted her friend was, the more she had to say.

Lenore entered the room, glanced at Garren holding her hand and smiled.

"Sit here, Lenore." She patted the edge of her bed. Multiple scratches covered Lenore's fair skin, but otherwise, she was none the worse for wear.

"I have something for you, Anna." Reaching into her pocket, she withdrew the antler pendant. A new strip of leather bootlace, purchased in the gift shop, turned it into a necklace again. Lenore slipped it around her neck.

"I'm so sorry for everything," she whispered.

"Stop." Lenore silently mouthed the word. "They gave me the okay to go home. I'll stop by your grandfather's cabin in the morning, and grab you a shirt.

You might get arrested if you leave here wearing the pieces of the one you checked in with."

"You'd have no shortage of escorts though." Bridget laughed.

"Did they find any sign of Brodie?" Chris asked.

"No, they said it's like he dropped off the face of the planet. I'm not even sure they believe there was a Brodie, and that we didn't make up the whole thing," Lenore said.

"It's all so unreal. You guys sure know how to throw a party!" Chris yawned. "But I'm done in. If you don't mind, I'm going to call it a night. Can we give you a ride home, Brie?"

"Hmm, maybe not. I'd love to, but my dad's waiting on me. I know crap's gonna hit the fan over my skipping and I want to get it over with." Bridget and Chris stood to leave.

"We'll wait in the car for you, Lenore," Chris said. "We'll be back in the morning, Anna. Stay out of trouble."

Lenore slid off the bed, walked over to Garren and reached down for a hug. "You did well, buddy. Are we still friends after the drop kick?"

"My kind of woman," he replied. "Hey, I wouldn't be here without you."

"C'mon, my turn." She held out her arms.

"I wasn't going to forget you, Anna."

When Lenore embraced her, she whispered, "Lenore, I didn't…"

Lenore whispered back. "Hush, I already know what you're thinking, Anna. I told you it wasn't that kind of dream. Besides, you saw him first, sister, but just in case, you might need this." She winked and placed something in Anna's hand. She stood and left with a mischievous smile on her lips, and a glow in her eyes.

"What was that about?" Garren asked.

"Oh it was nothing, just girl talk." She smiled, rubbing the raccoon bone necklace.

***

Floating and weightless, he shook his head in confusion. He listened, but the voice in his head was gone! Zachary, the dark man, was gone. He ran his hand over his chest. There was no bullet hole, no blood. Was it all a dream? No. He'd made sure that Aunt Diana had no recourse but to shoot him...to end Zachary. But where was he? Heaven? Or the other place? Please not the other place...

A quick bright light, like a flash from distant lightning, and a man stood before him. He no longer floated, but the gravity was different here...lighter.

"Who are you? Where am I?" he asked the man.

"My name is Adam."

The man held out his hand and he snatched it in a tight grip.

"We've missed out on so much, you and me. We have a lot to catch up on and I want to know everything. And we have eternity, Son."

A rectangular glow appeared behind the man. "What's that behind you?"

"A doorway they've opened to welcome you. The rest of your family is waiting there—even dear old Moll. Shall we go meet them, Brodie?"

Hand in hand they proceeded together, chattering away like long lost friends. As father and son passed through the doorway's embrace, it throbbed like a beating heart and closed soundlessly behind them.

The End

Author's Afterword

With this third book and the conclusion of the series, I'd like to respond to my readers' questions about the origin and historical accuracy of the characters and events in the 'Legends of the Family Dyer' trilogy.

***

Beginning with **'Sister Witch,'** the historical evidence is scarce and anecdotal due to a courthouse fire in the late 1600s. However, there's evidence of two Mary Dyers (Moll being a common nickname) arriving in Maryland during this period. There's a colonist's letter stating 'Moll Dyer has a countenance so ugly it hurts to behold her.' Further circumstantial evidence includes a road bearing her name, the infamous rock bearing her marks, and Moll Dyer Run— a small stream traversing what's said to be the site of the original Dyer homestead.

The legend of Moll Dyer, however, is considerable. She was known for her curative prowess, as well as her lack of social graces. She traded herbal remedies with local Native Americans and it's said she enjoyed their companionship over that of her own people. These traits, combined with catastrophic crop failure from drought, an outbreak of disease, and a superstitious citizenry, spelled Moll's doom. The colonists rose up against her, proclaiming her a witch.

On the coldest winter night in 1697, they formed a mob (encouraged by the colonial governor) and set Moll's cabin ablaze. She fled to the woods to escape her tormentors. Days later, a young lad, searching for his missing cow, stumbled upon Moll's lifeless body, bent over a large rock at the river's edge, frozen. When Moll's body was wrenched away, the rock retained the marks of her knees and palm. This 300-pound rock now sits in the courtyard of the county courthouse with a simple plaque proclaiming it 'Moll Dyer's Rock.'

Moll's story, 'Sister Witch' is a culmination of the known facts about her integrated with the ancestral oral traditions of long-time residents of the area. Disregarding paranormal elements, colonial life and associated historical events are accurately portrayed.

***

'**H**is **Father's Blood**' follows John Dyer, a fictional descendant of Moll Dyer approximately 100 years after her demise. Some local folklore regarding Moll's life (and death) states that a male family member was associated with her in the Maryland colony. Oral tradition is split on this point. Some local families' version claim Moll was alone in her colonial misfortunes; others name this shadowy male figure as either a brother or son. I accepted the veracity of the latter version in this, book two of the trilogy.

According to the son theory, Moll's scion left the Southern Maryland area and followed the displaced Native Americans northwest into the mountains along the headwaters of the Potomac River. The paranormal powers attributed to John Dyer are drawn from the legends of these mountains—originating from both early white settlers and the Native Americans of the area.

Moll makes an appearance toward the end, having never forgotten her family ties—even in death.

***

Fast forwarding another hundred years from 'His Father's Blood,' the reader is introduced to additional (unknowing) descendants of Moll Dyer. In this book, **'Sons and Brothers,'** the setting begins in the Dyer's ancestral home, a land not so drastically changed from Moll's colonial times. Moving from there into John's beloved mountains, we observe the disparate fortunes of the family after three centuries.

As in the other installments, Moll Dyer is the thread that flows through and connects the narratives. Transforming from pariah and accused witch into a protective entity and culminating here as a spirit guide, her story binds the Dyer family and this trilogy.

Moll and I hope you've enjoyed this sojourn into her world. I thank you for your support and wish the best for you and yours always, David W. Thompson.

About David W. Thompson

David W. Thompson is an award winning author, a native of Southern Maryland, and a graduate of University of Maryland, University College. David's love of the written word began early in life. He claims his first writing effort was "Dick and Jane" fan fiction when he was six years old-no doubt with a dark twist!

After his family and cheesecake, reading was his first love. It exposed him to people, cultures and ideas he'd never experience otherwise. Writing was a natural extension of this "out of body" experience as characters act as tour guides to their worlds, and their possibilities. He hopes to honestly convey the stories that they whisper in his ears.

When he isn't writing, Dave enjoys time with his family and grandchildren, kayaking (mostly flat water please), fishing, hiking, archery, wine-making, and pursuing his other "creative passion"- woodcarving.

For more on Dave, his current releases and upcoming WIP, check out his site at: https://www.dthompsonwrites.com/

Often bloody, habitually dark, always original!

Acknowledgements

To the many folks who've contributed to this book (some unknowingly), and names too numerous to mention… I thank you.

To my dear wife, Ter, for tolerating the lengthy periods I spend in the fantasy world of my characters—oblivious to the here and now.

To my good friend, Old Crow (AKA Larry O.) of beautiful Grant County, WV for allowing me to steal some of his more colorful mountain colloquialisms, as well as borrowing his Dad's tall tale about the Peach Tree Buck. I appreciate it, my friend.

To Lee and Patty, on the precipice of the WV Eastern Continental Divide, I appreciate your wonderful hospitality in allowing this flatlander to experience the deer camp tradition, unknown in my part of our great nation. Happy 50th anniversary!

To Jason Thompson of La Dolce Vita Photography Studios for the fabulous cover image.

To my publisher, Solstice Publishing for taking a chance on me from the beginning. Melissa, K.C. and Kate- you guys rock. Thanks to my wonderful editor Brian for the many corrections of my boo-boos, typos, and…

Thanks to all for making this novel (and the series) possible.

If you enjoyed this story, check out these other Solstice Publishing books by David W. Thompson:

Sister Witch

1st place winner of the Golden Quill Award for Fantasy and 1st place (Magical Realism) in the Ed/Pred reader's poll. Official Selection of New Apple and Reader's Favorite contests.

Moll Dyer wants to leave her troubles behind when she immigrates to the New World... but even an ocean cannot keep the Dyer family curse from following her! Wanting only to find peace, she fights injustice in a new land founded on tolerance, but ruled by bigotry. In 1607, the ancient enemy returns, and Moll takes a stand. 300 years later, is the world finally ready for Moll's story?

Life in the British colonies is tough on man and woman. Hunger, disease, Indian attacks, and drought test the resolve of the settlers daily. But troubles for the Dyers include another threat. In this land of religious fervor, devastating sickness, and persistent greed, can Moll turn back the evil alliance formed against her and her bloodline? Or will hell's bloody wrath extinguish her dream of a new life in the New World? How far will she go to protect her family and their world?

Faith despite Betrayal. Courage in the face of Injustice. The triumph of love.

The legend of Moll Dyer originated in earliest colonial Maryland. Despite 300 years of civilization, and the advent of scientific reason, Moll's name is still often heard there, especially around campfires late at night, or as a warning to misbehaving little people. Her spirit is often seen as a wisp of unnatural fog in the swampy woodlands near her homestead, with her half-wolf companion at her side.

https://www.amazon.com/gp/product/B076KR626G/

His Father's Blood

1st place in P&E's 2018 Reader's Poll for Magical Realism novel of the year. Literary Titan's Gold Medal for 2018!

The demonic force that's cursed the Dyer family for generations has returned even stronger! Defeated by Moll Dyer a century earlier, the demon Laris lays claim to another Dyer child.

Homesteading on Devil's Peak, skin-walking shaman John Dyer must fight to save his bloodline. Can the Dyers stand against the horrific desires of a centuries old demon? Can their faith in each other overcome the evil pitted against them?

This historically accurate epic follows John- scion of the Dyer family, and the great-great grandson of the venerable Moll Dyer-- in his quest for a new life, and a place to settle down and call home.

The fates conspire against the Dyers, and only their sorely tested faith in each other can overcome the evil set in place against them.

https://www.amazon.com/gp/product/B07CS7SSQW/